Crossroad

ANGELS CAN DANCE

A J Swann

This edition is published in Great Britain in 2015 by Landmark Regions UK Ltd.

ISBN 9780993405914

Publisher: Landmark Regions UK Ltd, Leamington Spa, UK
www.crossroad.website
Email: editor@crossroad.website
ISBN: 0993405916

For my son

Acknowledgements

THIS NOVEL HAS been many years in the making and acknowledgements due are legion.

In the beginning, when my urge to tell the story of Finn and his family first saw the light of day, I was supported and encouraged by various writing groups. In particular, I would like to thank the members of the Leamington meetings for their contributions and support as I took my first unsteady steps.

Thanks to the many readers who helped me hone and polish the final drafts. They include, but are not limited to: Kate, Claire, Rachel, Paula, Patrick and Lin…

Thanks to Loulou for your invaluable comments they helped me see the wood and the trees. To David for your proofread-come-copy-edit and for guiding me through the nightmare of unintended manual indents and use of straight and curly quote marks.

I am indebted to the professionals who checked out my medical references and in particular a consultant at the oncology department of the Birmingham Children's Hospital – thank you Bruce.

And, of course, I cannot close these acknowledgements without thanking my wife for her laser sharp insights, encouragement and unconditional support, thank you Helen. And finally, my children, Zoe, Anna, James and Robyn; one of the great surprises of my life has been the joy of discovering that these four incomparable beings have been my most worthy teachers, thanks guys.

If I missed a name please forgive me. Thank you all.

A J Swann
September 2015

Chapter 1

THE WOMAN IN the video, the woman who'd haunted his dreams and invaded his thoughts, was still sitting at the end of the bench, watching. Or was she waiting? Although their recent conversation had provided some clarity, Gabriel was still unconvinced.

He would never shake off the memory of their first encounter. Celia's prim and twin-set exterior hid a far more engaging and yet disturbing presence. Truthfully, he was not sure he had the energy to continue the dialogue. A recurring twinge reminded him that octogenarians shouldn't prevaricate. He decided to ask again, one more attempt. 'I give up. Why don't the same rules apply now?'

Celia pointed to the river. 'Ask your friend.'

The swan had reached the river bank no more than a few paces from where he sat. She circled coyly and found a spot where she could watch, her eyes fixed on Gabriel. *What is she waiting for?*

Both questions lingered, wrapping Celia's nonsensical suggestion. Her remark was the last of many one-liners that implied much and explained nothing. He was distracted from the task as Celia reached into her pocket, removing a familiar object. She placed it in their line of sight. Gabriel was intrigued on both counts: the swan's attention and the red box. How many years since his first encounters? Ten? Fifteen? Celia lowered her hand and her next comment was more to the point. 'You should prepare for your next journey.'

Gabriel's cane dropped from its perch against his knee. He steadied himself. 'Where, exactly, am I going?' He flinched, and then smiled as a butterfly replied, roused in his chest to an arrhythmic beat. He'd performed too many rehearsals to experience stage fright and was prompted to seek only reassurance. 'Will I see you again?'

'Maybe.' Celia moved closer. 'But this is my final gift in this lifetime. It will take you back, if you choose…' She feigned a new sensation by cupping her ghostly hand around his whiskered, grey chin, holding his gaze as the butterfly's movements slowed and then stilled, too still. Gabriel held out a shaking hand as she removed her parting gift from the box and placed it in his palm. The talisman glowed, its light streaming like some miniature light-house between his fingers. Gabriel felt his fragile hold on consciousness fade as Celia brushed her face next to his and whispered. As always, she had the last word.

'Go…'

Chapter 2

THE YOUNG DOCTOR Newman was exhausted. The internship at the local hospital was proving to be an endurance test. Stamina, rather than a trial of new skills, was the primary requirement. It was barely eight-thirty and already dark, autumn dark. He was tempted to sleep, but at twenty-two and unattached he had other agendas. Top of the list was the over-riding need to seek out company. A nurse had recommended a club near the city centre. It was an interesting place, no booze. A varied crowd gathered there, but not until the pubs emptied at eleven.

First he wanted the smell and taste of hospital washed away. He took a bath. As he reclined in the tub the temptation to indulge in an extended soak was frustrated by the worn enamel under his back. His attempts to get comfortable proved impossible, and the cold tap dripped. It was this latter irritation that caught him out, the frequency of the drips hypnotic, lowering his eyelids, bit by bit. Sleep advanced, covertly, like an extended blink. He was unconscious before his head slipped under the soapy water.

Before choking, before the inevitable startled awakening, he was visited by a memory, one that included an event yet to pass. The recollection was lost as he frantically resurfaced. Recovering, he dried and dressed. A nagging sense that something was missing, that this was a re-run, distracted his search for lost cars keys. Deja vous perhaps?

The Mini started first time, a miracle. It was a short drive to the club, located in a glorified shed opposite an industrial site. He cast around for a parking place and pulled in behind a beat-up Ford, a Cortina. He could hear music as he crossed the road and entered the building.

Inside it was dark and thick with cigarette smoke. The main room was used as a dance floor. A would-be artist, with more enthusiasm than talent, had painted Egyptian murals around the walls. Beyond was a coffee bar. He eased his way forwards, dodging dancers. He ordered a cola, scanning the fog in the hope he would recognise someone. Whether it was the cola, tiredness or the smoke battering his adrenals, he felt light-headed. The sensation was strong enough to be unsettling. He gripped the bar for support and gradually the vertigo eased. Too many long shifts, too much caffeine to cope with those long shifts, and yet the feeling that he was stepping outside his skin persisted. He felt more confident – on reflection less cautious – which was why the encounter, when it came, was welcomed and not entirely unexpected.

The fact that she had her eyes on him as she crossed the room was not the challenge it should have been. She was gorgeous: long dark hair, olive skin, and those eyes... He was captivated.

'Hi...' She moved closer. 'My friend, over there,' she said, pointing to a nurse from the hospital, 'says your name is Gabriel?' He nodded. 'I've always wanted to meet an angel,' she continued, smiling. 'You can call me Isabella.' She grabbed his hand and pulled. 'Let's see if angels can dance.'

Chapter 3

FIFTY YEARS LATER, Gabriel had good reason to remember the day they'd met. He stared at the car ahead. Meeting Isabella was a landmark moment in an otherwise unremarkable, but well-lived life. As the traffic edged forwards Gabriel recalled his mood that day. It was like he knew something significant was about to happen. Now an unwelcome change seemed inevitable, and he had the same feeling…

Why did the years spin away with such geometric enthusiasm? In spite of Isabella's illness Gabriel was determined to maintain a brave face, but his stoicism was tempered. An ending was approaching. He resisted the temptation to seek out and dwell on missed opportunity – why would he? It seemed churlish; thus far they'd led a charmed life. However, the walls were closing in and only one exit remained. He wrestled with the unwelcome choices he faced, filling his mind with the mundane, chasing away more pressing thoughts.

The call from his daughter, Beth, had complicated his planning that day and he found himself pushed, uphill, towards unwelcome territory. He was irritated and stressed. Why did he avoid saying "no" with such religious conviction? He depressed the clutch and pulled on the hand-brake. His fingers drummed the steering wheel, impatient as ever – it would be a long wait. To the left and right traffic streamed, blocking his exit. The windscreen was marked by the impact of various insects, a smeared battleground. Their kamikaze antics were lost to Gabriel, as was much else, including his grandson chatting away on the back seat. The boy's rhetorical nattering was another source of irritation, and he bit his tongue, certain that even if he did complain it would make no difference.

He waited for the lights to change. The road ahead was lined with cherry trees drawn by a recent warm spell into blossom. It was a picture-book vision. He drifted into an unlikely calm that stilled his mind, as if the passing of time had slowed and he could see, uninterrupted, the space between relentless minutes. His eyes dilated and his dancing fingers skipped a beat and stopped. Cherry blossom fell in a constant mist and for an instant he could follow the downward progress of each falling petal. The pink and white motes slowed until his entire vision was lost in the shimmering host. There was a moment of disengagement, when he forgot the cares that dulled and plagued his waking hours, and in their place he experienced a new sense of self, one that allowed him to share in a vision of the world with new eyes. He had a nagging sense he was returning to familiar territory.

'You can go, Granddad, they're green.'

Startled by his grandson's raised voice and the realisation that green lights required action, Gabriel eased out into the cherry blossom road, desperately trying to chase the receding vision. Of course he failed, and in the process of failing the full weight of his concerns returned. He drove on. Beth had promised to meet them at the toy shop and Gabriel was anxious – they were running late. Finn continued his rant from the back seat.

'But I don't have any money.'

'I do.' Gabriel tapped his pocket. 'And please be quiet, Finn, I'm trying to concentrate.'

The last of the cherry trees passed by, relegated to a peripheral blur. Flurries of displaced blossom followed their progress, unaware they had danced for a wider audience. For thirty seconds Finn was quiet, and then, 'It's left, Granddad.'

Gabriel, still trying to recreate his moment of bliss, sighed. 'What do you mean? It's straight on.'

The car pulled away, straight on. 'This is the wrong way-ay,' muttered Finn, in his unselfconscious, sing-song voice.

His grandson's certainty was unnerving. As they passed the town council offices moving in the wrong direction, the boy's comment was confirmed – they should have turned left. Gabriel clenched his teeth and turned left at the next traffic lights, with Finn's vocal approval this time. After a few more time-consuming twists and turns they arrived.

Finn was cheery in that irritating way in which the righteous, especially the almost eight-year-old variety, celebrate victory. 'See, I told you...'

Gabriel slammed the car door. Next time he would walk or wear ear plugs. 'Don't forget you only have five pounds to spend.' Finn ran ahead. 'Be careful. Stay on the path, and wait for me.' And of course he didn't wait. 'Damn,' said Gabriel, turning and depressing the remote lock on the car key. He was encouraged by the customary bleep and wink.

⊷⊨⊜ ⊜⊨⊶

The cry of an excited child brought him back. *Finn…* The boy was nowhere to be seen. Gabriel displaced his anxiety by blaming his grandson for disobeying instructions. He picked his way between the family groups entering and leaving the store and thought he could see Finn passing a box of Lego kits. He pushed his way through the crowd, limping slightly as his pelvis complained. In his mind he ran the litany: *For goodness' sake don't run off like that, I'll never find you…*

The store stretched out in all directions, an organised maze of shelving stacked with several hundred ways for Finn to spend five pounds. Finn always seemed one step ahead and out of view. Gabriel slowed as yet another pushchair barred his progress. He wanted to shout, to tell the curly-haired adventurer to slow down, but he needed a target for his instruction. His thoughts turned to Isabella. He hated being separated, even for a few hours. Gabriel was eager to leave, aware that visiting time started in less than two hours.

A rather portly woman with three screaming kids rounded the end of the aisle. Gabriel stood back to give them room. As they passed, the eldest of the brood, a surly-looking girl of nine or so, stuck a finger up her nose. When she noticed he was watching she withdrew the digit, a wicked expression on her face, and wiped it on her brother's arm. Gabriel's obvious disapproval was all she needed; she ran screaming to her hapless mother.

'That old geezer's starin' at me!'

Gabriel tensed, in no mood for a scene. *Where the hell are you, Finn?*

The harassed mother was having none of it. 'For God's sake behave. Get in front where I can see you.' She pushed her daughter away. The young girl rounded on Gabriel and threw him the middle finger. Gabriel was appalled. 'Dear God! Finn, did you see that?' No reply. 'Finn?' With the disappearance of the dysfunctional foursome the view ahead cleared. There was definitely no sign of his grandson. With a rising sense of panic he backtracked, one aisle, two... He couldn't see him. His anxious scurrying drew the attention of a security guard.

'Can I help?'

Gabriel explained Finn's disappearance. 'I can't find him. He's wearing a grey top, jeans, nearly eight. Has a mass of red curly hair, name's Finn.'

'OK sir, give me a minute, this happens all the time. We'll find him.' He unclipped his radio and reported the issue to the store's office. 'Yes, that's right, better tell Andy on the door. Stop him if he tries to get out. Cheers.' With a practised flourish he fixed the handset to his belt. 'OK, let's be systematic shall we? They're looking for the lad on the CCTV and he won't get past Andy, it's the only way out.' Gabriel wanted to do a bit of searching himself. He edged backwards. The security guard followed. 'So we'll start from the entrance and work our way across the store. If we stay in this intersection we'll be able to see up and down all the aisles as we go. OK?'

Gabriel was doing his best to ignore the sinking feeling in the pit of his stomach, and the hysteria that threatened to take control of his legs. He rounded on the guard. 'Can we start, please…?' Gabriel coughed, struggling to find his voice. 'I'm really worried, someone may have, you know, taken him.'

The guard took the hint and they managed a first sweep of the store in less than three minutes. No sign of Finn. A distorted call on the radio interrupted their search. The guard turned away from Gabriel and there was a brief, crackling interchange. Gabriel ran his fingers through his hair. *For God's sake, hurry up.* When it came, the response was reassuring.

'I think you'd better come with me.'

'Have they found him?' Gabriel's spirits lifted.

'Not exactly. There's something we need to show you on the CCTV, the manager will explain.'

Gabriel had a million questions of his own to ask. The guard steered him towards the office and seemed reluctant to offer any further clarification. They negotiated the checkouts and entered the room marked "Office". The only occupant, the manager, replaced his telephone as they entered the cramped quarters.

'Sorry about the amateur dramatics, but there's something we need to look into with you. Please take a seat, Mr…?'

'It's Newman, Gabriel Newman. Shouldn't we be looking outside?' Gabriel, apprehensive and anxious, could feel his impatience growing. The manager's condescending edge was not helping.

'Don't worry, no child with your grandson's description will leave this building on his own or with anyone else. However, there's something I'd like to clear up.' He pointed at the monitor. 'I'd like you to take a look at our CCTV. I realise you must be feeling anxious, but I promise this won't take long.' He swivelled his chair and punched instructions into a keyboard. 'This is the entrance where you came in.' He pointed to one of the half a dozen monitors that lined the office wall behind his desk. 'There's something I don't quite understand.' Before Gabriel could respond the image on the screen showed him coming through the doors, and where was Finn? 'As you can see, there's no sign of your grandson.'

'No, you don't understand, Finn had run on ahead. Rewind, he was at least ten yards ahead of me.'

The manager pressed the rewind button. As the image reversed, Gabriel watched himself disappearing back through the entrance. The recording continued digging back in time. A multitude of shoppers retreated from the store, none of which was a small boy in jeans with a grey top. 'I don't understand. He was just ahead of me.'

'We ran the recording back so we could get a look at Finn, know who we were looking for.' The manager reclined in his chair and cancelled the playback.

Gabriel was feeling decidedly uncomfortable. Finn's absence from the recording was inexplicable. Perhaps, he thought, he was hidden behind a group of adults, there must be an explanation. Whatever the reason, he needed to get out of the office and continue his search. He was about to speak out when he spotted an elderly woman on the CCTV monitor. She was staring at the screen, staring at Gabriel. She lifted her hand and placed a finger to her lips. 'What on earth…?'

'Excuse me?' The manager was watching him with an expectant look, but Gabriel was lost for words. He continued to stare at the screen: she could actually see him. She was smiling, an elfin look that itched inside his head.

'I'm sorry,' the manager continued, 'but your story doesn't add up. You came into the store alone. Is there someone we could ring, maybe the boy's mother?'

Gabriel had to get out, find Finn. The old woman's lips moved and a voice whispered between his ears. As he listened he couldn't avoid smiling. 'Of course, damn it, how stupid of me.'

'Sorry?'

'Finn's mother, my daughter, was following in her car. Before we came in Finn must have spotted her; they're probably in the pet shop next door. I'll call them.' He reached for his mobile, edging back towards the door. 'I'm sorry about this, I didn't see him after we got out of my car, I'd assumed he'd run ahead.'

The manager stood. 'No harm done. I'll keep a copy of today's recording, just in case.'

Gabriel retreated to the car park, and leaned against the car door. He reached for his chin, taking comfort from the grey, tailored beard. Even that repeated gesture was off-key. A small fragment, a crumb, slid under his index finger, a would-be reminder of the morning's hurried breakfast. He opened the car and sat clutching the wheel, door wide open.

'Dad?'

Gabriel shook his head, an inner fog confounding his attempt to deal with this new information. Someone tugged at his sleeve. All he could think of was the look of familiarity on the woman's face. How could she talk to him from a video screen?

'Dad, are you OK?'

When Gabriel raised his head he could see his wife. She looked younger, and what was she doing out of hospital? She leaned towards him.

'Dad, stop staring at me like that. It's me, Beth.'

Gabriel blinked, another tug at his sleeve.

'Look Granddad.' Finn, most definitely Finn, was holding a plastic bag filled with water. Inside a small goldfish patrolled its domain.'

Gabriel eased his grip on the steering wheel. 'Finn, how…? They don't sell fish in the toy shop.' His wife look-a-like seemed to share his confusion.

'Dad, we bought the fish in the pet shop, next door.'

Finally, the penny dropped, the mist cleared. It was his daughter, not Isabella. A rush of rational justification filled his mind. The whole episode had been a mistake, but so real. 'Beth. I thought… I mean, you really look like your mother.'

Beth smiled in a worried sort of way. 'We couldn't find you. Finn said you were following so we went to the pet shop.'

Slowly, his tired mind made sense of the scattered events. 'Damn, I thought Finn had gone into the toy shop. Sorry, in a bit of a state. How stupid, sorry.'

Chapter 4

HER FATHER'S CONFUSED state of mind worried Beth. She was pleased when he agreed to go to the hospital in the same car. Beth could pick hers up later. Finn's goldfish was safely stowed in the boot. Beth glanced at her father as they drove; as usual he'd insisted on driving. His strange behaviour in the car park was a worry. He looked worn out. She'd seen that faraway look on his face before, as if something had captured his attention and he was unwilling, or perhaps unable, to let go. Not surprising really, considering the stress he'd been under for the past year. There was precious little black remaining in the mass of grey hair, swept back and resting on his shirt collar. He had a strong face and it was marked now. Unselfconsciously, she rested a protective hand on his shoulder.

As the journey progressed, Beth's attention turned to other concerns. She shifted in her seat. If her calculations were correct she was ten weeks late and the swelling in her belly felt real enough. She'd caught after all. Patrick was delighted. Her husband embraced the Catholic breeding ethic and would happily father a dozen. One of their few differences of opinion was Beth's insistence on taking the pill after Finn was born. As far as she was concerned, one was enough. Of course, it was not the only point on which they disagreed. He was a good man, and Beth could see how Finn had taken the best features from his father: a lively intelligence and his shock of auburn curls. She was saved from the slippery slope that inevitably led to disappointment, or worse, resentment, when Finn pushed at the back of her car seat.

'When will we see Grandma?'

'Soon. Maybe fifteen minutes if we get parked.'

'Some things never change.' Gabriel pulled the car to a halt, lights on red.

'What do you mean?'

'When will we be there? You and Grace would repeat it like a mantra. Used to drive me mad.'

Beth ignored the jibe. Grace, her younger sister, how she envied her lifestyle. By comparison Beth felt trapped. She eased the tension of the seat belt across her lap. *And now this...*

'It'll be good to get Isabella home.' Gabriel tapped his fingers on the steering wheel. 'Hopefully, the transfusion today should keep your mother stable for a few weeks.'

Beth didn't add to her father's statement, it seemed rhetorical and sounded like his GP voice. It was odd that his diagnostic banter should persist – he'd retired from general practice over five years ago.

A prickly sensation crawled across the back of her hand. She scratched, conjuring her mother's face. Her father was right, she did favour her mother's looks: tall, dark-haired. The Italian stock had been kind. A reluctant smile crossed her face. She could still remember the thrill when Patrick's eyes had taken her in for the first time. What a curse, familiarity. They eased into the hospital car park.

'We're here, Finn.' Beth took a deep breath. *We're here...*

~⊶⊷~

Finn didn't like his granddad's hand, it was sweaty. And why the rush? No one seemed to be concerned about his goldfish locked in the car, and he was far from happy with his mum's feeble excuse. *And how come goldfish have germs anyway?* His mother was following and both grownups looked miserable. The hospital corridor seemed endless; the green, cushion-tiled floor squeaky underfoot. Finn tried to match his granddad's stride and was obliged to add hurried steps. The unsteady dance annoyed him. Another grey door blocked their way. Finn, impatient as ever, pushed with his free hand and was disappointed when a new and longer corridor stretched out before them. He rounded on the adults, pulling his grandfather's hand to stop.

'Which room is it, Granddad?'

'It's the door with number seven on it, down there.'

Finn was relieved to have a target. He jerked his hand free and legged it.

'Finn, don't run...' His mother's receding plea was ignored. Finn pushed the door and disappeared. *Grandma will know.* As the door closed he stared – she was fast asleep and all was not well.

'Grandma!'

No response.

'Grandma, wake up!'

This time she stirred. Finn stood by the door, finger extended, pointing.

'Hello Finn, where's Mummy?'

At that precise moment his mother was the last person on his mind. He continued his insistent jabbing.

'What is it?' On cue, his granddad opened the door and saved Finn from further explanation.

'Oh shit!'

Finn giggled, in spite of the apparent emergency his granddad had said the "s" word.

His grandma looked cross. 'Gabriel, for goodness' sake…'

'It's your hand, you're bleeding.'

She looked and lifted her right hand from its resting place, a very red and sticky pillow.

Finn watched as his granddad pressed a button at the side of the bed and then pulled something from the back of his grandma's hand.

Finn's mother bent down and whispered in his ear. 'Let's wait outside while Grandma's hand is sorted.'

'Beth,' said his grandma, smiling at Finn, 'bring the boy back when they've finished with me.'

'Sure.'

'And Beth?'

'Yes Mother.'

'How's the new one?'

Mysteriously, at least from Finn's point of view, his mother smiled and stroked her stomach. 'Everything's fine.'

What new one, and what's fine?

A nurse appeared and smiled at Finn as they left the room.

'What's fine?' Finn had no patience with uncertainty. He waited for an answer.

'What do you mean?'

They were back in the squeaky corridor and Finn's head was full of questions. 'And why was his grandma's hand bleeding?' A thought crossed his mind. 'It was that thing in her hand.' Finn's insights piled in. 'I saw Granddad pull it out...'

'It's a surprise.' Now Finn was confused.

'What is? How can Grandma's hand be a surprise?'

His mother giggled. 'The reason everything is fine is a surprise. Your dad and I, we'll need to tell you later.'

Finn stopped walking. He felt cheated. 'But that's not fair, I want to know now, and how come Grandma knows?' His mother knelt on one knee so her face was level with his. Finn liked her eyes, they were interesting: one was brown and the other green. Absently, he wondered if she knew. Maybe he should say something? Instead he did that thing with his face that made her smile, a sort of engaging openness that nearly always meant he would get his own way. His mother's reply was a kicker.

'Why don't we find a café, have a drink, some chocolate?'

Instantly, a whole raft of gratifying possibilities flooded his mind.

'And crisps, and...' He hesitated. This was dangerous ground. 'Coke, I want Coke.'

'Now you know that's not allowed.' Finn did know, but he flipped over his winning card.

'Well, I'll ask Grandma what "fine" is,' he said. 'And she'll tell me.' He thought of adding 'so there' but kept that up his sleeve for later.

The half-smile that followed nailed it. He'd seen it before, a grownup's way of letting you think you were winning when really they were going to do things their way. He folded his arms, ready for a fight.

'Come on. Let's get you a can of orange and some chocolate, and then we'll see if Grandma's hand's better.'

In his mind Finn was happy with the outcome of the exchange, so much so that the relevance and impact of the unexplained words was suddenly unimportant.

→──◉ ◉──←

The nurse lifted the dressing and inspected the wound. 'This may need stitches.' She frowned, glancing at the empty bag hanging from the drip stand. 'We may have to start again with a fresh unit.' She taped a clean dressing over the wound and removed the soiled pillow. 'I'll get a doctor.'

Gabriel was puzzled. 'You must have caught the line while you slept. Strange you didn't wake.' Isabella, screwed up her face and he was quick to pick up the signal.

'How many Co-codamol did you take?'

Isabella sighed. 'Help me sit.'

Gabriel embraced his wasted partner, avoiding pressure on the scar tissue. The skin on her cheeks had a strange dry feel. As he leaned forwards to share a kiss, a lock of her hair came away in his hand. The grey curl floated to the floor. She gripped his shoulders, holding him close.

'We should prepare the family. I'm not sure how much longer I can bear this.'

Gabriel eased back. 'They must… they must know what to expect, the girls are not stupid.'

'Beth perhaps, Grace I'm not so sure. In any event it would be a relief to talk openly, even Finn should know. I hate all this pretence,' she said.

'Why don't I ask the girls over, on their own, to talk things over? I'll tackle the registrar when he comes and make sure you're home tomorrow.'

'That would be good, a relief.' She picked at the ring on his finger. 'How are you coping, Doctor Newman?'

Gabriel considered sharing his experience in the toy store, but only for an instant. When Isabella's illness had progressed, he'd made a decision to keep his anxieties and problems to himself. Isabella was not only his wife, she was his best friend, his confidant, and now, his patient. He couldn't share the upsetting experience of that afternoon. He'd had precious little time to process the episode himself. Feeling uneasy and suddenly isolated he lowered his eyes – Isabella would see he was hiding something.

'It's not going to be easy. What can I say?' A silence settled between them. Isabella seemed to make up her mind.

'There's something else I'd like you to do for me.' Gabriel risked a look – she was smiling. 'I'm going to contact Lorrianne. I'd like her to stay if she's agreeable.' Isabella paused and Gabriel could see she wanted a response. Lorri was Isabella's sister, ten years younger, but even so they were very close. 'I'm tired of hospitals. I'd like to manage at home if you can bear it.'

'Of course.' He'd been dreading this moment. 'I'll tidy up the spare room.' Gabriel knew that if Isabella wanted Lorri she was contemplating an ending. He rallied. 'Be good to see her again.'

Isabella held his gaze. 'I think I need to keep you busy.'

Gabriel relaxed. This was more like it, familiar territory. He made a mental note to sort out the laundry, and listened as Isabella filled his week ahead with purpose.

Chapter 5

FLASHING LIGHTS DISTORTED the text as Riikka attempted to read, points of light that drifted in from the outside, at the peripheral limits of her vision. She squinted, clutching two envelopes, willing the migraine to hold back. Miraculously, her eyes cleared and she could focus again. The first envelope contained her payslip, addressed to Rick. Riikka was tired of explaining the origins of her name. *Didn't everyone know it was Finnish?* So she introduced herself as Rik or Rikky. *But no "c" for God's sake!* Her mother was the Finnish influence, a second-generation import, but they'd always lived in the UK. Her father was a journalist and thoroughbred Englishman. Riikka yearned for a proper English name; plain old Jane would do. Anything that didn't require an explanation. That's an interesting name...

Since she'd finished university she'd taken on two part-time jobs. She knew it was a cop-out, a tame option. She'd turned down her friends when they'd suggested a year out travelling. Tempting, but she was knackered and broke. She was postponing a decision; soon she would have to choose a serious career. She continued to sort the paperwork on her desk, musing about possibilities for the weekend. Jonathan was visiting, taking a break from medical school. They'd first met a year before at a friend's party. Lust at first sight.

Meanwhile, one more envelope and then home time. She puzzled over the name – Doctor Newman? She'd taken the offer of a short-term summer job at the local health centre. During the three weeks she'd been there she'd not come across a Doctor Newman. The redoubtable Irene would know.

'Irene, who's this?' Irene took the letter and her face softened.

'Silly drug companies, still sending Gabriel junk mail. Doctor Newman, I should say.' Riikka was amazed, Irene was blushing. The woman blustered on. 'He retired five or six years ago.' She handed the envelope back. 'Doctor Campbell takes his mail, such as it is.'

Irene was pointing, wistfully, at a framed photograph on the wall next to her desk. An elderly man holding what looked like a ticket. Riikka was taken by his expression. She liked the look of Doctor Newman. His face had character, a face you would remember.

'The partners and staff paid for a cruise, so much better than a clock,' continued Irene. 'The poor man's not had the time to enjoy himself since.' She paused, the sort of pause that encouraged enquiry.

Riikka obliged. 'Is he not well?'

Irene lowered her voice. 'It's his wife, she has the cancer, and it's not looking good.'

'I see.'

'Doctor Newman was a born healer, not like some as pass as doctors these days.' Irene raised her eyebrows. 'He was sorely missed, I can tell you...'

The exchange left Riikka in no doubt that Irene had a soft spot for this Doctor Newman. Interesting. Nevertheless, her work for the day was done. She closed down her computer terminal and picked up her car keys. The migraine was bouncing back, niggling at the space between her eyes. She needed to get home, take pills, drink tea and sleep. She still remembered her first migraine, walking home with the sun in her eyes, barely sixteen.

'Bye, Irene.'

⋆⇒◉ ◉⇐⋆

Riikka shook her head. Why had the car stopped? Her attempts to restart the vehicle had failed and she was starting to panic. She knew she was supposed to do something, but since she'd joined the rush-hour traffic the pain in her head had become merciless and thinking was a challenge. She turned the key again to no effect. In the mirror she could make out traffic, backing up. There was nothing else for it, she would have to get help. The helpless woman driver was not a role she wanted to play.

There was a tap on the passenger-side window. Riikka squinted as the late afternoon sun streamed around a woman's face. *What a relief.* She reached across and opened the door.

A well-manicured hand reached across and helped Riikka flick the gear stick into neutral. 'Take your foot off the accelerator and clutch, try the ignition again.' Riikka disengaged her tensed feet and twisted the key. The car started. The woman settled into the passenger seat. Riikka jerked her head back in surprise as the same well-manicured hand smoothed the hair from her forehead. The movement intensified the pain. 'That's some headache? Yes?'

Riikka nodded. *How on earth…?*

'Shall we go?'

'I think I can manage.' Even as she spoke a rather uncomfortable feeling spread downward from the back of her head. It wasn't the car that was the problem. Nausea joined the pain and Riikka gripped the steering wheel to steady her nerves. 'I think I'm going to throw up.'

The stranger continued to soothe. 'It will pass, don't worry. It will take a minute or two for me to settle in.'

Settle in where?

'My name's Sarah, I'll make sure you get home.'

Pins and needles started at the source of the migraine and spread the length of Riikka's body. Instead of discomfort and hysteria she started to feel a weird sense of disengagement. The car started to move. Riikka had no idea how she was driving. She could see her hands moving the wheel, changing the gears. She was anticipating junctions, but it was not her driving. They came to an abrupt stop. She was home and dimly aware that the car door had opened. She removed the keys from the ignition and found that she could negotiate the steps to her bedsit. The headache was beyond painful. She needed medication and was confounded by the other woman's chatter inside her head. *What's she saying?*

'I'm afraid this is going to be a challenging process.'

'What process? I need my pills.'

A quick search of the kitchen drawers revealed the much-needed pain relief. Riikka took two of the butter-coloured tablets and lurched towards the sofa. She rested her head on a comforting lap. Her visitor spoke again.

'Difficult for me too. We've been chosen you see, not enviable roles.'

A hand continued to stroke her hair. It had been a good while since Riikka had felt someone bring physical ease in that way. She was unconcerned by the strange conversation and let her legs curl as Sarah continued to talk. The newcomer continued her exposition as Riikka slipped into a deep sleep.

⇥ ⇤

The next morning Riikka woke, shivering. She sat bolt upright and regretted the movement – the headache was still loitering. She half expected to see Sarah. She discarded the woollen throw and tottered to the window. Outside she could make out a late frost on the ground-floor kitchen roof. Riikka rubbed her head. After a quick search she found her car keys and shamefully flicked through her purse. Nothing seemed to be missing. The front door was locked. She almost looked under the bed. *She must have let herself out? But the door, did I lock the door?*

She needed more pain relief and a hot drink. The kettle blew its whistle and she left the tea to brew, rummaging in her bag. The antihistamine would slow her down but she didn't want another episode like yesterdays. *God, it was so embarrassing!* She was unsure, irritated, and beyond that vaguely terrified by the journey home. Parts of the trip she could remember: the queue of traffic, the car stalling, Sarah turning up. *Thank God it was a woman and not some smarmy white-van man.* Did she really drive home? And the conversation, what had Sarah said? Riikka's head started to ease as the chemicals did their job. She rationalised, speaking to the empty room.

'Well, whoever you are, thanks.' She raised her cup.

Her eyes lighted on the doll. Vasi was her name, and the toy was the only thing that Riikka connected with her mother who'd died when Riikka was barely four. The doll came with a Russian story book: Baba Yaga and Vasilisa the fair. Although Riikka was sure her mother had read the story, only a vague memory remained. More recently, Riikka had downloaded a translation from the internet. It was an odd tale, like a Slavic *Cinderella*, only the witch was a bad sort rather than a benevolent fairy godmother. In the story, Vasilisa was given a doll by her mother that helped her through various trials set by the witch. Riikka picked up the doll and considered. Her life thus far had been fairly uneventful. She made a mental note to quiz her father on the subject the next time they met.

She stepped out of her clothes and into the shower. At least no work that day. What she needed to do was shop.

After dressing, a quick examination of the fridge and kitchen cupboards left her little choice, unless she wanted to drink water and eat bagels all weekend.

⇥⟡⟡⇤

Riikka fingered the key. She'd never noticed before, but the round end of the Yale had a faded tartan pattern. She was facing the door, the same sad, grey paint peeling from the woodwork, but she couldn't turn the key. Was she going out, and therefore closing the door, or returning and opening the door? She stood and fretted, trying to empower the key to decide, in or out?

What the fuck is going on?

The feel of the bag hanging from her left hand seemed significant.

For God's sake, shopping, how stupid. I'm going to the shops…

She'd walked a hundred meters towards the local supermarket when the bag had more to say – her fingers were burning. She stopped and set the brown carrier on a low wall. A quick inspection revealed vegetables for the coming week. Riikka joined the bag on the wall, feeling faint.

I've already been shopping!

She sat trying to figure out what had happened. Why couldn't she remember? The bag was full – a visit to at least two shops – and yet she couldn't recall a thing. Her mind was a complete blank. Riikka's thoughts drifted as if some unknown wind had caught her sails. After a serious night out the sensation – a cerebral version of the whirling pits – would have been easy to explain. But a visit to the shops? She was starting to feel apprehensive about her state of mind. She had to get home.

When she turned the key this time there was no confusion. She placed the bag on the kitchen table and tried to make sense of the experience, convinced that the headaches were to blame. Was it just migraine, perhaps Jonathan would know?

She started to unpack and realised she'd visited more than the greengrocers. Hidden beneath the bags of new potatoes and carrots was a small package, beautifully wrapped. Riikka removed the paper and stared with fascination at the object within. It was a bottle of nail varnish – no big deal – but black? She never wore black nail polish, in fact she never wore nail polish. Although her fingers were long and the nails manicured, she had no patience with the process: the painting, the chipped paintwork, and the vile smell of nail polish remover.

'Pick it up.'

Curiosity, encouraged by the unnoticed instruction, guided her hands as they reached for the bottle and unscrewed the cap. Again the voice.

'Why such a prude?'

Riikka licked her lips.

'Try it. Let *me* try it.'

She sat, and with an altogether different look in her eyes, kicked off her shoes and discarded the raincoat. She watched as first one and then another nail changed to a deep black. The rest followed. She stared at the transformation, mesmerised. Her hands had assumed an unsettling, vamp-like quality. The cool air of the kitchen raised the hairs on her arms. Her thoughts drifted, remembering the last encounter with Jonathan. She shivered as her dress and then underwear joined the raincoat on the floor.

Chapter 6

FINN WATCHED HIS latest friend circling a glass bowl. Freddie the fish definitely seemed to know when Finn was watching. He would wriggle to the side closest to Finn and stare. Finn liked to talk. The fact that Freddie could not was of no consequence. Perhaps he could hear, or perhaps he would know what Finn was thinking? Finn hoped so. He liked his fish. He liked a captive audience. Which was why, when Freddie did speak, Finn was surprised, but rather captivated.

'Hi Finn…'

He was amazed – the goldfish hadn't moved his mouth and yet he could hear what he said.

Freddie spoke again. 'Why are you staring?'

This time Finn was not so sure. Was the voice Freddie's? And if not…?

'And you've got it wrong.'

Tentatively, still watching his fish, Finn replied. 'What's wrong?'

'I'm a she.'

Finn narrowed his eyes. This was an unexpected turn of events. 'So? Some girls could be called Freddie.'

'Not me.'

A fish with attitude. Finn was intrigued.

'And I'm not a fish.'

With a flip of his tail – Finn was having none of this girl stuff – Freddie coasted to the far side of his pond and nibbled at a piece of descending food.

'Well the man in the shop said you were a boy.'

'He was right, Freddie is a boy.'

'But you said you was a girl.'

'I am, apparently.'

Finn was getting bored.

'And my name's Cissy.'

Finn giggled, who ever heard of a goldfish called Cissy? No sooner had the thought popped into his head than the hairs started to rise on the back of his neck. He was sure someone was standing behind him. He whirled around. Nobody there, and he could hear a girl chuckling. Perhaps Freddie was a girl?

'You are silly.'

Finn stared at Freddie, who was still busy at the far side of the bowl.

'Here I am.'

A very large face appeared behind Freddie.

'See, I told you…'

Finn leapt backwards, almost falling over. It was a creepy face, like one you would see in the fairground, in the funny mirrors. Further speculation was cut short as a young girl stepped out from the other side of his room divider.

'Where did you come from?'

'I'm not ready to answer that, not yet. Let's just say we're going to be friends.' Finn was fascinated. He thought. *How come she sounds like a grownup and yet she's shorter than me?*

His mother poked her head around the door. 'Finn, are you OK? I could hear you talking.'

Finn was mortified. How could he explain Cissy? 'Well...'

Cissy was still there, smiling.

'Are you chatting to your fish again?' said his mum, looking straight through Cissy. 'Anyway, the reason I came up was to tell you that we're going to Grandma and Granddad's house. Your aunt Lorri will be there soon.'

Finn was still lost for words, although thoughts tumbled about inside his head. *But what about Cissy? Perhaps Mum's pretending she can't see her.*

'We'll be going in half an hour.'

Finn nodded, the suspense awful. When would she see Cissy? His bedroom door opened again. It was his dad this time. Finn's anxieties redoubled.

'Shall we?'

Finn was split. Ordinarily, his father's remark would have pricked his interest. Shall we what? He was more concerned that both his parents were in his room and neither mentioned Cissy. She sat on the floor, in full view, smiling like a Cheshire cat.

His mother nodded. 'Do you remember at the hospital when I told Grandma it was fine?'

Finn remembered right enough.

'Well,' she turned to his father, 'we've got some important news to share with you.'

His parents were grinning, which was stupid. What was there to laugh about? Finn didn't like this at all. He dropped his gaze and stared at Cissy's feet – she was wearing odd socks.

His mother's hand cupped his chin and gently lifted his face. The suspense was unbearable, Cissy and now this.

'Why don't you tell him, Patrick?'

Under normal circumstances Finn would have been dancing on the spot, excited and curious.

Finally, his dad put him out of his misery. 'Mummy's expecting a baby. You're going to have a little brother or sister.'

Finn was gob-smacked. For an instant he forgot the odd socks. Nothing in his previous seven years had prepared him for this. He'd assumed he was an only one, not a twosome. He shook his head.

His mum was frowning. 'Aren't you pleased?' Finn shrugged his shoulders.

His dad came to his rescue. 'Give me a minute...'

'Well don't be long.' Mum said. She looked put out as she left the room.

Finn sneaked a look at Cissy. She was still there. 'Don't be a dork. You're going to have a baby sister.' She tipped her head to one side. Finn had no time for this obsession with girls, and suddenly realised Cissy had spoken.

Apparently, his dad was unable to see or hear his uninvited guest. He was adopting his Sunday best, sympathetic dad look.

'So, Finn, just because we're having another baby doesn't mean anything else will change.'

Who are you kidding? Finn thought.

'You'll still be our special boy.'

Finn cringed. His dad was prone to making soppy remarks. He tried to force a smile as this usually stopped his parents saying something reassuring. 'Will it be a girl?' He was still chewing over Cissy's assertion.

'No crystal ball I'm afraid, the baby could be either. Would you like a brother?' Finn nodded. 'Anyway, you'll have plenty of time to get used to the idea.' His dad checked his watch. 'You'd better find your trainers, we'll be going soon.'

As his father left, Finn closed the door. He was concerned that Cissy would follow his dad and she may not be invisible outside his bedroom. Finn was in shock. The double whammy, Cissy and then the baby stuff. He had no enthusiasm for the new baby thing. Why did they need another child when they had him? The question was ripe territory. Finn rounded on Cissy. 'How come they didn't see you?'

'Because I'm your imaginary friend.' Cissy raised her eyebrows. 'You're the only person who can see me.'

This latest revelation was too much. He'd heard of imaginary friends, but only small kids had them – he was nearly eight. Cissy seemed to read his mind. 'Like your dad said, you'll have plenty of time to get used to the idea.

Finn spotted his trainers under the chair, but when he turned to reply Cissy had gone. He glanced upward – Freddie was still watching.

Chapter 7

Isabella was intent on making the most of the time she had left. Unfortunately, pain demanded analgesia and medication had an unwelcome side effect. Like an autumn fog it limited the view ahead. She wanted to be present to the world. She'd no idea what she was listening to – one of Gabriel's CDs, pleasant enough, but she needed to stay alert. Now that she'd made contact with her sister she was impatient. So much to say. They'd talked earnestly enough when the cancer had first appeared. They had agreed on no drama; Lorri would wait for her call. She heard the doorbell ring.

'At last.'

Voices in the hall below and then the sound of stomping feet on the stairs. Isabella sighed, she recognised the sound. Finn burst into her room.

'Hi Grandma.' Isabella winced as Finn scrambled onto her bed. 'I thought Freddie could talk, but it was a girl, and...' Finn snuggled up to whisper. 'She's called Cissy. And,' he said, wide-eyed, 'Mum's making a baby.'

Isabella eased the excited young man away from her sore side, trying to untangle Finn's threads. She had no idea who Freddie and Cissy were, but was relieved that Beth and Patrick had told Finn about the baby.

'How lovely. Would you like a baby brother or sister?' Isabella smoothed her bedding and waited, knowing it would be a brother desired and a sister he would get.

⤙▬◉ ◉▬⤚

Gabriel watched his daughters chatting in the kitchen. Both had inherited their mother's Mediterranean looks, but there the similarities ended. Beth, the eldest, was the one who coped and Grace simply enjoyed herself. He'd often thought they would be more fulfilled if they shared their genes. His thoughts turned to Isabella; it was good to have her home. True to her word she was keeping him busy. Instead of dithering – should he do this or that – he had a to-do list. What a relief. He'd even managed to rationalise the episode in the toy shop. Obviously he'd been under a lot of stress, not enough sleep. Gabriel was content with his own counsel. He was back on track and would make the most of the time they had left.

The bark from a failing exhaust made him jump. A minute later the doorbell rang.

'I'll get it.' Gabriel's cry was challenged by the rush of small feet. Finn was grinning as he raced his grandfather to the front door and was at full stretch, struggling with the latch. They opened the door together. It was Lorri.

She hadn't changed. If anything she looked younger, hair even longer, white shot through with a wild grey. She was at least ten years younger than Gabriel's approaching seventy-fifth, and could have passed for fifty, and her eyes... She turned them on Gabriel: green, sharp, direct, enquiring.

'Where is she?'

'In our bedroom.'

'Great.' She kissed Gabriel, no polite peck on the cheek. She tasted briefly of fruit. 'You holding up OK?' Gabriel knew Lorri had no time for pretence.

'It's been tough.'

She laid a hand on his chest. 'I've been thinking about you.' She increased the pressure on his chest. 'But I've been driving for three hours and I need to pee. So if you'll excuse me.'

Gabriel reached for her bag. 'Let me take that.'

Lorri released the handles. 'Thanks.' Finn stood back to let his aunt pass. She reached into her pocket and withdrew a bar of chocolate. 'Here you go.' Finn retreated, mumbling a muted thank you. 'Are the girls here?' asked Lorri.

Gabriel pointed to the kitchen and stood aside as Lorri made for the stairs.

'I'll be down to say hello when I've seen Bella.'

Gabriel was about to follow when a familiar voice spoke, somewhere between his ears.

'Be still, you're about to take a break.'

He shook his head. *What...?*

⊷═◉ ◉═⊷

Lorri didn't wait for a response to her knock. She opened the bedroom door, anxious to see Bella. She was lying on the bed, thin, but eyes still bright and welcoming.

'Lorri, it's so good to see you.' Isabella struggled to her feet and they hugged. 'Thank God you're here.'

Lorri helped her sister to sit. 'I should have come earlier.'

'None of that, this is what we agreed.' Isabella swung her legs back on the bed. 'I'm starting to feel separated from all this,' she said, waving expansively at the room. 'I think it's time to consider a dignified exit and you're the only person who I can discuss it with.'

'Has the witch been tormenting you?'

Isabella laughed, a dry, throaty chuckle. 'Grandmother is never far away. I'm not sure I'll need much help, especially from Grandma Lucca.' She gripped Lorri's hand. 'There's something I can't quite fathom. If I hadn't got this wretched condition, maybe I could figure it out.'

'So, where do we start?'

'No idea. I was hoping we could spend some time together, see if anything...' Isabella paused, stuck for words. She hated the expression but it was the best she could do. 'Shows up?'

At that precise moment Grace opened the door, looking agitated. The waxy grin she directed at her mother was not reassuring.

Isabella's instincts sharpened. 'What's wrong?'

'Nothing, I wondered if you'd like a drink, and Dad wants to show Lorri something.' She twisted the doorknob. 'Downstairs.'

Lorri and Isabella exchanged glances. Lorri spoke first. 'Maybe I should go and see what he wants.'

⤞═◉ ◉═⤝

Downstairs, Gabriel was standing with Lorri's bag at his feet, immobile and apparently asleep. Beth was holding her father's arm and looked petrified. She whispered as Lorri approached. 'I've never seen him like this before. You don't think he's having a stroke or something?'

Lorri shook her head. 'Take it easy. His legs would've folded...'

Lorri held a finger to her lips. Gingerly, she squared up to Gabriel. Even though eye level was sternum level she could see his eyes were closed and rolling under the lids. *Well, looks to me like he's gone travelling.*

Grace stepped into the hall, supporting her mother.

'Lorri, what's going on?' Isabella limped towards her sister.

'Seems like you got your wish, something has showed up.' Lorri stood back. 'I thought you were the "walker"?'

'Walker?' Beth took her mother's free arm.

'Sleep walker. Lorri means your father's sleep walking.' Isabella frowned and shrugged off her daughters' support. 'Let me see.'

Lorri marvelled as her sister shuffled towards her husband. She cut quite a figure: pink slippers, a nightgown that would have flattered if she'd been carrying another thirty pounds.

'Gabriel.' Her voice had a tender edge. 'You can't sleep here.' No response. 'Why don't you walk with me?' She took his hand

and he moved. They walked towards the sitting room. Isabella cast a backward glance. Lorri smudged the moisture under her eyes and reached Isabella just as she stumbled. Gabriel trotted on and sank into his favourite armchair. His family watched in amazed silence as he purred softly, sound asleep.

--»)═◉ ◉═‹«--

Gabriel was still walking. One minute he'd been striding towards the stairs with Lorri's luggage in his hand and then this. The cross-over had been instant, and he'd no sense of his immobile, recumbent self. He was vaguely aware of the wrought-iron gates as he entered the park. He walked on, each step matched by a swing and tap as his cane beat the ground, his marching drum. Each footfall assumed the tick of a metronome, the rhythm emptying his mind. Dreaming or not, he was content to follow the path, his journey thinning the veil between him and the ghost inside.

Soon he was striding between avenues of cracked willows lining a river. The twisted branches were thick with new growth. In the distance a familiar object came into view. Taking his time he reached the bench and smoothed the worn oak, awakening other memories. This was their seat, a quiet corner, a refuge, a place where they would come to still the doing part of their lives and be together.

Familiarity washed over him. He pulled a bag from a side pocket of his jacket. The fact that he knew it would be there seemed unremarkable. Time stretched out as he tossed broken bread towards the river. Whether an instant passed or a lifetime, it was a tactile sensation that marked change. A stiffening breeze raised goose bumps on his arms. Gabriel squinted as the sun cleared the tree line ahead. Time to go.

His wandering attention was taken by swans. One in particular headed in his direction, threading between anxious moorhens. Reaching the bank she left the water, opening her wings, the power of the movement spraying water from her wing tips. Sunlight caught the droplets, making rainbows, another cherry tree moment. This time there was no distraction, no need to add meaning. Gabriel's mind was finally stilled.

'It's almost like she's talking.' A well-dressed woman stood at the end of the bench. He recognised the face even though her comment made no sense.

'I beg your pardon?'

'Would you mind if I sat? Gravity has a rather painful effect on my joints.' She didn't wait for permission and sat smoothing her skirt. 'The creature seems to know you.' Gabriel, confused by the woman's remark, missed his cue. 'Perhaps you should enquire when you get back.'

Gabriel shuffled his feet to ease the grip squeezing his bladder. *Back where?*

She spoke again. 'It's a question of seeing.' Gabriel did not see. She laid her hand over his, her touch cool and smooth like worn silk. She increased the pressure, holding him still. The need to pee dissipated. 'Don't forget.'

Gabriel's stick clattered as it fell to the floor. His attention snapped to at the sound, rather like waking. He freed his hand

and bent to retrieve the cane. Gingerly, he withdrew the stick, avoiding bird droppings. When he eased back the woman had disappeared, and then he remembered. The face, he had seen her before, on a security screen.

Chapter 8

LORRI SIGHED. IT was getting late and Gabe showed no sign of waking. Her mind wandered. The room was almost dark, a vague glow from the kitchen spilling along the hall, creating a relaxed gloom. The house had a closed-for-business feel: watchful, but pregnant with the absence of talk, of padding feet. Even appetite and bodily functions were required to slumber, unless, of course, you were charged with watching a dreamer.

She'd known that the call from Bella would come, but when it did her spirit had sailed ahead. She was anchored, there was no other place she would rather be. Bella had promised she would send word when she was ready, and she had. Lorri smiled as she mused. Initially, Bella had insisted she keep away. At times Lorri had felt like a shade obscuring the inevitable. Now she was here they could make friends with the Grim Reaper and face Bella's gateway. When she'd received the call she'd felt apprehensive. She was, after all, going to lose her sister, the mother she never had, her best, best friend.

Her thoughts returned to her slumbering brother-in-law. The timing of his sleep walk – what was that about? What was going on? The object of her sojourn still purred contentedly in his favourite chair. Bella wanted to know if he dreamed. More to the point, the sisters wanted to know what he dreamed. What was it about sleep that turned the incumbent into such a spectacle? Gabe was not an unattractive man, but in sleep he'd assumed a clichéd posture: open-mouthed, chin resting on his chest – no drooling, thank the Lord – all far from flattering. Gabriel's head jerked upwards. Lorri's hope that he was waking was quickly dashed as his whiskered chin resumed its position, nodding against his chest.

Lorri and Bella had always been close. Their mother had died shortly after Lorri arrived and they'd lived with their grandmother. Grandma Lucca had terrified the girls in the early days. In time they became accustomed to her strange ways and had grown to respect her insights.

Lorri considered her options. Grandma Lucca had taught them how to step into their own dreams, and with practice, into each other's. Maybe she should take a peak? Of one thing she was certain: if Gabriel was dreaming she doubted he was a dreamer. Lorri had no issue with the apparent conflict, that she was both certain and doubtful, as she attached a different meaning to the two states of consciousness: dreaming and being a dreamer. Aware of her promise to Bella to stay awake, her eyes began to close, but not to sleep.

⋅→▆◉ ◉▆←⋅

Upstairs, Isabella was wide awake and impatient for news. *Surely he'll wake soon?* The pain in her chest and hips was an irritation she could bear tonight. Waiting, on the other hand, created suffering that depended on others for analgesia, and that she could hardly bear. There were too many loose ends. She desperately wanted to pursue an ending and knew the way, but first she needed answers. She was afraid, and not because she was dying. She was pregnant with notions that needed a shape before she left, and Gabriel was hiding something.

'You OK Mum?' Isabella was startled. Grace pushed open the bedroom door and approached her bed. 'Your light is on...' She eased her mother forwards and reversed her pillows, a tender act. Grace always remembered the little things, the feel of cool linen against a hot back.

'Well, what can I do? Drink? Pain killers?'

Isabella shook her head. She reached out. 'Sit with me.'

Obediently, Grace sat and waited.

'When you were little so much of you was hidden.' Isabella paused. 'You were like seeds, I'd no idea what you'd become.'

Grace tipped her head to one side. Her lips closed as she stifled yet another reflex to gather air.

'Now I feel I've seen who you are.'

'So it's not me that's keeping you up?' Grace said.

Isabella smiled. 'No dear. Not you.'

'Who then?'

'I'm not sure. Grace,' she said, her voice losing its motherly edge, 'you know I'm...'

Grace laid a slender finger across her mother's lips.

'Of course I know. We just don't talk about these things. Stiff upper and all that.'

Isabella was speechless. *Is this my Grace?*

'Anyway, we've all got to go sometime.' Grace turned her head away.

She's smiling!

'Sorry Mum, that was crass.'

Isabella was laughing. 'Well, well...'

Grace took encouragement from the reaction. 'You're a hot topic. Beth and I have been speculating for months.' Grace reached into her pyjama pocket and withdrew a tube of lip protector. She twisted the base. 'Shall I?'

Isabella nodded, pursing her lips, struggling to hold back a grin as Grace puckered her own lips as she worked.

'So, what's missing?' Grace added a final flourish.

'Well, it's a feeling I have, that something is brewing – I can't really explain.'

'Like the seed thing?'

'Exactly, that's it, clever girl. The feeling wants to be more, but what?'

'Is it anything to do with Dad's weird sleep thing tonight?'

'Partly.' Isabella sighed. The conversation was straying into difficult areas. 'Actually, I want to know if he dreams, and if his dreams are...' She struggled for the right word. 'Relevant?'

'I thought you were going to say he needed the rest.'

Isabella ignored the wry comment. 'Do you remember my stories, when you were kids, about my dreams?'

'I remember the ones when you were an owl. I grew up thinking how fab it would be to fly.' Grace wrinkled her nose. 'I never had dreams like that.'

'Well, I believe dreams can tell you things. The drugs have stopped mine.' She smiled. 'I was rather hoping your dad would have them for me. Silly really.' Isabella gripped her daughter's hand as a different cramp set in her belly.

'What is it?'

'A number two I'm afraid.' She slipped her legs from the bed. 'And as punishment for being such an irreverent daughter, you can help me.'

⇥ ⇤

It was early morning and still dark when Gabriel woke. His first confused reaction to waking was location – the armchair was no bed. And his neck hurt, the tentative twists and turns were agony. The discomfort, real as it was, did not distract him from the dream. The well-dressed woman on their bench was the face on the video screen in the toy store. He felt out of place, as if certainty had taken a quick step ahead and he couldn't catch up. He gripped the arm rests, reassured by the familiar feel of worn fabric. He slipped his finger into a split seam, gathering reassurance from the well-known lair. The initial calm on waking was stripped away as a figure appeared out of the semi-darkness.

'Lorri, why are you here?'

'I promised Bella I'd wait with you. After I arrived you sort of fell asleep. So we sat you here and Bella insisted that she speak with you as soon as you woke.'

Gabriel attempted to take in this new turn of events. He could remember Lorri arriving. He remembered bending to pick up her bag and then nothing until he woke in the chair.

Lorri filled in the gaps. 'I won't kid you Gabe, you fell asleep standing in the hall. It caused quite a commotion. Isabella led you to your seat where you promptly fell into a deep sleep.' Lorri reached across the side table and flicked on the table lamp. They both squinted as the room leapt into focus. 'The thing is,' she continued, inching forwards, 'Bella and I attach a lot of importance to dreams…' She waited.

Gabriel was in no mood to share his possible insanity with anyone, especially Isabella. He was content to deal with his own problems. Lorri, she was too close to her sister, and would likely share anything he said without a care for his promises. He said nothing.

Lorri smiled, a grin that suggested she knew otherwise. 'You did dream?'

How was it, he thought, that women were so adept at framing questions as accusations? Now any response would sound defensive. He coughed to clear his throat. 'Well, yes, I did, but nothing of consequence.' Before the words left his lips he knew what Lorri would say next, and she did.

'In which case, if it's of no consequence, would you mind sharing it with me?'

'But why? It was literally a walk in the park,' Gabriel sighed. 'And some old woman was sitting on a bench telling me about swans.'

'And that wasn't interesting?' Her eyes sparkled. 'What did she say?'

Gabriel crossed his legs, the twisted formation jumping up and down. 'Listen, can we save this 'til later? I really need the bathroom.'

'Tell you what, you sort yourself out and then let's go and see Bella.'

⟶⟩⟨⟵

Washing his hands, Gabriel reflected. What was he getting so fussed about? He was stressed in the store and must have associated the woman on the screen with his own thoughts. For God's sake, how could he hear someone on a video screen talking inside his head, it was ridiculous. And the woman on the bench, come on, it was a simple association, working out his anxieties. He splashed water on his face and stared at the reflection from the bathroom mirror. He felt better.

Much to his dismay Lorri was busy chatting to Isabella as he tentatively opened the bedroom door, hoping that his wife was safely asleep. His settled demeanour shifted towards edgy.

'Gabriel, come, sit with me.' Isabella had obviously taken over as inquisitor. Gabriel felt a growing irritation at their interest in his dream, and there was a vague notion, a lingering doubt, that there could be meaning that eluded him. More to the point, he was desperately trying to script a response so that they, unlike he, did not connect the errant dots: the episode with Finn and the lady on the bench. For a doctor grounded in cause and effect, symptoms and diagnosis, his recent experiences were a step too far into the crack: the gap that we step over as we keep crazy at bay – even if he could justify his experience as a reaction to stress. He sat on the bed, relieved to see that Isabella appeared to be pain-free. He reached forwards and placed his hand on her face then forehead.

'So, how am I Doctor?' She chuckled.

'Well enough I think.' He didn't wait for a reply. 'Lorri says the pair of you are interested in my silly dream. What on earth could be as dull...?' He ran out of steam. Implacable, he thought. That's what they were, the pair of them, waiting. 'OK. What's going on? Why the morbid interest?'

The girls exchanged a knowing look.

'Because it's unusual?' Lorri ventured.

'Falling asleep on your feet? You have to admit it's a bit strange,' said Isabella, gazing at Gabriel, a knowing look passing the top of her reading glasses. 'And we like our dreams. Sometimes they tell us things.' Isabella pressed into her pillows then lifted her hands, palms uppermost.

No pressure, I see... Gabriel took a deep breath, why was this so difficult? 'OK. I was walking in the park, by the river, and came to our bench, and an old woman came and sat next to me. That's it.'

'What did she say?' Isabella this time.

'That a swan was trying to tell me something.' He was losing the story line.

Lorri leaned forwards. 'When you woke you were muttering about a face, someone you'd seen before?'

Gabriel had no idea he'd spoken. In any event this was the connection he did not want to follow. He shrugged. 'No idea.' He knew the lie was a mistake.

Thankfully, the door opened and Grace walked in. 'You guys do know it's four am?'

Gabriel turned, willing Grace to say more. She addressed her father. 'Well, well, the sleeper awakes.'

Isabella took up the baton. 'There's root ginger in the fridge Grace. Could you cut a chunk and boil it with a slice of lemon for me?'

'Sure. Anyone else?' Shaking heads.

As Grace disappeared Isabella turned to her sister. 'Thanks for waiting with Gabe. I think I should get reacquainted with my husband.' Lorri took the hint.

She kissed Isabella. 'See you both later.'

Gabriel was aware, a new skill, that an unspoken communication had passed between the women. Isabella closed her eyes. The door latch clicked as Lorri left. Light from a single lamp threw shadows across the room. Outside, Gabriel could make out the first sounds of the dawn chorus. *What am I supposed to say?*

'Tell me more about this woman, what she said.' Isabella patted his hand. 'Humour me, and tell me where you'd seen her before.'

'I've told you already, and I've no idea where I've seen her before.' The lie repeated.

'So you don't remember saying that to Lorri?'

Gabriel shook his head.

Grace appeared with the tea. She placed it on a bedside table and glanced at her father. 'This looks tense. I'll get some sleep...'

Isabella warmed her hands on the mug. 'Sometimes, when we dream, there's something worth remembering, something important.' She sipped, tentatively. 'I have a feeling that you'll remember soon enough.'

Gabriel felt like an eleven-year-old, out of his depth.

Isabella held out the cup. 'You should try this.' Gabriel shook his head. He was too dismayed by his unwillingness to face his demons to respond. Isabella, apparently, had no such qualms, she lifted him from the hook. 'Such a serious face, let me tell you why dreams can be important and then you can hold my hand while I sleep.'

⇥🞂 🞀⇤

Isabella attempted to conjure light to speed up the first signs of day. She was impatient. There would be no sleep, only the gradual awakening of her body as the analgesics cleared her system. Her mind was sharper, but pain was its growing obsession, it left little space for contemplation. She could feel the opiate fog dissolving and with it the barrier that held her imagination at bay. She concentrated, focusing her vision on a point midway to the opposing wall. *Where are you?* The effort required to hold the meditation was exhausting. A stooped form emerged from the semi-darkness.

The figure advanced to the end of the bed. Isabella relaxed a little as her grandmother's presence approached, offering respite from her aches and pains. For a brief moment the world, her cancer, even her husband's breathing, ceased to be, and she was at peace.

'You are foolish to call me back. You should save your energy for the living, not the dead.'

Isabella hesitated. 'I'm lost, Grandma Lucca. There's something holding me here and I'm too sick to make sense of it.'

'Let your sister hold that candle.' Before Isabella could respond her grandmother continued. 'All I can see is that this one is possessed.' She pointed at Gabriel's sleeping form.

'I've never heard you use that expression before. What do you mean, possessed?'

Catarina Lucca smiled at her granddaughter. 'Always the questions. Talk to Lorrianne, and for now, sleep. You've wasted enough energy on this tittle-tattle.' Her image faded. 'We'll be together soon enough.'

Miraculously, sleep did follow. Not a deep sleep, rather a waking sleep, a day dream. Isabella was aware that at some point morning had arrived and Gabriel was no longer in the room. She needed the bathroom. Grace, her minder appeared, hair twisted, yawning.

'Thought I heard you stirring.' More yawning followed. 'Shall I boil up your ginger and lemon concoction?'

'Bathroom first, then tea would be great, and toast.'

'Wow, the patient is much improved today.'

'I believe I am. God knows why. And could you ask Lorri to come and see me as soon as she surfaces?'

⊶ ⊷

Between them the sisters made some sense of Gabriel's ramblings. Since she'd conjured her grandmother, Isabella had felt less anxious and was content to let Lorri talk.

'My instinct is that we should back off. The older woman Gabriel encountered seems a benign character and I'm pretty clear that Gabe's seen her before, but he's not ready to let that cat free,' said Lorri. 'I'll keep an eye on him. Don't worry.'

Isabella was not used to passing off responsibility, even if the volunteer was her own sister. 'In that case,' she said, 'can I make an unreasonable request?' She waited.

Lorri stared. 'You need my permission?'

Isabella dropped her head. 'Would you spend some time with Gabe, afterwards…?'

Lorri reached out and held her sister's hand. It was cold. 'Of course, you don't need to ask.' Lorri paused. 'I'll support Gabe, no problem.'

Isabella felt something release inside and any resistance she may have harboured to hold back the cancer's progress melted away. 'Then I can leave.'

Chapter 9

GABRIEL LEFT THE house early in no mood for more third-degree. He left a note on the kitchen table and set off for town. He needed time to think. The sun was up early and he took the footpath around the local golf course. It was no short cut, but he wanted exercise and then breakfast. It was almost June and the dawn chorus had long since faded. On the shaded sides of the greens the grass was still greyed with dew. He took a deep breath. *This is more like it.*

The temptation to rationalise his behaviour in the past few days – to dismiss the odd events as figments of a tired and stressed imagination – was compelling. Unfortunately, the diagnostic habit was hard to kick, and then there was the old woman. "What ifs" chattered their conclusions as he picked up the pace. Thankfully, his clicking hips were merely a background scratch that day. The air was still fresh and free from the warmed pollution waiting in the town centre.

Eventually, the path joined a back road into town and in the distance he could see shop keepers lifting their shutters to accommodate early deliveries. He could hear their muted banter as they fiddled with locks and alarm key pads. Gabriel was intrigued by a plastic fly screen flicking back and forth across the entrance to a second-hand shop. His grandparents had mounted a similar barrier above their back door. He stopped. *Gabriel, you mind them boots before you ventures inside...* The sound of his grandmother's voice drew him on, he could almost smell his favourite, a home-made corned beef pie.

Gabriel checked his watch: eight-thirty. The door was open so he ventured inside. The lights were on but no sign of the owner. A single, battered strip light made little impact: it was gloomy and smelt of old shoes and damp. He found himself searching through a box of post-war cigarette cards: well worn, with faded pictures of cricketers and flags of the Empire. They slipped between his fingers, extinct brands, Wills, John Player, all triggering memories of school. He could still remember how to play with the cards, flicking them across the playground to knock over a single card leaning against the wall. The associations deepened. Now he could see, almost reach out and touch, the sandstone sills, deep groves worn into the stone by generations of boys sharpening pen knives. How times had changed. In the past knives were tools: for skinning a rabbit, gutting a fish or plain and simple whittling.

'Can I help?'

Gabriel looked up. The shopkeeper had a careworn expression, as if life had dealt him the wrong cards.

'You can have the box for a fiver.' He gave Gabriel a knowing stare. 'Wait a minute...' The remark was strangely drawn out. 'Aren't you the good doctor? Doctor Newman?' He raced on. 'Bless me. You looked after my Mary…'

Gabriel, his mind frantically disengaging from memories that were far too clear and present, replied. 'I'm sorry, I'm retired now.'

'You shall have these as my gift.' The old man pulled a used Tesco bag from his coat pocket, promptly dispatched the cards and handed over the bag. 'Please, take it, least I could do…' He took a shuddering in-breath, the process disrupted by feelings. 'She died you know, of course… I expect you don't recall?'

Gabriel was almost back; he gazed absently at the crumpled bag. A face popped into his mind, an emaciated, middle-aged woman with emphysema. 'Mary Gardner?'

'Yes, that's right. She struggled at the end. Horrible it was, couldn't catch her breath.' The forced smile returned. 'Still, small mercies…' He gripped Gabriel's arm. 'I was going to make a cuppa, could I tempt you?'

Gabriel backed out of the shop, making excuses. He needed light, fresh air and breakfast. He spotted the door of a café opposite, the number eleven stencilled on a glass panel. The solitary occupant, a young woman, stopped her table cleaning as Gabriel entered. She offered an empty smile.

'Sit where you like, I'll be over in a second.'

He took a table with his back to the door but a view of the street. Eventually, the waitress wandered over.

'Ready to order?'

He thumbed the menu. 'Yes, I'll have a black coffee and the scrambled eggs with toast please, brown toast.'

'No problem. Anything else?'

'Do you have a newspaper?'

'There are copies of the nationals,' she said, pointing towards the bar. 'I could fetch one if you like?'

Gabriel flinched. Would she have said that ten years ago, five even? 'Yes, that's kind of you. *The Times* or *Independent* would be fine, thanks.'

The waitress trotted off and returned with the broadsheet. Sometimes, he reflected, ageing seemed to jump out and bite. He really didn't feel that much older. He smiled. Many of his contemporaries would expect and appreciate that sort of consideration, content to settle back and let life happen. He flicked open the paper and gradually the café started to fill. The eggs, when they arrived, were perfect, not overcooked. He was interrupted by a polite cough.

'I'm sorry to intrude.'

Gabriel removed his glasses and was confronted by a young woman.

'Would you mind if I shared the table with you?' She looked around the crowded café. 'It's rather full.'

Gabriel moved his paper. 'Of course, please...'

The waitress arrived with tea and Gabriel resumed the crossword. He peered over his reading glasses; his table companion was apparently searching for something in her bag.

'Could I use this?' She lifted a sachet of sugar from his saucer. 'Can't find my sweeteners.'

'Yes, help yourself.' She had extraordinary nails, long and painted black. Gabriel couldn't take his eyes from her hands as she slowly ripped the top from the packet and poured the contents into her cup. She smiled, a mischievous, worldly grin.

'Look, I can see you're having a quiet read. Tell me to shut up if I'm disturbing you.' She continued stirring her tea. 'The thing is I think I know you. Is it Doctor Newman?'

Gabriel folded the newspaper and stilled his bobbing knees. *Damn waterworks.* 'Yes, it is, but how did you know?'

'I have a part-time job at the health centre; Irene showed me your picture.'

'How extraordinary.' Normally, Gabriel would have made excuses and left. He'd had a lifetime of unwelcome banter with patients he'd bumped into. Perhaps this young woman was different, and in any event Gabriel was not averse to a distraction.

She reached across to shake his hand, and he gripped the manicured fingers. 'My name's Riikka.'

'And no Doctor Newman please, I'm Gabriel.' He folded the broadsheet. 'So, you're working at the surgery?'

'Yes, part-time, I've just finished university.' She opened her bag and pulled out a key-ring. 'My other day job is selling books.' She dangled the keys. 'And it's my turn to open the shop this morning. Can't be late...' `

'I see.'

'I work not far from here, Hamiltons, on the high street.'

Gabriel found himself relaxing. Riikka had no doubt been filled in by Irene on his domestic challenges, but even so... The conversation was refreshing, and surprisingly so. Small talk was not his forte, he'd always avoided the type of convivial banter that seemed so attractive to most people. Today, somehow, it seemed the perfect antidote to the stress that had mounted up in the past few months. For the first time in many years he rediscovered a fondness for speaking without a clear intention to make a point, or solve a problem. He could somehow distance himself from recent events and pretend. Gabriel wanted the conversation to continue even as evidence suggested otherwise: Riikka drained her cup and checked her watch.

'Sorry...' She brushed her hand against the arm of a passing waitress. The girl stopped and smiled. She touched her arm again. 'Can I have my bill please?'

'Sure, give me a minute.'

Riikka opened her purse. 'Thanks for letting me sit with you.' More hesitation. 'If you call in at the bookshop be sure to say hello.'

The waitress returned and left her bill. Riikka placed a few coins on the table. 'I'd better go.' She stood.

Gabriel struggled to his feet. 'I've enjoyed our chat.'

'Me too, and don't forget to call in if you get a chance.' She hesitated. 'I'll be sure to tell Irene that we've met. She'll be jealous.' The Cheshire cat was back. 'Bye now.'

As she made her way to the door, Gabriel's mind drifted. He picked up the partially read newspaper. Another half an hour and he'd better make tracks. Grace would need to go before lunch and he'd no idea what plans Lorri and Isabella had hatched. The café emptied as breakfast regulars were drawn back to their jobs or shopping lists. He removed his reading glasses; perhaps it was time to leave.

'Still tongue-tied?'

'Good heavens.' Before he could add another word the elderly woman commandeered the opposite seat.

'Be a dear, order me a coffee would you.'

Gabriel was still dealing with disbelief. The woman on the video, the woman in his dream, she was sitting in front of him.

He lifted his hand to attract the waitress, who wandered over.

Gabriel pushed the table menu towards his second, uninvited, guest. 'What would you like?'

'Same as you please.'

The waitress seemed to be in a hurry, scuffing her nose to disguise the smile on her face. She lifted her pad. He ordered two coffees.

'So that's two black coffees?'

'Yes please. Thank you.' He turned his attention to his visitor. The waitress disappeared into the kitchen and could be heard laughing with the kitchen staff.

'Sorry, I think I missed your name?' Gabriel said.

'You could call me anything really. What about Celia?'

The experience of seeing someone he'd rationalised as fictional, as a dream fragment, was unsettling. Actually, it was way beyond unsettling. Gabriel shifted in his seat as two cups appeared as if by magic. Unable to speak, he slid one of the coffees across the table.

Celia ignored the proffered coffee cup and withdrew a small red box from her pocket. She placed it on the table and pushed it towards Gabriel. 'This time I'd like you to watch me leave.'

Gabriel looked on with disbelief. 'But your coffee, why did you ask me to order the coffee?'

'To make a point.'

Jesus, what does she mean? 'You're not making any sense. I don't understand...'

'Now you're on the right track.' She placed her elbows on the table and leaned forwards. Her eyes were spectral, not the worn and milky gaze of an aged person, but bright, piercing. He could not look away. 'Understanding breaks the conversation.' She tapped the side of her nose. 'And I am leaving.' Celia stood and stepped away from the table, moving towards the door.

The box, she'd forgotten her wretched box. 'Celia...' A few of the remaining customers looked in his direction. 'Your box?'

She stopped and called back. 'You're confused, Doctor Newman, possession is key. It's not my box.'

Gabriel struggled to his feet as she disappeared through the door. He half spoke a wasted question. 'How did you know my name?' He gathered up the box and was still staring at it when the waitress ambled over.

'Will there be anything else?'

'No, I'll have my bill please.' He placed the box on the table. His bladder was not going to be denied this time. He needed the loo.

⟶⊨⊚ ⊚⊨⟵

Gabriel sat and stared at graffiti on the back of the cubicle door. He read the inane words, the crude invitations, praying, hoping that the world would re-form in a more familiar shape when he emerged. His moment of solitary contemplation was broken by approaching voices. The outer door opened. Any prayer he may have sent was not heard, far from it...

'Hear what Pattie said?'

'About the old geezer?'

'Yeh. Wish I'd seen it, ordering for himself and his imaginary friend, and shouting at the door.' More laughter. 'Well, takes all sorts.'

'Guess so.' The voices faded with the wail and protest of rusty hinges. Silence. Gabriel sat dumbfounded.

⋯▸┥═◉ ◉═┝◂⋯

Gabriel was appalled. He'd made a hurried exit from the café and walked slowly, needing time to think. He was offended and perplexed. How could ideas coexist that were so obviously contradictory? She'd sat there talking, surely he'd not imagined... Gabriel drank in the everyday, grateful to a passing bus for not taking flight or shrinking like Alice. He couldn't believe Celia was a figment of his imagination, his mind driven to find an explanation.

There was no way he could go back and challenge what he'd heard. Coming after his confusion in the toy store it couldn't be a coincidence, or could it? Thankfully, his professional persona was ready to pick up the threads, to look for an explanation and then a solution. He ran through the possible candidates, giving scant attention to the most likely: dementia, or less savoury personality disorders. Instead he settled on stress; after all, he'd had plenty of justification. He determined that he would have to talk to someone. The time for single-handed heroics had passed.

He ran over his "symptoms" again, searching for an alternative cause. Voices in his head, apparent hallucinations, narcolepsy, at least his memory seemed OK. It must be a stress reaction, he concluded. In any event he would have to get help, but who? He'd have to hold himself together, he couldn't possibly tell Isabella or the girls. He was not ready to talk to his ex-partner at the practice, not yet. Which leaves? It would have to be Lorri. There was no one else he could trust.

A vehicle tooted, breaking his line of thought. He stopped. A small figure jumped from the back door of the car as it pulled into the curb ahead. It was Finn. Patrick leaned from the passenger window.

'Couldn't restrain him I'm afraid. Is it OK if he walks with you? We're going to your place to relieve Grace.'

Gabriel waved them away. 'Sure.' It seemed his other preoccupations would have to wait.

Finn danced towards his granddad, chatting away. 'We saw you, Granddad, me and Cissy.'

'Cissy?' Gabriel couldn't help smiling, the boy's face was full of life. 'Who's Cissy?'

'She's my friend.' Finn lowered his voice. 'But no one else can see her, just me.' Finn skipped ahead. He turned, signalling his granddad to stop. 'She said that we should walk with you.'

'Well that's very thoughtful of Cissy.'

Finn cocked his head to one side, apparently listening to his friend. 'And,' said Finn, as Gabriel watched his face transform again, mischief in his eyes this time, 'she says you don't need to worry.'

Gabriel grabbed Finn's hand and made progress towards home, his grandson's remarks too close, too much.

Lorri was sorting laundry when they returned. Patrick and Finn disappeared with a substantial shopping list. Beth and Grace decided to walk to the bus station. Grace was a public transport advocate, which left Gabriel and Lorri facing each other across the kitchen table. Gabriel was evidently preoccupied. Lorri, as usual, cut to the chase.

'What's on your mind?' She moved her head so she could see his eyes, no escape. 'Shall we start with the old woman in your dream? Where had you seen her before?'

Gabriel looked up. 'Can I... I mean, can you and I speak in confidence?'

She sat back. 'What do you mean – secrets?'

'I am worried about something, but I don't want Isabella...' More silence.

Lorri refilled their cups. 'I think you'll find secrets, confidences, will twist and scratch. Once you let the cat out it's best to let it run.' She paused. 'I would never intend to say or do anything that would hurt you or Bella.' She smiled. The man needed encouragement. 'Bella is stronger than you think. She's facing her challenges head-on. Life really is too short…' She watched him gather his thoughts and willed him to be brave.

'I had seen her before in the toy shop when I thought I'd lost Finn.' Gabriel shuffled in his chair.

'Lost Finn?' Lorri was curious.

'I drove to the retail park to meet Beth. She wasn't there when we arrived so I followed Finn into the store, and then lost him. I mean I thought I did.'

Lorri decided to bide her time. She had more questions but they would wait. There was more, she was sure of that.

Gabriel sat, chewing over his thoughts, and she could see he was reliving the experience.

'The thing is, I really thought Finn had gone into the shop. I saw him, for God's sake. I had the store security look for him, I was pretty frantic. And then the store manager showed me the video – me entering and no Finn… And then I saw this Celia.'

Lorri leaned forwards. 'Celia?'

'The woman in the dream.' Gabriel clenched his fists. 'She was on the bloody video, the security video. I could hear her speak inside my head. She told me Finn was next door with his mother.'

Lorri was engaged now, this was more like it… 'Is there something else Gabe?'

She watched as he drew in a nervous breath. 'She turned up yesterday, I was in a café. She asked for coffee, gave me a box and then left.'

Lorri bit her lip, holding back a torrent of insights.

'The worse thing was I overheard two lads in the gents, joking about this old fella that was ordering drinks for an imaginary person and talking to himself. It was me. Do you see?' Lorri was unsure what she could see. 'Where's the box?'

'I left it...'

Lorri sighed. 'Listen.' She gathered her thoughts. 'I've no idea who or what Celia is, but she's not exactly a bad guy. First of all she gets you out of a difficult predicament in the store, then she offers you a different viewpoint in the park, and finally she gives you a gift and demonstrates that her relationship is with you, and not the world at large. She wanted you to know that. She wanted you to get found out.'

Gabriel seemed to realise something. 'She said that. She said she was "making a point".'

'And,' said Lorri, tapping the table, 'you have to go back and get that box.'

Gabriel looked nonplussed. 'But won't that be a fiction as well? How can someone imaginary leave something real? And anyway I can't possibly go back.'

Lorri stood. 'Time I checked on Bella.' Gabriel shifted in his chair. She continued. 'I suggest you clear up the kitchen and as soon as Beth returns, or the boys, you and I are going to have a quiet coffee in town.' She turned on her heels and headed for the stairs.

⤙▩ ▩⤚

As they approached the café, Gabriel was unsure he could step inside. Thoughts buzzed around his head like bees in a hive with no exit. Lorri was keen to see the box, but how could there be a box if Celia was unreal, a figment of his imagination. Lorri had slipped her arm through his as they walked. He found the gesture comforting. Her hair was tied back, the extended pony-tail bobbed in the summer breeze. Why was she doing this? Why didn't she feel, as he did, that the balance of his mind was disturbed? An enterprising worker found a chink in the hive's shell, the thought escaped. 'Am I going insane?'

Lorri's head dropped and she laughed. She turned her green eyes to face his hound dog, wrinkled stare. 'You're the doctor, what do you think?' She pulled him to a halt and faced him.

'It's not funny,' he replied. 'If I'd had a patient who'd had my recent experiences I would be concerned.'

'But you're not a patient, and I get that you are concerned. Don't you doctors have a base line that folks have to cross, before you send for the white van?'

'What do you mean?'

'Apart from getting yourself in a state in a toy store, and talking to yourself in this café. Oh, and falling asleep on your feet.' She giggled. 'You do sound a tad bonkers.' Gabriel wished she would take him seriously. 'OK,' she continued, 'did you at any time place yourself or anyone else in harm's way?'

He considered her remark. 'Not exactly, but I don't know how to deal with this, this woman.' Now he was smiling. 'Am I not a little long in the tooth for imaginary friends?'

Lorri gripped his arms, lifting her petite frame to kiss his cheek. 'This is corny, but I can't think of a better way to offer you peace of mind. You need to suspend disbelief.'

Gabriel struggled with the phrase. The maze of ripples on his forehead gave him away.

'It will be hard for you Gabe,' Lorri said as they continued their stroll. 'I can't say too much as it will likely confuse you even more. However, for what it's worth, I will support you, whatever weird and wonderful experiences you may have.'

The exchange had calmed his internal chatter. They rounded a street corner and his heart skipped a beat. 'Oh God, we're here…'

⊶⊷

For the second time that day Gabriel found himself sitting in number eleven.

Lorri reached for the menu. 'Let me order.'

The waitress, the same waitress, came over and took Lorri's order. Gabriel was sure she was smirking. Lorri, apparently, was not missing a trick.

'Was that her? Did she serve you?' Gabriel nodded, grateful that Lorri was keeping her voice down. 'When she comes back ask her if the box was found after you left this morning.'

He tried desperately to think of an excuse to leave.

Lorri touched his leg with her foot. 'Here she comes.'

The drinks arrived and the waitress seemed reluctant to leave. The young woman reached into her apron pocket. 'The thing is,' she said, staring at Gabriel, 'when you went this morning, you left this.' She withdrew the crumpled Tesco bag and placed it on the table. As she weaved her way between adjoining tables Gabriel's first reaction was relief, at least his visit to the curio-shop had been real enough. Lorri peered inside the bag and lifted her shoulders. No sign of a box.

'Sorry.' The waitress had returned. 'There was this too.' She placed the small red box on the table and walked away.

Chapter 10

BARELY AWAKE, RIIKKA caught a glimpse of her face in the small mirror perched on the bedside table. The eyes that stared back were unsettling. For an instant she was looked on by the reflection: someone foreign and unforgiving. She reached out and turned the glass away.

This is stupid.

She couldn't shake off the feeling that there were thoughts in her head that belonged to another. She'd slept fitfully and for the first time regretted that she lived alone. Even though she preferred it that way, company, at that particular moment, would have been appreciated. The nagging sense that something was adrift, not quite right, would not go away. She stared at the unaccustomed clutter in her bedsit as she lay waiting for the alarm to proclaim the day. That too was odd. Today was the third day she'd cheated the clock. She never did that, and there was the sex thing. She was not exactly a prude, but pyjamas were *de rigueur*. So why was she waking naked and sore?

She kicked at the discarded nightclothes as she padded into the bathroom. She sat on the loo facing the only full-length mirror in the flat and quickly closed her legs, a reaction to the disturbing notion that the recurring other was looking back.

Shit!

Riikka stepped into the shower and stood, head back, under hot rain. Gradually, the heat and feel of water resolved her anxieties. The process was stimulating. One more day at the bookshop and it was the weekend. A wicked smile spread across her face as she remembered Jonathan's last visit. They'd managed an ambitious coupling in the same cubicle. She turned to face the tiled surface, pressing against the unyielding and cool ceramic; in her imagination she created a lively Jonathan. The fantasy progressed and she was unconcerned that her visitor was directing. She was lost...

⋆⊷⊶⋆

Riikka was summoned to the manager's office as soon as she arrived at the shop.

Tommy Smith stared at the ceiling. 'This is a request, Riikka. It's fine for you to decline.' The smirk on his flabby face said otherwise.

'But I have no empathy with kids. Surely one of the other staff, any of the others, would be more suitable?'

'So what's it to be?' Tommy stood. The buttons holding his shirt together strained as his corpulent belly settled above his belt. Even with her rising interest in matters physical she had no desire to speculate further.

She capitulated. 'Fine, so when do I start?'

'Next week. Draw up a list of the slow movers in the children's section. I'll call the hospital and arrange for your first visit.'

Riikka hated being a victim. There was definitely no choice about Tommy's request. She turned and left the room and was busy listing titles when Sarah made an appearance. Riikka waited. She'd resolved that the voice was actually an aspect of her own personality, and one that had a label, Sarah. Even so, surprise made her drop the book she was holding. As she bent to gather the paperback, Sarah spoke. 'I'm afraid we have to go off-line for a minute or two.'

'What do you mean? You make me sound like a computer.' Riikka placed the book on the shelf, rationalising the experience – she was irritated by her own thought processes. The feeling that she was displaced, in the rabbit hole again, intensified.

'Hopefully your colleagues will know what to do…'

Riikka rallied. 'Even supposing what you say is true, don't you think I should be given some choice in the matter?'

'That's a chestnut we'll have to debate later.'

<hr />

Riikka couldn't understand, the taste and smell was foul. It was mixed with exhortations for unknown, missing resources and alternated with pressure on her chest. The rubbery sensation and dead air returned. Riikka desperately needed to remember something. The unpleasant intrusions were unwelcome and she couldn't figure out why her eyes would not open. She could feel bile rising in her throat to meet an uninvited presence. A voice, a male voice, sang out. She couldn't make out all the words.

'Where the hell is that…'

For a time there was a pause in the sour wind and drumstick beating her chest.

'Time to wake.' Sarah was back and purposeful. 'That gross bag of shit is about to hit on your tonsils again. Don't you think it's time to wake? Just a suggestion.'

The reboot was taking an age and Riikka was lost, the dots most definitely disjointed. 'Why can't I remember?'

'Listen, will you go back. You may be unconscious but that man's breath is turning our stomach.'

Riikka felt it this time. Someone was holding her nose and winding a tongue across the back of her throat. This time there was no resistance. Her gorge rose and voided into the opposing cavity.

Paramedics saved the day. Entering the shop at that precise moment they assumed that Tommy was the patient. The other staff members explained. Riikka was helped to a sitting position and connected to a portable ECG monitor. A member of staff tentatively handed a towel to Tommy, who staggered to the toilet.

The room was cleared.

'Would you like to take this off?'

Riikka nodded and helped the rather good-looking medic remove her soiled shirt. He folded a regulation blanket around her bare shoulders.

'ECG is fine, blood pressure's fine. Any aches or pains?'

Riikka shook her head.

'We'll have to take you in. To make sure we haven't missed anything.'

My God he's gorgeous.

'Let's see if you can stand and we'll get you settled into the van.' He disconnected and packed the ECG and his companion disappeared with the holdalls. He held out his hand. 'Take it steady, you may feel a bit light-headed at first.' He helped her stand and she leaned into his body, feigning the vapours. 'Whoa, I think we'd better wheel you out.'

Riikka straightened and gripped his arm. 'I'll be fine, honestly, if you could perhaps support my weight.'

The staff at the hospital were attentive enough, although Riikka lost interest when her medic disappeared. After almost an hour a doctor arrived. She read the notes clipped to the bottom of Riikka's bed and proceeded to test her reflexes. 'How do you feel?'

Riikka wanted to get home. 'I feel OK. No idea what happened. I blacked out...'

'Can you remember how you felt before the incident?

A nagging suspicion that she needed to watch her words was underlined by a familiar voice.

'Careful, no will do fine.'

Riikka hesitated.

The doctor persisted. 'Was there something?'

'No, I was cataloguing books for the children's hospital and then I woke puking into my boss's face. Embarrassing.'

The doctor smiled. 'For the record I think he may have over-reacted: the mouth-to-mouth routine. Smelling salts may have been more effective.' She sat on the side of the bed. 'Is there someone you could stay with for a couple of days? Your notes say you live alone.'

'Do I have to? I prefer my own company and my boyfriend's coming down for the weekend. Actually, he's a medical student… ' The doctor took the bait.

'In that case you can go, but be careful, any sign of light headedness and you should get medical attention.' Their conversation was interrupted by Tommy's voice.

'… if I could see how she is? I'm her manager.'

The curtain parted and a nurse's head appeared. 'Your manager's here. Can I show him in?'

Riikka could almost feel her blood pressure rising. She was half dressed and in no mood to see Tommy in her present state. 'Tell him to wait for me outside.' She turned to the doctor. 'I have a problem.' She lifted the soiled shirt from the plastic carrier left by her medico.

'We have a supply. We'll find you something.'

❖

Before she left the hospital Riikka determined she would not let Tommy off the hook. The journey back in his car proved to be physically uncomfortable and predictable – he was the sort of person who liked to have the upper hand.

'Well I must say you gave us quite a turn.'

Riikka could tell he was expecting an apology. She decided to go on the offensive. *What the hell.* 'What happened exactly?'

'You passed out. I heard a commotion and then saw you on the floor, pale as a ghost. I swear you weren't breathing…' Tommy paused, presumably for dramatic effect, then continued. 'I yelled for someone to call an ambulance and waded straight in with CPR. I can tell you I was terrified.'

'So, I guess you saved my life?' Riikka's sacrificial pawn suckered him out.

'Well, you know… Needs must…'

The son of a bitch wants me to thank him!

'Did you by chance check my pulse?'

He swore as a battered Mercedes cut in ahead. 'To be honest I can't remember, it all happened so fast. Being the shop first-aider I had to dive in, no time to lose. Never thought the training would come in so handy.'

Riikka stared at the puffy face and swollen lips. A vague and disturbing sensation roiled in her stomach. *That's your game. Handy was it?* She took a deep breath. 'The tests were pretty conclusive.' She waited.

'Tests? Conclusive?'

'According to the paramedics and the hospital doctor I fainted. I guess you must have missed my pulse and shallow breathing?'

He fingered his collar. 'Wait a minute, I did my best. Better to err on the side of caution.'

Riikka decided to up the ante. 'I take it that's the nearest I'm going to get to an apology?'

'Apology! Now see here...'

Riikka cut in. 'Of course, I could always lodge a complaint with my staff rep.'

Tommy Smith took a hypothetical step back and made a critical mistake. 'As I remember,' he said, 'you were unconscious until you vomited in my face.'

'As you weren't unconscious, do you remember tonguing me in your efforts to clear my airways?' Riikka gave him no time to respond. 'It was your unsavoury breath and unusual mouth-to-mouth activity that made me vomit.'

This time there was no response. Riikka noticed Tommy's hands tighten as he gripped the wheel.

'Can I suggest,' she said, pausing for effect, 'that you be a little less "rushed" if there's a next time? Also, from now on your card is marked. By this time tomorrow every woman who works in the store, and that means everyone, will know what you did.' Riikka reflected. 'And it might be a good idea if you have a second member of staff trained as the shop medic, perhaps a woman this time?'

The rest of the week passed without further mishap. Riikka didn't tell a soul what had happened, but she was amused to see an announcement pinned to the staff notice board when she next turned up for work: *Volunteer wanted for first-aid training.* Tommy had put it about that he'd been traumatised by the recent emergency and wanted someone else to share the responsibility. *Bingo*.

⌖

Riikka's fingers tingled as she tidied the bedsit. She fished spare pillows from the dusty airing cupboard. It was Friday afternoon and Jonathan was due about six.

He arrived on time and she was not disappointed. He'd acquired designer stubble and their first kiss was an interesting experience. The hair around his lips was surprisingly soft. She stroked his chin.

'This is new.'

He grinned. 'Had no time to shave. It'll have to come off soon as it's starting to itch.' He held her at arm's length.

'You look different.' His rucksack slipped from his shoulder and he gazed around the bedsit. 'Where shall I dump this?'

'Anywhere.'

He yawned. 'Sorry, not bored, promise. Hospital placement has been a bitch. They treat student doctors like slave labour. I can't tell you how good it is to get away.' He reached into his pocket, grinning. 'Let's catch the cheap drinks. It's only six-thirty.'

Riikka found her thoughts drifting. She was more interested in his pockets. *Stop staring…* 'Yeh, why not, give me a second.' She dashed into the bathroom and closed the door, giggling furiously.

⌖

Much later, several drinks and a curry later, Riikka was approaching her limits. The sex had started well enough, but was turning into an endurance test. What she desired was slipping away as Jonathan began his pre-climax moans. *Too soon!* Her orgasm drifted ahead, chased by thoughts and distracted by the monotonous pounding between her legs.

'Oh my God...'

She sighed, now he was having a religious experience. She resigned herself to a rerun in the morning.

'You give up too easily.' It seemed that Sarah shared her concern. Sarah's voice, of course it was her "voice" – even Riikka knew that multiple personalities didn't converse and schizophrenia definitely didn't run in the family. 'Let me show you a different approach,' continued Sarah, her hand descending. Jonathan, it seemed, was oblivious to the added strokes as he pursued his own golden glow. Meanwhile Riikka experienced a strange opening sensation. It was unlike anything she'd felt before. Her thoughts were cut short by Sarah's next instruction. 'Stop thinking.'

An overwhelming, remote energy mingled with more familiar sensations. Their mutual cries of pleasure were cut short as in quick succession Jonathan stopped moving and Riikka passed out.

⇢⊨⊙ ⊙⊨⇠

Sarah took her hand. 'There, you made it.'

Riikka gazed in amazement. She was floating next to Sarah in a green sea, safe enough, but the sky, it was filled with a rising moon. But not the familiar moon, this moon was planet-sized. Pale ochre and grey-blue clouds shifted across its surface. 'Where the fuck am I?'

'Good question. However, how you got here is a much better topic for conversation.'

'Christ, Sarah, what happened? I was having a leisurely fuck for God's sake and now I'm... Where am I?'

'Your mind is taking a break. You won't remember this chat; well, most of it won't be remembered, so let's make the most of it.'

'But what about Jonathan?'

'He's fine. His body is contentedly curled up next to yours having notched up a first – you came together. He is not so flimsy that he takes full credit for the accomplishment, but you'll find him a very happy person when he wakes.'

'This is crazy.'

'Off-world perhaps, definitely not crazy, and its uncommon knowledge you're experiencing. So relax...'

There was a quality to floating in the sea, a quality that rendered the unknowable known. It was like being held, cradled, effortless. Riikka could cope with relax. She felt expansive and willing to suspend curiosity.

'Your Taoist sages have come closest to explaining what's happened,' continued Sarah. 'In their tradition women are yin and gather subtle energies, whereas men are yang and expend energy.' Sarah closed her eyes. 'Bring the two together and, ironically, your most pleasurable, shared physical activity, sex, is the closest you get to the source of these energies. You are the nearest I have to a battery charger. Without your help I cannot access all this...' She gazed at the horizon. 'In fact, without your help a significant event will not occur. As it happens you are an adept – in a past life you would have been considered a wizard. I helped, that's all, helped you boost the process.' Sarah turned to face Riikka. 'Right now, your mind is trying to make sense of an experience that makes no sense. This ocean and that planet are not necessarily real, they are the explanation your mind creates to puzzle out its relationship to something that is beyond thought.'

Riikka gazed at the rising orb and could almost see the folds of space that supported its tumbling motion. Curiosity fought its way back. 'But why me? I don't understand...'

Sarah took her hand and rolled it into a closed fist. 'There'll be times when you'll need to make use of this experience, to draw on the energy that abounds in this place.'

Riikka closed her eyes and allowed the illusions manifested by her senses to cease. She surrendered to the warm, enfolding care of the ocean. Breathing and any evidence of a beating heart were lost, irrelevant, as she drifted into an extended moment in time. Knowledge came at a rush, not byte by byte, but all at once. She experienced, in that time-sheltered place, a link with Sarah and her companions, and beyond that, to the source of knowing that mapped all possibility. When her mind's insistence on progress and explanation broke through, all Riikka could hear was Sarah's familiar voice.

'And there's a bonus – from now on, no more headaches.'

Chapter 11

Finn sprinkled fish food into Freddie's bowl. He had a sudden thought – do fish drink? The notion was disconcerting. As far as he could tell the fish bowl didn't seem to be running out of water, and yet, surely, Freddie needed to drink?

'Fish are different.' Cissy's assertion, vague on detail, was enough for Finn. He felt tired and flopped onto his bed. Cissy seemed concerned. 'You OK?'

Finn shrugged his shoulders and yawned. Cissy was sitting cross-legged at the bottom of his bed. 'Sure, I'm tired…' The yawn triggered another coughing fit. A weird rattling sound followed each wheeze.

'That doesn't sound too good.' Cissy stretched out her legs and placed her feet next to Finn's, sole to sole. There was no sensation of touch, but he realised that when Cissy "touched" it was not the usual sort of touch. When she made contact he felt better somehow, like the difference a deep breath of fresh air made, or waking after a good sleep.

'How do you do that, make things better?'

Cissy made her not-going-to-answer-that-one face. Instead she simply said, 'Because I can.' She continued, changing the subject. 'I hear your mum is going to have a baby.'

Finn shook his head, did he have no secrets? 'So?'

'Well, how do you feel about that?'

'OK, I guess.'

Cissy resumed her Buddha pose. 'So you'll have a real live friend soon.'

'What d'you mean?

'When your sister arrives.'

Finn was gambling on a brother, but... 'Anyway, you'll still be about?'

It was a question that remained unanswered as Finn's mother shouted from the bottom of the stairs disrupting the dialogue. 'Bed-time Finn. I'll be up to run your bath in a minute, and remind me to give you your medicine.'

⊷⊨◉ ◉⊨⊶

There was one thing that Finn hated more than feeling sick and that was being sick. He gazed at the mess on his duvet. The spasm of coughing that woke him threatened to return. Cissy stood by his bed.

'I feel bad.' He shifted in the bed, a half-dazed look on his face as he attempted to lie down. Horizontal was not a healthy option. The fluid in his lungs moved, ably assisted by gravity. Finn was sweating and still feeling sick. He fought back the impulse to clear his throat, knowing that was how the bad stuff started. He opened his eyes, Cissy was still there. 'Make it go away.' Finn had realised some time ago that his imaginary friend was not much help with practical matters.

Much to his amazement she pointed to the door. 'Best to get some real help...'

He abandoned his attempt at ignoring the smell from his sheets, folded back the soiled bedding and padded towards his bedroom door. 'Mum, I've been sick,' he shouted. No response. The shout triggered another coughing fit, and he shivered. His rather over-productive efforts rekindled the gagging reflex. This time he dropped to his knees and heaved the remains of his supper onto the carpet. The door opened and light from the hall streamed into the room.

'Finn... Christ!' His father removed his bare foot from the sticky puddle. 'Beth, I need a hand.'

After much fussing Finn was back in bed, sitting with an old washing-up bowl on his lap, a towel covering the changed duvet. His father had washed his feet and was drying out the cleaned patch on the carpet.

Finn's mother sat next to Finn on the bed. 'Here, try to drink some water. We've spoken to Granddad and he says we need to get medicine inside you to bring your temperature down, but I'd like to make sure you're not going to be sick again.'

Finn sipped half-heartedly. 'Do I have to? I want to sleep.' Cissy tutted. Finn was getting a little irritated by his friend. He glared across the room. *Whose side are you on anyway?*

His dad yawned and slumped in the old armchair in the corner while his mother poured a spoonful of the sticky goo.

'Have to make do with liquid paracetamol I'm afraid.' Finn winced – he hated the pink syrup. 'Granddad's coming over in the morning with something better.'

'It'll make me sick again.' The threat fell on deaf ears. He swallowed two spoons' full and glared at his mother.

'Coo-eee…'

Finn couldn't resist smiling. Cissy was standing right in front of his dad pulling the most amazing, funny face. She jumped backwards, at the same time as his dad stood and tripped over Finn's discarded clothing. He walked towards the bed. Finn giggled.

'Glad to see you've regained your sense of humour.' His father yawned again. 'I'm off to bed.' He kissed the top of Finn's head. 'Shout if you feel sick again, we'll leave the doors open.'

Finn nodded. As soon as his parents left the room he placed the stained washing bowl on the floor. Cissy came and sat by his feet. Gratefully, the hot, sick feeling was going away. 'Why did you jump back when Dad stood up? Aren't you like a ghost to grownups?'

'Guess so, but your dad may have felt something and I didn't want to risk that.'

'Like a spooky feeling?' Finn was intrigued. 'Anyway that was a brilliant joke face.'

'Close your eyes.'

'Why?'

'I want to talk inside your head.'

Finn, too tired to be curious, closed his eyes. He was pretty sure that all their talk was inside his head anyway. 'OK then.' He waited.

'I have to explain something complicated so listen carefully.' It was unusual for Cissy to sound so serious. 'It's about free will.' Cissy reconsidered her words and continued. 'I want to copy something, something inside.' Another pause. Finn could hear, remotely, his clock ticking. 'The thing is, what I want to copy is protected, kept safe so it can't be messed with.'

Finn was struggling. 'What's kept safe? Don't understand.' He ploughed on. 'And how can you copy stuff inside me?'

'I told you this wouldn't be easy.'

Finn, eyes tight shut, relaxed, this was his best friend ever talking. 'Do it, I don't mind.' He could feel Cissy weighing his words before her final whisper.

'OK, no more talking...'

Finn could usually sense when Cissy was with him, even when his eyes were closed. He could see her most of the time, but often it was more like she was a dream, or a thought in his head. Now that feeling spread until he couldn't figure where Cissy started and he finished. A weird tingling followed Cissy's progress as she searched. He could make out the moment when she found what she was looking for and that she was waiting. At the same time he knew what free will was: not like understanding, more a sudden knowing. In an act of total selflessness Finn lowered his shields, the barriers that protected everything that he was, from the chaos that chattered beyond. He felt Cissy's presence expand to protect him as she worked, and before he drifted into real sleep, as she left, he felt like he'd done someone, somewhere, a real favour.

Gabriel and Lorri sat either side of Isabella's bed. With Lorri's encouragement Gabriel had bitten his lip and recounted his recent, odd-ball experiences. The three stared at the small red box, the only physical evidence of Gabriel's adventures.

'Now I feel much better.' Isabella tapped the box. 'What fun you will have lifting the lid on this mystery.' She gripped Gabriel's hand. 'And in future young man, be courageous...' Gabriel half-smiled, realising that Isabella was not impressed with his innate caution.

Lorri picked up the cube. There was a fine groove running around four sides that suggested a lid, but their joint efforts had failed to budge it. It was heavy too, perfectly symmetrical, each side five centimetres long. Lorri was stumped. 'It feels like it's filled with metal or rock. Maybe it's solid, not a box?'

Gabriel fell back on his let's-change-the-topic strategy. 'Finn was telling me about his imaginary friend, Cissy. I was tempted to tell him about mine.'

'Maybe you should.' Lorri pushed her chair back. 'Mind you, I like mystery, somehow living with a mystery is so much more satisfying than living with no mystery. Don't you think?'

Gabriel frowned. 'Not too sure about that.'

Lorri stood, addressing her sister. 'Bath time?'

Gabriel followed suit. 'And I should make tracks too. Beth rang earlier, Finn was sick in the night. I said I'd pop over. I'll say goodbye before I go.'

Lorri had taken on the role of companion nurse. Gabriel was much relieved. He seemed to have more time for the occasional walk, and God forbid, reading. Isabella had flourished under her sister's care. The cancer continued to make advances, but she was still at home and Gabriel was hopeful they could manage without further extended hospital visits. The Macmillan nurse visited twice a week and made sure that Lorri and Gabriel were updated on Isabella's condition. All three were resolved that Isabella should finish her journey at home.

He could hear them talking in the bathroom as he mounted the stairs. Lorri was busy sponging down her sister's back as Gabriel eased open the door. 'I'm off. He held up his battered home-visits case. He no longer prescribed drugs, but couldn't bear to part with his bag of tricks. 'I won't be long.'

Lorri caught his eye. There was no need for words. He would advise Beth to keep Finn away from his grandma until the infection was under control. 'I'll see you soon.'

Isabella flicked water at a fly showing too much interest in her feet. 'You be careful too, I don't want you in quarantine.' She blew him a kiss. 'Give my love to Finn.'

Sometimes, Finn thought sleep time was better than awake time, especially when Cissy was with him. She'd finished her copying so they were having a rest together. They were looking out to sea, he loved the sea, so big. He spotted a white tanker, the superstructure sparkling in the sun, making knots towards the horizon. He felt like a part of him was sailing with the boat.

Herring gull cries drew his attention to a small fishing boat, closer to land, the scavengers eager to share the hard-won catch. Finn could smell the salty air and hear the faint chatter and shrieks of the gulls as they fed. Cissy stirred.

'Whatever happens Finn, don't be fooled by your thoughts. Nothing ends.'

Finn was amazed by his friend's silliness at times. Everybody knew that minutes pass, days end. Finn clicked his fingers. 'See, the click ended…' He felt proud of himself. *So who's smart now?*

'The click didn't end, it changed into silence.'

A rather disturbing notion wriggled into Finn's head. 'If Grandma dies what will she change into?'

'What do you think?'

'Will she be a ghost? That might be scary.' The ball of thought unravelled further. 'And what about you, and me?' Finn could tell she was smiling, which chased away some of the fear that was sneaking about.

'The click doesn't worry about not being a click, it enjoys being what it is.' Cissy sat and made her smart face. 'And when it's not a click, then whatever it becomes it can enjoy being that too.'

Finn sighed. The conversation was getting way too difficult. A mist rolled in from the sea, rubbing out the ship, the fishing boat and the seagulls' squawks. It felt cold and it was getting dark.

'Perhaps you'll have new insights,' Cissy said.

Finn had no idea what "insights" were, he hoped they were exciting. He could hear a voice, his granddad's voice, and then the visions, of the sea, of the mist and his concerns melted and he opened his eyes.

--⊨⊙ ⊙⊨--

'Morning, Finn.' His granddad was holding his stethoscope and rested it against Finn's chest. 'Deep breath please.' Finn obliged.

'I was dreaming about the sea.'

His granddad removed the ear pieces. 'Sit up for me, sunshine.' He lifted Finn's Superman top and tapped his back with his fingers.

'Well, what do you think?' Finn's mum was sitting in Finn's corner chair.

'I think Finn would benefit from antibiotics. Unless I've lost my touch, his chest is congested. Ring Irene at the surgery and ask her if Robert could pop over and see him. A short course should do the trick.' Gabriel gave his stethoscope to Finn who promptly donned the ear pieces and listened.

'Where's it 'gested Granddad?' He struggled with the word.

Gabriel shifted the position of the acoustic head. 'Take a deep breath and listen carefully.' Finn did.

'It gurgles a bit.'

'That's right. The bottom of your lungs, where the air goes when you breathe, is filling up with fluid. Antibiotics will kill off the bacteria, little bugs that are making the rattle.'

Finn took another breath and smiled.

Gabriel retrieved his instrument. 'You should get up and move about, drink lots.'

'What about his temperature?' asked Finn's mother.

'Ah, yes…' Gabriel reached into his bag. 'Won't hurt to give him a couple of these every four hours until the antibiotics kick in. See if you can get him to eat fruit, but no dairy, for a couple of days.' He winked at Finn as he handed the pack to Beth. 'These are the ones that disappear in water.'

'My favourite,' Finn whooped. 'Better than pink stuff.'

—>═◉ ◉═<—

The house was quiet when Gabriel returned home, too quiet. He dropped the car keys on the hall stand and took to the stairs. Lorri was closing Isabella's bedroom door; when she saw him approaching she lifted a finger to her lips and pointed downstairs.

Lorri filled the kettle and turned to face her brother-in-law. 'The Macmillan nurse has barely left, she came with the oncologist. Bella wants a few minutes alone.' Gabriel sat down. 'Bella's liver and kidney functions are failing. The cancer seems to be metastasizing.' Lorri pursed her lips. 'We have to prepare the family. We need to figure out a way that Bella can say her goodbyes without it turning into a weepy.' Gabriel couldn't speak. 'She has enough to cope with.'

Gabriel gazed at Lorri, trying to take in what she was saying, but was unable to grapple with the notion that finally he and Isabella were going to be separated, and permanently.

He was still holding his worn case. He placed it carefully on the kitchen table. Somehow the instruments that he'd put to such good use seemed redundant. Death, it would seem, was about to have its day.

Lorri handed Gabriel the hot drink. 'She's expecting you. I'll make sure you're not interrupted. Ignore the phones. This is your time...'

Gabriel sat with Isabella for almost two hours. Little was said. They accustomed each other to the notion that her life was drawing to a close. Plans were made and Gabriel agreed to make the calls.

'You should contact the girls later today. I've written letters for the grandchildren and given them to Beth.' Isabella smiled. 'I'm assuming the second will be a girl. Call it intuition, or more like wishful thinking.' She handed him a small envelope. 'It's just a little something from me, for afterwards.' She paused. 'Apart from Lorri and our family there's no one else I want to see.'

'And after tomorrow? What then?'

Isabella drew in a shallow breath, which hurt. 'I'm going to be fitted with a morphine pump, so I can regulate my own pain relief. When that's done, easy on the fluids, no drips. According to the doctor who came this morning the internal damage is progressing pretty rapidly.' She ran her fingers through the grey curls above Gabriel's collar and tipped his head so she could see his eyes. 'I won't be here next week.'

Chapter 12

GABRIEL WOKE, HE presumed, to another unremarkable day. This fiction, that always seemed to follow waking, lingered. He noticed sunlight exploring chinks in the bedroom curtains. His mouth was dry – snoring again? *Wonder if I kept Isabella awake?* Gabriel groaned and rolled into the duvet as the shutters that held back the rush of memory flew open. In a few hours he would have to face his family and Isabella's funeral.

The familiar collection of objects lining the shelves and walls offered little consolation, frame after frame a reminder of a past with no future. One photograph in particular caught his eye. He'd taken it on some eastern Mediterranean beach, a stop-off on their retirement cruise. Isabella sat on white sand. She was wearing a cotton dress, a beautiful deep pink. She was staring at the camera smiling and for some unaccountable reason she was holding out her hands. They were cupped together, sand streaming between her fingers, the falling grains caught for posterity by the admiring shutter.

He closed his eyes, demanding a different outcome. What he wanted to hear was Isabella's cheerful voice and be reminded of the next task, but those chances had passed. With no sight his other senses sharpened; he could pick out Isabella's fading perfume. There was a growing conflict between the things that provided some measure of comfort, and were yet the cause of his present discomfort. Breaking the grip of the bed coverings he released an arm and, reaching forwards, smoothed the far pillow. The tender gesture was not enough.

Feeling like a trespasser he slid across the bed and settled into the chilled and absent space. From Isabella's vantage point he noticed her slippers almost hidden beneath the dressing table. He couldn't imagine that they would ever be moved. The emotions that this simple vision inspired were too much. Gabriel threw back the duvet and grabbed his towel from the radiator.

In the bathroom he fumbled with the tap, splashing cold water on his face. He drew a deep breath to steady his nerves. Hands smaller than his had discarded the Marigolds resting on the tiled windowsill, the yellow fingers barely covering a jar of cream. He closed his hand to a fist, willing the associations to stop. Water dripped from his chin, the forgotten towel within reach. Tears, the first since Isabella's death, were tempered by the soft touch of blue cotton. Gabriel wept, ignoring the chimes from the downstairs clock.

⋅⊷⊷⊷⊷⋅

Grace was the first to arrive. She parked away from the house and was in no hurry to leave the car. She glanced at the bag perched on the passenger seat. The daily itch began. *Not yet. Not yet.* Gritting her teeth she removed the key from the ignition. *Better make a start. I hope Dad's OK.* She glanced at her watch. Beth had promised to meet her at nine. Grabbing her bag she stepped out of the car, gathering her thoughts.

She opened the front gate, the hinges still complaining. Her childhood home was not the same: the neglected pathway, long ago a playground, seemed changed, as if her mother's departure had taken the joy from her memories. Grace sighed. She trod carefully, reliving an old obsession, avoiding cracks between the over-weathered flag stones. Walking slowly towards the house she was haunted by the vague sound and feel of tossed slates, of hops and squeals of laughter. The carefully laid paving had long since lost its playtime utility, couch grass and dandelion the victors. Gardening had never been her parents' strong suit.

The pack of nicotine whispered. Just one, she thought, before it starts, before you need to face your father's grief, and your own. She paused as the shades from the past joined in the call: how will we manage, how will Dad manage? It was as if all possibilities had been reduced to unknowns. Grace unconsciously railed against the call to delay. She pressed the doorbell and waited, stale chimes breaking the spell. *Come on, Dad, Lorri. Surely they're awake.* Grace opened her bag and rummaged. *Bollocks, where's the wretched thing?* Eventually, the key was found and the front door eased open.

'Dad? Lorri?' Grace pulled the key from the Yale lock. The house seemed deserted. An unopened letter lay on the floor. She bent to retrieve the envelope.

'Hi Grace.'

Startled, Grace was confronted by Lorri standing at the foot of the stairs, twisting her feet into ankle boots. 'Sorry about the doorbell, couldn't get this damn boot on. Your dad's in the bathroom. I'm going for a quick walk, clear my head.' She took the envelope from Grace's hand and gave her a quick hug. 'I won't be long.'

Grace held on to Lorri's arms. 'How is he?' she whispered.

'Pleased that you're here, and living the nightmare…' Lorri grabbed her coat. 'Difficult day for all of us I guess. Where's Beth?'

'On route.'

Her father interjected, calling from the first floor. 'Is that you Grace?'

'Yes, down here.'

Lorri headed for the front door, whispering, apologetic. 'Only be thirty minutes, promise.'

Grace dropped her bag and keys on the hall stand. *Why do I always do that?* She shouted up the stairs. 'Have you eaten yet?'

Her father stumbled down the stairs still wearing his preferred night-wear: tee-shirt and boxers. He was wiping his face with a towel and Grace could see he'd been weeping. She repeated the question.

'Have you eaten breakfast?'

He shook his head. 'Not yet.'

'OK, I'll make breakfast, then you really must shower. We have two hours before this place turns into Hotel California.'

Grace marched into the kitchen, removed her jacket and grabbed her mother's kitchen apron. She opened the fridge. 'Did Beth get the shopping in?'

'Yes, came over last night. We could have managed, but you know how your sister is.'

Setting a pan on the hob, Grace composed her face. She really wanted that first cigarette.

'One egg or two?'

⭰⭤

After breakfast Gabriel retreated to complete his ablutions and Grace decided to lay out suitable clothes for her father. She contemplated the row of neatly ordered suits and shirts. In the bottom of the wardrobe six lidless shoeboxes displayed footwear, mostly unworn. She lifted a pair of black brogues. Next, a dark-blue suit and white shirt from the rails and a black necktie. She laid them carefully on the bed.

Gabriel coughed politely from the door. Grace smiled to herself. 'Dad, why don't you wear these new shoes?' She followed her father's gaze as he scanned the ordered display on his bed.

'For God's sake Grace, enough.' He steered her out of the room. 'I remember how to dress.'

'That's more like it. You're much more attractive when you're feisty.' She kissed his cheek. 'And you smell better too.' *And, by God, he's smiling.* Grace wandered back to the hall, picking up her bag. She toyed with the unopened pack of cigarettes.

Her daily attempt at giving up was going to fail early, and in her estimation for good reason. She stood outside and sent her absent sister a text message.

Where are you?

The first drag dropped her anxiety levels by half. *Christ, I'll never be able to give this up.*

⊶⊷

Gabriel and Grace were sitting in the kitchen drinking coffee when the doorbell rang. It was the caterers. Soon the large dining room table was covered with a starched white cloth and enough food to sustain the mourners. Grace set out glasses and arranged bottles of drinks in the kitchen. And still no sign of Beth. She noticed her father struggling with a pile of plates and walked over to help.

'You look great Dad. The blue suit is perfect. Good choice.' Grace checked her watch. 'Think I'll prop the front door open, save us doing the doorman thing all morning.'

Grace stood on the front step while her father rearranged the lounge furniture. Now that he showed some sign of coping her thoughts returned to her mother. She was haunted by the memory of Isabella's empty stare at the end. She and Beth had only popped out for groceries. As soon as she entered the bedroom Grace knew her mother had gone. She was relieved that her suffering was over but plagued by feelings of regret, about times when she'd had the opportunity to visit but was distracted by other concerns. She was aware that the process of compromise she juggled with every day left her unsatisfied and now regretful. Maybe she could've handled things differently?

The smell of honeysuckle enticed her back. She was ready to say goodbye and it was a beautiful autumn day. For a brief moment Grace could almost taste her mother's absence. It was the small things she missed: her smile, always at the right time; her touch, never in anger; a womanly pride in her daughter's achievements – all gone.

'Glad to see I'm not the only one lost in thought. Unusual to see you so reflective.'

Grace took comfort from her father's touch, their roles suddenly reversed. She leaned into his shoulder. 'Guess we all miss her...'

A car slowed as it approached the house. Gabriel tapped Grace's hand. 'Isn't that Beth's car?'

⋯⊷⊶⋯

Beth braced herself. Her father and Grace were waiting at the front door. She passed a hand over her extended belly, searching for movement within. *One step at a time.*

'Dad, you don't need to avoid my bump.' Beth was amused by her father's posture as they hugged. 'And you look really smart.'

Finn shouted from the front gate. 'Granddad!'

Her father waved in Finn's direction and kissed Beth lightly on the cheek. 'Go on in, I think we're all set.' He headed out to meet his grandson and Beth strode inside, followed by Grace.

'Could have done with your help earlier, where have you been? Dad was in a right state.'

'Well he's not now.' Beth flexed her aching back. 'I had a bit of a scare when I woke up, a slight show.'

'You should have said. For God's sake sit.' Grace pulled out a kitchen chair. 'Should you even be here?'

'I've told no one so please don't say anything, especially to Dad. And yes, I do have to be here.' Beth wrapped her arms around her sister's waist. 'And sorry for being late.'

Before they could continue Finn burst into the kitchen. He buried his head between them. 'Granddad says I can have a biscuit.'

⇥⊫⊚ ⊚⊨⊣⇤

Lorri drank in the warm air. She'd totally underestimated the effect it would have when Bella passed away. Her sister had always been a part of her life, somewhere within reach. Now she was gone. Her absence was odd, unacceptable, and yet... Lorri spread her fingers, running them through the leaves of a privet hedge as she walked. *Save a place for me honey.*

She felt blessed that they'd had so much time together. Truly, there was nothing left unsaid. Bella had been right though, there was something haunting the Newman family and it was not Grandma Lucca. In her final week the sisters had decided they could not, should not, interfere. Gabriel's behaviour, his companion Celia, all seemed to be following some sort of plan, to have a purpose. In the end Bella was content to release her concerns, and Lorri felt their weight on her shoulders as she walked.

Her promise to watch over Gabriel was made with an easy conscience. He was a natural healer, and thank the Gods was totally unaware he had such raw talent. Whatever the fates were weaving she was glad to be watching over him, at least for a while.

She missed the sea, and the gales blowing rain through the lochs. Strolling through a suburban landscape, obliged to tread pathways determined by traffic flow and the boundaries of private property, was no substitute. The air moved close to her cheek. A wren darted ahead, alighting on a gate post. Lorri smiled, engaging with the tiny creature. It was a good sign. Wren apparently thought so too, she led Lorri to the corner of Gabriel's street, dancing from bush to tree. With a final flourish she bobbed a curtsey and left. Beth's car passed as Lorri made her way back. She shortened her pace – they would need time together.

Chapter 13

THE SUMMER WAS almost gone and still Riikka hesitated. She was content, dividing her time between the surgery and the bookshop, but she needed to ease the drift away from a career decision. Jonathan's visits were becoming more frequent. At some point soon, describing their relationship as "early days" would be stretching the truth. She checked her watch. The London train was due in ten minutes.

She'd received a call from her father the previous week. In recent years he'd worked abroad, specialising in Middle East issues, and was making a rare flying visit to wind up a property sale. According to their hurried conversation he was intent on taking an appointment with Reuters based in Beirut. He'd requested the visit. She'd been surprised by the call. They'd never been particularly close. As the train drew in Riikka felt apprehensive. Her childhood was spent with a variety of relatives after her mother had died. Her father had never made much effort at parenting; his excuse was always the demands of his job. So why get in touch now?

She hardly recognised him as he stepped from the train. He was dressed like a colonial, a faded cream suit and black tee-shirt. He was tanned, and his face broke into a smile when he spotted her.

'Rik. Wow, you look terrific.' He dumped his backpack and Riikka accepted the hug.

'How was your trip?'

'Fine.'Riikka waited for the "but". With her father there was always a "but". 'The thing is, my posting to Beirut has been brought forward. I fly out tomorrow so I'll need to take the last train back tonight.' He retrieved his bag. 'Sorry, I was hoping to spend more time with you.'

Riikka grabbed his arm. 'That gives us time for lunch. No sweat...' They headed for the car park.

The journey back to her flat was broken by small talk and extended silences. The man sitting in her car was a stranger, and although Riikka was prepared to be civil, she had no great expectations for their limited time together. In some respects, that was preferable.

They were part way through lunch when he reached for his bag and removed a package. 'I wanted you to have this. It's mostly your mother's old photos, birth certificate... There's also a notebook.' He seemed reluctant to let go of the package. 'I found it all when I was clearing out my London flat. I should have given you this years ago.'

'What's in the notebook?'

'Its gibberish mostly, your mother liked to flow write, stream of consciousness stuff. I thought you'd like to have it.'

Riikka took the bundle and placed it on the bookshelf with Vasi. 'I'll take a look later.'

'Good grief, you kept the doll.' He stood and lifted it. 'Do you remember the story? Your mum used to read it to you.'

Riikka shook her head. 'Too young. Too long ago. I'm surprised you remember.'

She watched his head drop as he carefully replaced the doll. 'When your mother died I sort of fell apart. I couldn't cope…' The look on his face was wretched. 'The other reason I wanted to see you was to apologise. I was pathetic.' He raised his head. 'This will be my last posting overseas. Maybe when I get back from this tour we could spend more time together?'

Riikka was embarrassed. The last thing she wanted was this late-comer parent. She had to say something. 'You don't need to apologise. I never had a father so what is there to regret? If there is any hurt it's well buried.' She pushed her plate away, aware that her response was telling, and even if unintentionally so, hurtful. Her father's expression was pained. 'I'm sorry, that didn't come out too well. For sure, get in touch when you're back in the UK.' She reached across the table and held his hand. 'Could you tell me about Mum?'

⤙⟡ ⟡⤚

Riikka stared at the screen, scrolling through online requests for repeat prescriptions. Although she'd felt nothing at the time, the conversation with her father had been unsettling. She'd managed to be polite. He had seemed to want more, but she couldn't conjure affection. She'd been grateful for his recollections about her mother, but her notebook was something else. The "gibberish" described an internal landscape of her feelings. It was fascinating. She couldn't stop thinking about it. In an odd sort of way her father's brief visit had deepened her interest in both parents, and the interest had lifted the denial: she could sense the long-buried regrets.

The phone rang. Doctor Campbell wanted the prescriptions for signature. Riikka could see that Irene was preoccupied. 'Irene?'

'Dear me, did you say something?'

'Could you pass over the prescription requests, Doctor Campbell wants the file.'

Irene handed over the paperwork. She seemed agitated. 'Could I ask a wee favour?' She didn't wait for a reply. 'It's just that Doctor Newman's wife passed away last week, a blessing no doubt – poor woman - and I'd like to attend the funeral, but I don't want to go alone. The rest of the staff don't know the family.' She lowered her voice. 'And I don't want to go with Doctor Campbell…'

Riikka was surprised that she'd been singled out for the invitation. Having met Gabriel Newman, and with the benefit of Irene's previous comments, the news was not entirely unexpected. Even so…

'When is it?'

'Tomorrow, mid-day.' Irene fussed with the pile of patient records on her desk. 'Of course if you don't want to go it's fine. It's very short notice.' More fussing.

By chance Riikka had swapped a shift at the bookshop, so she could go. 'Sure, be glad to.'

Irene positively gushed. 'Are you sure?'

'Absolutely. Shall I pick you up here, say eleven?'

'The service starts at twelve so that would be perfect.' Irene looked as if she'd won the lottery. 'I hate going to these occasions alone.'

Riikka's thoughts drifted. 'Actually, I bumped into Doctor Newman in a café a month or two back. I recognised him from the photograph you showed me.'

'My word… Did he have much to say?'

'Not really, we passed the time of day.'

'I see.' Irene sighed. 'He has the gift that one. His patients were always loath to see another doctor if his list was full.'

Riikka switched her attention to the pile of prescription forms. She wondered how Gabriel was coping with his loss. On reflection, she was not too sure if she wanted to go to the funeral. It felt like an intrusion.

Chapter 14

FINN PULLED HIS father's arm, determined to find out why his mother was so quiet. As far as he could remember he'd not been especially naughty that day. He was sure she was upset. He'd watched the arrival of lots of people at his granddad's house that morning and needed to know what was happening. His father was talking to a man wearing a black dress and a white collar. Finn remembered him from his grandma's church and decided that he didn't like him. He pulled his father's arm harder.

'What is it Finn?'

Finn whispered. 'Why's Mummy sad?'

'Because it's your grandma's funeral today.'

'But why's funeral sad?'

His mother walked over and interrupted. 'Patrick, could we run through a few things with Father Conway in the back room? Dad wants to go through the order of service one more time.'

Finn interjected. 'But Dad's telling me about funeral.'

'Sorry Finn. Give your dad five minutes. We need to sort something out with Granddad.'

'But that's not fair, he was talking to me first!'

Grace appeared and took Finn's hand. 'As your mum and dad are busy why don't we talk about it, about funerals?'

For a young man accustomed to seeing the world as a series of wants and their instant gratification, his aunt's offer was appreciated. He watched his parents leave the room and kicked at the edge of the carpet.

'It's not fair. Dad was talking to me first.'

'Listen, why don't you sit on Grandma's stool and I'll get us a drink.'

Finn nodded and ambled over to the tartan footstool. He made a sorry sight, chin on hands, head bursting with questions. While he waited he decided to play his favourite game, being invisible. He sat on his throne convinced that no one could see him. He tried out a few tricks to test his theory: blowing a raspberry, pulling faces. Well below any adult's line of sight he was ignored, the subdued chatter in the room drowning his histrionics.

Finn's mind returned to its key concern: what happened at funerals? He sort of knew it had something to do with Grandma's death but Grandma had explained dying and she hadn't seemed upset. Finn clasped his hands between his knees, wishing that death was a story. He slipped back into daydreams, especially reading his favourite book with Grandma. He imagined snuggling between the covers of her big bed and opening *The Snowman* once more. She always brought the pictures to life and Finn was transported, again, to a winter garden. Perhaps, he mused, people were like the Snowman, maybe they melted when their story was over.

'There you go. Sorry it took so long.' Aunt Grace sat, taking up residence in his grandma's chair.

'So, how are you doing?' She leaned forwards.

Finn liked his aunt, she always seemed calm and interested. She was wearing a black dress. He pointed to a silver bird pinned to the collar. It was an owl.

'Your grandma gave me this when I was eighteen.' She fingered the small broach, then sank into the chair and gripped the padded armrests. 'Now what was it you wanted your dad to tell you?'

Finn felt a bit embarrassed, but decided to come out with it. 'What's funeral mean? Mum's sad and Dad says it's because of Grandma's funeral and I don't know what funeral is.'

'Well, it's a time to say goodbye when someone dies. To celebrate who they were and then...' She hesitated. 'Then their body is buried.' She added quickly, 'That's what your grandma wanted, to be buried.'

Finn was horrified, he knew what buried meant and had an idea that death was permanent, even so he had to check it out. 'But what if Grandma wakes up, how will she get out?'

'Steady Finn. You don't wake up when you die.' Finn was about to ask another question when his mother interrupted again.

'Cars are here. We leave in five minutes everyone.'

Grace helped Finn stand. 'Let's talk later shall we?' They joined the press of visitors heading for the front door. 'Come on, let's get this over with.'

⊷▰⊷ ⊶▰⊷

Gabriel was surprised to see so many familiar faces when they arrived at the church. He was approached by family and acquaintances including his ex-partners from the practice. After the first round of handshakes and commiserations he noticed a friendly face standing inside the church entrance. He walked over.

'Irene, what a nice surprise.' He leaned forwards and kissed her cheek. Irene's face flushed, too overcome to speak. It was only then that he recognised her companion. 'Goodness, didn't expect to see you today. Is it Rikky?'

'You have a good memory Doctor Newman. I think I mentioned that I work with Irene.' Riikka stepped forward and shook his hand. 'I'm so sorry to hear of your loss.'

'Thank you, and its Gabriel.' He smiled. The informality seemed too much for Irene.

'And of course my condolences Doctor Newman.' This time there was no repeat of his first name.

'I should go. I'm to be a pall-bearer. Perhaps we'll have a chance to talk another time.' A second kiss for Irene and an engaging smile from Riikka as he turned and rejoined his son-in-law by the hearse. Together they listened to the instructions on the lifting and carrying and watched as the oak casket was drawn from the back of the vehicle. It was lifted shoulder high by the funeral director's staff, one at each corner. Gabriel took up position in the centre, opposite Patrick and rested a shaking hand on his son-in-law's shoulder. They took some of the weight. Gabriel tipped his face and rested his cheek against the smooth timber.

'Right gentlemen, let's proceed.'

They carried the casket and laid it on a stand before the altar. Beth and Grace took up position either side of the casket with Lorri standing behind. During the course of the service each offered a short eulogy.

Even though she was a failed Catholic, Isabella had requested a church ceremony, and had discussed the service with the priest and Gabriel. After the minimum of required prayers and formalities it was time for Gabriel to offer a final address.

He avoided the steps to the pulpit and stood next to the coffin, deserted now. He faced the congregation, willing him on, willing him to loosen the dried tongue and bring Isabella to life in their mind's eye once more. Instead he gripped the polished oak and an unsteady silence descended on the church.

Gabriel raised his eyes and rested them on Lorri's face. There was no urging or upset. In its place was a pool of calm that reached out and slowed Gabriel's racing heart. He smiled and Lorri smiled back.

'I've struggled to find words of my own to speak to you today. He paused, reaching into his pocket for the lines of verse. 'Isabella wrote this for me. I'd like her words to be the last today.' Gabriel stroked the casket. 'Hope I do them justice...' He unfolded the paper.

Beguiling: your first look.
A glance, a mark.
When time's tyranny parted –
A beginning...

Strange how, in that beginning,
In chapters unread,
A quiet shadow drifted, unnoticed,
Our ending…

And between now and then,
And my becoming to you,
I am enough. Content to have danced a lifetime's worth;
With angels.

Gabriel folded the paper and returned the glasses to his top pocket. Addressing the absent soul he opened his mind to the memory of her voice and the silence of her passing.

⊷⊷⊷ ⊷⊷⊷

Finn watched the box holding his grandma as it was lowered into the ground. He edged backwards and bumped into a tall lady with dark hair. She placed her hands on his small shoulders and kept them there. From his lowly vantage point he could see a copse of trees in the distance. Cissy was sitting there on the end of a bench. She waved. Finn looked away and then back again. Cissy smiled and pointed to his left. Out of nowhere his great aunt Lorri appeared and took his hand. She bent and spoke with a soft voice.

'Come and stand next to your granddad, and say goodbye to your grandma.'

Finn glanced back at the trees. Cissy was gone. The tall lady nodded and Finn walked with Lorri to the graveside. He stood by as his granddad and great-aunt threw a red flower into the grave. Lorri handed Finn a rose and directed him to follow their example. He tossed the flower and then leaned forwards, peering into the hole. The three blooms made a pattern on the coffin lid, a triangle.

⊶⊷

Riikka was strangely moved by her brief contact with Gabriel's grandson. It would seem she was not the only one to be stirred by the experience.

'We're all here now, all the players.' Riikka was inclined to ignore her alter ego, but Sarah was not for keeping quiet. 'Strange how a remedy forms from such disparate sources.'

You're speaking in riddles again…

'So watch.'

Irene drifted away as the ceremony drew to a conclusion, speaking earnestly to two young women by the graveside. Riikka assumed they were Gabriel's daughters. She was content to watch.

A young girl about Finn's age and an older woman approached. The girl spoke.

'There are three of us you see.'

Riikka frowned. *Sarah?* And then, out of nowhere Sarah joined them. She spoke next.

'Don't go flaky on us and for goodness' sake don't say anything.'

Riikka could feel the skin tingle down the left side of her face. The older woman spoke.

'I'm known as Celia, at least I am in Gabriel's mind, and this little person is Cissy, Finn's imaginary friend.'

Sarah completed the riddle. 'And I'm your imaginary friend.'

The tingling sensation was spreading down her neck and left arm. *What's happening?*

'We wanted you to see that we are connected,' continued Sarah. 'And that therefore…'

Riikka picked up the thread. *So are we…* The thought seemed to open a curtain. The unlikely trinity parted and Riikka's attention was drawn to a woman standing by the graveside; nothing remarkable, except she was wearing a bright pink dress. She turned her face in Riikka's direction. She looked out of place, alive in a sea of black. Riikka couldn't move. She knew, instinctively, who the woman was: the realisation slipped through disbelief like a hot knife in butter.

'You all right dear? You look as if you've seen a ghost.' Riikka's eyes switched to Irene's concerned face. She nodded. 'I was miles away, sorry.'

'We should go, let the family pay their respects.'

'Yes, of course.'

Riikka followed Irene's lead, turning to take a final look at the graveside party. Gabriel and his grandson were standing next to a woman with long greying hair and his daughters. There was no sign of the imaginary trio or the pink lady. Riikka's rational side was scrabbling for an explanation. She did feel a connection with Gabriel and Finn, and her vision (if that's what it was) simply confirmed this. There was a different and emerging aspect of Riikka that knew, was certain, that meeting Cissy and Celia was more than a projected confirmation of vague feelings. And as for the rest? Was that really Isabella?

Chapter 15

PATRICK WAS CONCERNED. He was glad the funeral was over. He knew Beth wanted to be with her father, but unless they'd got their dates wrong, Beth was almost full-term. He could see that she was preoccupied, anxious. She must have uttered 'I'm fine' a hundred times that day, but he was not convinced. The little one was on its way and he was ready, watchful.

When they finally said their goodbyes to Beth's family Patrick was relieved. The journey home was uneventful and much to his relief Beth and Finn went straight to bed. The house was suddenly quiet. Patrick stood on the landing unsure what to do next. He could hear Beth's soft purring as she slept. His action man, driven-to-do-stuff psychology shut down and he felt exhausted, and yet his feet remained rooted to the landing boards as options drifted lazily around his head. He couldn't remember the last time he'd had a few minutes to himself. The thought was provocative. He made a bee-line for the drinks cupboard, and to be on the safe side, poured a small Jameson.

The whiskey burn was glorious. He raised his half-empty glass in salute to his growing family. He knew that Beth had plans for her life, and the pregnancy had been a setback. He resolved to make the most of the new baby, spend more time at home. He'd already organised paternity leave and was working on his employers to allow him working from home, at least a day a week. Although Isabella's illness had affected Patrick, truthfully, he'd been more concerned, especially in the past few weeks, by its effect on Beth. He shook his head. It was sad that they had to deal with her mother's loss when the baby's birth was so close. He relished the arrival of the baby. They'd resisted the temptation to find out its gender at the twenty-week scan. He felt sure it was a girl. The new life unravelled in his mind, so many possibilities.

Patrick's own life as a child was a confused scrap book of memories. He was the youngest of seven. His parents, Catholic Irish, had resolved that the family should follow their father's need for work to England. Both parents had passed in their early sixties. He missed his brothers: all seven siblings were boys. That was another item for his wish list, to make more time to keep in touch. The bed creaked in the room above and Patrick could hear Beth's progress towards the bathroom. He emptied the glass, yawned expansively, and headed for the stairs.

⋯⟞⧟⧢ ⧢⧟⧠⟞⋯

Beth drifted between sleep and awake, shifting her considerable belly in an attempt to get comfortable. The baby moved and Beth ran her hand across the tight, stretched skin following the outstretched hand or foot. She needed to pee, again.

Almost beside herself with tiredness Beth levered herself to a sitting position and stared at the yellow streetlight framing the curtains. Her back complained as she stood and plodded across the landing. She'd almost reached the bathroom door when her waters broke.

'Oh shit!'

Quickly, she pushed back the bathroom door and drew up her tee-shirt, one of Patrick's. The remaining trickle of fluid spotted the pan. This was no false alarm, she was going into labour. Beth pulled on the light and squinted, she would have to work quickly. Finn had arrived in three hours, this one would be faster. A knot of anxiety formed in her throat. She needed to get Patrick awake and drive her to the hospital quickly. Her first task was to rouse her husband without throwing him into a complete panic. She pulled the soiled tee-shirt over her head and threw a towel over the puddle on the landing floorboards.

'Patrick. Patrick wake up.' Beth sat on his side of their bed, naked apart from a clean towel clamped between her legs. She shivered.

Patrick mumbled. His drowsy response was not what she needed, neither was the back of his head as he rolled over.

'Patrick, for God's sake, wake up...' In desperation she switched on his bedside lamp and shook his shoulder. 'My waters have broken, wake up!'

He sat upright, his hand shading his eyes from the lamp. 'Jesus, what...' He stared at Beth's naked form and in particular the towel between her legs. 'Christ, it's started, why didn't you wake me?'

-->==◎ ◎==<--

Finn dreamed about the funeral. Only in the dream it was different. He was watching the whole thing from a distance sitting on a bench with Cissy. She seemed quiet.

'Finn,' said Cissy, shuffling closer, 'something is going to happen and soon.'

Finn sighed; losing his grandma was enough something for one day. 'Such as?'

Cissy avoided a direct response. 'When it does happen I won't be able to visit you as often.'

Finn turned to his friend, alarmed. 'What do you mean?'

'I can't say, but I wanted you to know that it wasn't because I don't like being with you.'

'So, don't then.' Finn scuffed at the gravel beneath their seat.

'Do you remember when I copied something inside you?'

'Yes…'

'Well, what I copied needs to go somewhere else and I have to go with it.'

The dream state dulled Finn's upset. He half accepted what Cissy said. His fatalism was similar to the shock felt from a fall, a bruised head: unwelcome, but inevitable. In spite of her assurance that he would still see her, the part of him that demanded the exclusive attention of his best, special friend could not shake off the feeling that he was being abandoned. He wanted someone to blame.

'Grandma said I'd see her again.' Finn twisted the sleeve of his jumper. 'She said she'd wait for me.' He rounded on his friend. 'If Grandma can die and wait for me so can you. I can wait. Don't leave it too long.'

Cissy raised her head. She hesitated, uncertain. 'I can't promise when I will see you again. The thing is you may not recognise me.' Any further discussion was interrupted by a loud voice.

'Finn, wake up.'

⤙⊜ ⊜⤚

The call from Beth had plunged Gabriel into a fit of activity. He'd had less than four hours sleep. The news was expected but untimely: he couldn't believe that this was happening on the same day he'd buried Isabella. Lorri emerged from her bedroom rubbing her eyes.

'What's happening?'

'Beth's gone into labour and they want me to meet them at the hospital, to look after Finn.'

Lorri, wide awake now, followed Gabriel down the stairs. 'What can I do?'

Gabriel pulled on his coat and found his car keys in the jacket pocket. 'Could you call Grace for me, tell her to come to the hospital?' Gabriel stalled at the front door. 'Beth's waters have broken so she'll deliver sometime soon.'

'Why don't I ask Grace to come here and we'll get a taxi over?' She straightened the collar of Gabriel's coat.

'You're a gem. I'll call if there's any news.'

He made good time and pulled the car into the hospital parking space at the same time as Beth and Patrick arrived. He took charge of Finn and the small rucksack dangling from his hand. He kissed Beth. 'Good luck. We'll be waiting.'

Beth bent to give Finn a hug. 'Be good for Granddad. As soon as the baby arrives your dad will come and get you. 'She wrinkled her face like someone with toothache. 'We'd better go.'

-->═● ●══<-

Beth and Patrick were allocated a small waiting room. Beth changed into a hospital gown.

'Well here we are then.' Beth stared at the ceiling as the midwife chatted away. She completed her internal examination. 'Cervix is not fully dilated.'

As the midwife left the room Beth's eyes rested on her husband. 'Do me a favour. Nip outside and ask Dad to call Grace would you? I'd like her to be here if she can make it.'

Patrick smoothed back her hair. 'All organised. Lorri is going to call Grace and they'll both be here as soon as they can.'

The next contraction was challenging. Beth gripped Patrick's hand. Two hours passed and the contractions were pretty well continuous.

'Holy fuck!' Beth's face twisted as she tried desperately to avoid pushing. 'Patrick, get the midwife. I need to push.' *Dear God, Mum, where are you?*

When Patrick returned Beth was howling like a banshee.

'Now, now dear, early days yet,' said the midwife.

Beth was having none of it. She pulled the gown over her belly and spread her legs. 'Now tell me I can't fucking push.'

The midwife stared with disbelief; she could see the top of the baby's head. There was no time for transfer to the delivery room and within ten minutes, and accompanied by the anxious attentions of nursing staff, the baby arrived. It was a girl, and she passed her first medical with flying colours.

'Please, let me see her.' The swaddled bundle was handed over and Beth gazed at the tiny face. Patrick looked completely smitten. Beth kissed her daughter. 'Fetch Finn for me…'

⭑⭑⭑

Finn was bored and his granddad was no use, he was reading a paper and yawning. Finn edged his way along the row of chairs, looking for something to do. Cissy's head appeared from behind a vending machine. He crept over.

'What are you doing here?'

'Same as you, waiting for your sister to arrive.'

'Well that's not true, it could be a brother.' Finn was not sure which he preferred.

'Don't you think it's amazing, a completely new person is about to start breathing instead of floating around inside your mum.'

Finn had given little thought to the baby-making process. Cissy made it sound like the baby was a tadpole. The thought made him feel a bit queasy.

'Let's go and wait with your granddad. He'll have a fit if he thinks you've gone missing.' Finn was confused. Missing what? 'Come on, Finn…'

He followed Cissy as she made for the door where his parents had disappeared. Playing safe, he crawled under a table looking for his bag. Looking out from his spot he could see Cissy step back from the door as it opened and his dad appeared.

'Come here Finn.' His dad held his shoulders. 'You have a baby sister and your mum wants to see you.'

Finn reached for his granddad. 'You too.'

Gabriel stood. 'Congratulations Patrick, is everyone OK?'

Patrick held onto Finn's hand. 'Mother and baby are fine. The little one is in good shape. Would you mind waiting Gabriel? Beth wants a few minutes with Finn.'

Gabriel stepped back. 'Of course, come and get me when you're ready.'

Finn followed his father through the doors. Cissy was standing next to his granddad, waving. The door closed and Finn passed into the chaotic wonderland of new-borns. Three things registered with Finn as the doors closed behind him: sounds and smells and no Cissy. She'd gone. They passed rooms with babies screaming and tired-looking mothers fussing. There were women with huge stomachs still waiting for their baby to come. And the smells: the antiseptic whiff of hospital mixed with the scent of warm milk and soiled nappies. They reached their destination. His mother looked tired, but very happy. Finn, embarrassed, took her hand – it was hot.

'Look Finn, it's your baby sister.'

With trepidation he glanced at the small bundle nestled in his mother's arm. He dashed around to the other side of the bed. Carefully, he moved the blanket that hid the baby's face.

'Be gentle, Finn.'

The wrinkled prune opened her eyes. Finn stared. Her eyes were black. He had an odd feeling that something was loose inside his head. The sensation was weird. As he watched, the baby's eyes seemed to turn a bright blue. He blinked and they were black again. 'Wow…' His initial reserve melted and was transformed. For the first time in his life Finn discovered he could do something rather wonderful. He fell in love.

Chapter 16

AFTER WEEKS OF delays Riikka finally received the go-ahead to deliver the first batch of books to the children's hospital. A porter followed her to the car park and loaded the books onto a sack truck. She was apprehensive, and cold. It was October already. When they arrived at the oncology department she struggled with the entrance key pad.

'Let me do that.' The porter punched in a combination and they entered the ward.

Riikka was immediately struck by the children's drawings lining the walls. A young girl, about nine, ambled past. Her chest was distended. Riikka averted her eyes, conscious that she was staring. They arrived at the nurses' station and the duty nurse pointed in the direction of an anteroom. 'Julia Reeves, the play specialist, is expecting you.' The porter led the way.

Julia – Riikka assumed it was her – was hooting with laughter as they entered the playroom. She was engrossed in a game of snakes and ladders with three happy-looking kids. The porter unloaded the boxes and took his leave.

Julia raised her hand, ready to throw the dice. She apologised. 'Sorry, in the thick of it as you can see. Keep landing on the snakes' heads.' She winked. 'Give me a minute.' She rounded on the children. 'Looks to me like Craig has won this game.' A young man attached to a drip beamed. 'And I need to talk with this nice lady who's brought us some new books.' The children glanced at Riikka and then the pile of boxes. 'Take yourselves off and wash your hands, it's time for lunch in ten minutes.'

A silence settled on the room as the children left. Craig, the last to leave, was dragging his drip-stand into the ward. Julia seemed in no rush to speak and Riikka felt awkward, out of place.

'I'm from Hamiltons, the bookshop...'

Julia held Riikka's arm as she stood. 'Give me a minute.' She closed the door. 'I know who you are dear and I guess you know I'm the play specialist for this ward?'

Riikka nodded.

'First things first, thank you so much for the books, and, more importantly, your offer to help out.'

'Well actually, my boss said I should stay and stack the books for you. That's all really.'

Julia smiled. 'The thing is these kids are quite capable of placing a book on a shelf. Not that they would be unhappy if you did it for them.'

'I'm not sure I understand.'

'What they really need is company. Playing or reading with a sympathetic adult provides an opportunity for them to check out their status with a grownup. Often that's not possible with their parents – too close.'

Riikka shifted uneasily; this was not what she'd signed up for. 'Surely that's a job you should be trained to do?'

'You underestimate the power of listening. Children are adept at taking responsibility. Our job is to keep out of the way: read a book, play a game.' She grinned and picked up the board. 'I assume you know how to play this?'

⊶⧟ ⧟⊷

Riikka's conversation with Julia had lasted the best part of an hour. Much to her surprise she'd agreed to spend a couple of free afternoons each month working with Julia as a volunteer. She was bemused. Why did she agree? Sarah offered an explanation.

'Must be on track I'd say. And don't say anything. A hospital is not the best place to be seen talking to yourself. Riikka had not heard from her cerebral pen-friend since her dramatic appearance at Isabella Newman's funeral. Sarah continued. 'We think,' – Riikka assumed "we" included Sarah's two associates – 'that you should tackle Finn and Gabriel about their alter egos.'

Riikka was incredulous. *You expect me to have a real-world, speaking-type conversation with Gabriel Newman about his supposed imaginary friend? What was her name, Celia?* Riikka could hear laughing inside her head.

'What strange and limiting taboos. Wouldn't it be more interesting, and challenging, to discuss non-ordinary events than to discuss the weather or your aching back?' Sarah powered on. 'You'll find that Finn is more than happy to talk about Cissy. You should start there.' Riikka waited, for an instant her thoughts on pause, and then... 'And please don't patronise the boy. Finn is special. Listen to what he says. And when you've spoken to Finn...' Riikka had no idea how she would ever broach the subject with Gabriel.

Riikka realised she had stopped dead in the centre of the hospital reception. She sat on a nearby seat and pretended to look for something in her handbag. *This is crazy.*

'Actually it's more like hard work. You've no idea how difficult it is to separate myself and speak like this. To be honest, exploring your tactile experiences while I have a chance is what I'd rather be doing.'

Riikka glanced at a white-coated man crossing her field of vision. For a second she was sure it was Jonathan. She nearly cried out, and then she realised what Sarah would rather be doing...

'Why don't you ask him? He seems eligible.'

Good grief Sarah, why are you so obsessed with sex?

Sarah responded quickly enough. 'It's all connected, remember the battery charger conversation?'

Riikka sat on a red plastic chair as the memory of her time in the off-world sea was switched on. *I'd forgotten about that.* She needed answers. *Are you saying sex, my love-making, is some sort of refuelling process?* She waited. No response from Sarah. Eventually, she came to an uncomfortable conclusion: that her question was rhetorical. She stood and made her way to the exit. Outside there was a chill to the air and a welcome sanity in the rush of pedestrian traffic. She had learned from previous encounters with Sarah that she always arrived uninvited and left in much the same way. In any event, Riikka was losing faith in the notion that Sarah was a figment of her imagination. She was less certain that Finn or Gabriel would have the remotest idea what she was talking about, even if she were silly enough to introduce the subject. One thing she had determined, almost a eureka moment, was the idea that thinking was not a premeditated activity: she did not have thoughts. Thoughts, if anything, had her.

⟶▭◉ ◉▭⟵

The next day, as Riikka descended to the ground-floor sales area of Hamiltons, she was surprised to see Gabriel Newman. She stopped, adjusting a display stand on the half-landing. She couldn't help thinking about Sarah's comments. How on earth would Gabriel react if she asked him, 'I hear you have an imaginary friend too. Actually, I've met her.' The thought made her smile. She half expected Sarah to comment.

Of course, it was bullshit, a continuing drift in her out-of-control thinking processes. If she did speak she would be confronting her own imagined mental frailties. There was no chance she would open that particular box of tricks. Gabriel was still sorting through end-of-line thrillers when Riikka coughed politely. 'Gabriel?'

'Hi, I was hoping I'd catch you in…'

'Listen, I hope you don't feel that I was intruding, attending your wife's funeral. Irene was anxious to have a companion.'

'There's really no need. To be honest it was good to see you, someone unconnected, if that makes any sense?' He returned the book he was holding to its resting place. 'Thought I'd try to find a new author, something different.'

'I'm afraid I stopped reading when I finished my degree last year.'

'And now you work in a bookshop?'

Riikka was about to respond, but was distracted by the arrival of the corpulent Tommy, standing behind Gabriel, arms crossed.

She leaned forwards, lowering her voice. 'I take my break in an hour. Could we meet for a coffee? I can't talk now. Duty calls…'

'Yes, that would be excellent. I'll meet you outside in an hour.'

'Great.' Riikka drifted away, trying to ignore Tommy's military expression.

Wanker.

⟶➤◉ ◉◀⟵

Riikka stared at her reflection. Did she need to be concerned? Was she over-cooking the signals? She had no desire to bed the good doctor. She was as practised as most women in the art of the downward glance, avoiding eye contact. She had developed a non-committal smile for men who were, well, definitely not desirable; a smile, a kiss, the inevitable daisy chain that led to bed or disagreement. Why was she even thinking like this? Gabriel seemed a decent man. The truth was, the face in the mirror, in the cramped ladies' room, was interested. No, that was not quite right, when she was in Gabriel's company she felt the ghost of that transcendent event, when she'd floated away in water that touched inside, when Sarah had proposed unlikely links, and she'd stared with the same eyes at a blue and ochre moon.

She snapped the lid on her lipstick and disengaged from the wrong-sided face. The image, her train of thought was ridiculous. She grabbed her bag from a nail doubling as a coat hook and left the shop. He was there, and he looked pleased to see her.

In defiance of her instincts, Riikka kissed him quickly on his tanned and whiskered cheek. She grabbed his arm. It lacked the muscular tension of a younger man, her searching fingers finding bone. 'Well, where shall we go?' Gabriel seemed nonplussed so she removed her hand. 'What about the bar opposite? I've actually finished for the day and I need a drink.'

He still seemed lost for words. 'Sounds good,' he said, 'but I should warn you that I'm not used to drinking before six. Old habits, never knew if I'd be called out…'

They strolled over to the bar and took a table by the window.

The conversation had an unsteady start. Riikka was in no hurry to impress or otherwise. She sat back, engaging in small talk, sipping a beer. 'How is your grandson? He seems quite a character.'

Gabriel smiled. 'He's a monkey right enough. Actually, I have two grandchildren now. Beth went into labour last week, a baby girl.'

'Congratulations, is everyone OK?'

'Yes, perfect, except she is rather noisy and I don't think Finn is too impressed.' Riikka eyed her empty bottle and Gabriel's one-third empty glass. 'I don't know why but I always seem to rush the first drink. I'm going to have another – are you ready?'

'I'll skip this round. Don't have the capacity these days, but thanks for offering.'

There was a queue at the bar and Sarah joined in. 'You should relax. Trust your instincts.' Riikka was horrified. *He's just buried his wife. There's no way I can talk about Celia, or you for that matter.* Sarah ignored the thought. 'Live a little more recklessly, see what happens.'

Riikka paid for her drink and returned to the table. She could almost feel Sarah nudging her ribs. 'I've taken on a voluntary job, helping out at the children's hospital.' Riikka edged closer to the table. The change in body language bolstered her confidence as she carefully lifted the corner of her box lid. 'One of the kids, in fact one or two of them, seem to have imaginary friends.' Riikka took the plunge. 'I wondered if Finn…? It's all new to me, I don't know the best way respond.'

Gabriel's expression changed as she spoke. Sarah was quick to underline this reaction. Riikka experienced another thought-bound jab in the ribs. 'See, perhaps the good doctor is ready to confront his demons.'

Gabriel coughed and toyed with his drink. 'As a matter of fact Finn does, her name is Cissy.'

Riikka felt her vision shift. The realisation that she had seen and been introduced to Cissy prior to Gabriel's revelation broke her remaining grip on the certainty that Sarah and the rest of the brood were no more than unwelcome ideas. The anchor that held her world view in place was hauled in and for the first time the vast expanse of other possibilities rushed to show their hand. Her mind, unable to deal with the sudden change in perspective, did what all computers do when overwhelmed – it rebooted.

⇥ ⇤

Gabriel was too slow to reach Riikka as she slid from the chair. He quickly adjusted her crumpled form so her airway was clear. He could feel a pulse and she was breathing. Quite a crowd had gathered.

'I'm a doctor, would you mind standing back. She needs air.'

'The doc is right. Move back please.' A tee-shirted waitress knelt next to Gabriel. 'Should we call an ambulance?'

Gabriel spotted the first-aid bag in her hand. 'Any smelling salts in there?'

She unzipped the red holdall. 'Never thought this would come in handy.' She handed over a small plastic bottle.

Two passes under her nose and Riikka's eyes opened. 'Shit, what's that smell?' She tried to sit, her head spinning. 'What happened?'

Gabriel helped her back on her chair. 'You fainted.'

Riikka's head dipped. 'Could I have a glass of water please?'

⇥ ⇤

Fifteen minutes passed and Riikka was sitting on the same chair, no further blackouts. The crowd had dispersed, no more drama... Gabriel had reverted to type and continued to tease a response. 'Are you sure this has never happened before?'

She placed the empty glass on the table and seemed to reach a decision. 'Yes it has, at work a few months back. I had a similar fainting fit. I was checked out, at the local A&E, no apparent cause.'

Gabriel was about to suggest a check-up when he was pre-empted.

'I did see my GP,' she smiled, 'your ex-partner as a matter of fact. He ran some tests, all seemed to be well, and now this...'

'I would see Robert again, explain what happened today.' He drew his beard to a point, resisting the temptation to ask more searching questions.

Celia picked up his thoughts. 'Remember falling asleep on your feet? Isn't that like fainting? And you'd just mentioned Cissy...'

Gabriel found Celia's interjections irritating, especially when he was attempting to have a conversation with someone who needed his help. He snapped back. 'Damn it Celia, pipe down...'

Riikka looked up. 'What did you say?'

She didn't wait for a reply. The weight of her concerns – what was real, what was unreal – was suddenly shared and lifted. She couldn't wait to speak. 'There's something I need to tell you.'

Chapter 17

Cissy was unprepared for the feelings she'd experienced when she first linked with, and then separated, from Finn. He didn't have, or had not yet formed, adult prejudices. He still reacted without undue consideration of past events. In particular, he did not avoid experiencing feelings, or, more interestingly, did not shirk from taking responsibility for them.

Cissy's time with Finn had been illuminating. Finn forgot things, or he remembered, but his memories were tainted – they included shades of associated experiences – and therefore became new ideas. As far as Finn was concerned, they were true. Consequently, Cissy was able to experience a constant stream of new thoughts and the sensation was intoxicating. Although her recollection of the wider consciousness was fading, she knew that it would be impossible to develop these expanded notions in the wider continuum where knowing had long outlived the use of time and, therefore, the unknown could not exist. From her new vantage point Cissy listened to Finn's conversation with his mother.

⊷⇒ ⇐⊶

Finn was staring at his baby sister. 'Billie is such a stupid name.'

His mother disagreed. 'It's not. I think it's a great name, something different.' She detached Billie from her breast. 'And anyway, if she doesn't like it she can always use her middle name.'

Cissy could sense Finn's struggle with this new information. 'What's a middle name?'

'Billie has three names: Billie Maeve Carey.'

'But that's even worser, who'd want to be called Maeve?'

Cissy assumed that Finn would not be outdone and the next question was no surprise.

'So what's my middle name?'

'Patrick, after your father. You have a grand name: Finnbar Patrick Carey.'

Finn was mortified. 'What's Finnbar? My name's Finn…'

Although the exchange was amusing, Cissy needed to withdraw. She had new lodgings and was required to keep a low profile. No direct action this time. The new partnership would last a lifetime and dialogue would have to wait until much later. Finn's continuing discussion melted away as she became aware of Billie's pressing concern, to be reconnected with the food supply.

→⊨⊙ ⊙⊨←

Celia watched Gabriel as he held the red box. It was real enough, but inside was a different matter. There would come a time when the gift would serve Gabriel as he faced a final choice, but right now it was a distraction. Since Isabella's death it was evident that Gabriel's vitality was failing and it was necessary that this situation be reversed if Gabriel were to play his role in the coming months. Sarah and Celia had agreed a process they could orchestrate together. It would need to begin soon.

'Why such a morbid interest in the box?' Celia had discovered that Gabriel responded better if she spiked her comments. It was an effective ploy to disengage his mind from other concerns.

If you have such an intimate connection with my thoughts, why ask?

'Because, silly man, what I can see will not help you.' She pressed on. 'The box was used to unsettle your mind. The dilemma it posed was simple enough: how could it exist when I did not?' She could sense his agreement. 'And yet its existence was confirmed. Isabella, Lorri and the waitress, all of them could see or touch the offending item. Perhaps the lid will lift when you're comfortable with this apparent contradiction?'

Maybe. I'm still struggling to see the sense in it all. Even Riikka having similar experiences doesn't explain why. What is going on?

Celia was unable to answer his concerns directly. 'But at least you are asking why. Isn't that where change and transformation start?' She withdrew as Lorri approached. Time to expand the circle.

⋯⊨◉ ◉⊨⋯

Sarah was amazed at the speed with which Riikka adapted to her presence. And Riikka could see.

Why are you showing me this? Riikka was sitting in the hospital library-cum-playroom, listening to a small girl reading from a new book she'd delivered. She was aware that Sarah was making herself present. In a not altogether pleasant way her vision had shifted, somehow out of focus, the child sitting before her looked more like an egg, a shell of shifting light. There were areas where the luminosity was drawn inwards to darker still circles. Riikka blinked, she was feeling unbalanced. Thankfully, the child resumed her more recognisable form. The darker circles, she assumed, were the child's tumours. Riikka shifted in her seat and gripped the wooden table, willing a more familiar reality to return.

For God's sake Sarah, why the Rocky Horror Show?

Sarah struggled to maintain the conversation – this new visual experience was kicking up quite a storm – she would have to be quick. 'You lifted the lid, so, you must deal with the consequences. That was not my doing, it was all your own work.' She paused to give Riikka a chance to catch up. 'What you should consider is what this child is about to say…'

Riikka was distracted by the remark and then by her young companion. 'Rikky, what does this say?' Small hands twisted the open book so she could see, a tiny finger stabbing at the page.

'Understanding, sweetie, it means knowing something.' She wanted to say more, but the words wouldn't come.

'I get it, like you see something that you've never seen before, and then someone tells you what it is, and then you understand.'

Riikka found herself choking up. 'Exactly, you've got it. You understand. You know.'

Chapter 18

LORRI WAS FINDING the close proximity of her grieving brother-in-law a little claustrophobic. She was used to living with people who were open to less-formal behaviour. The lack of these accustomed freedoms had been denied for long enough. If she was going to keep her promise to Isabella things would need to change, free up. Lorri could hear her sister's response to the thought.

Good luck with that one…

Lorri was a missionary without a mission. It was time to change things and lift Gabriel's thick skin; or maybe she should take a break? He was too attached to a conventional world view and as far as she could see it was not doing him much good. Bella had left them in the spring and it was now approaching winter. He was still walking around the house looking for her ghost. She could tell that he was unwilling to let go. He would stand moony-eyed with an ornament in his hand, or some other artefact that reminded him of the past. If not for his own sake, he would need to cut the cord. Lorri could sense that Bella was reluctant to sever her less-worldly attachment to her tormented husband and that was not good. She couldn't influence the shade that was her sister, but she could help Gabriel. It would require conversation then action.

'I wonder if I could ask a favour.'

'Sure.' His face lifted expectantly.

Why was it some men delighted in being of use? 'I'd like to take you out for dinner tonight, my treat.' She watched his reaction carefully. 'Could you bear to eat Chinese? I was looking at the menu outside the Cantonese place near the station, what's it called…?'

This time he was quicker off the mark, engaged in the idea perhaps? 'The Emperors. I'd love to.' He reflected. 'Bella didn't like Chinese food…'

Lorri relaxed. Her guess was right, this would be a new experience. He wouldn't be gazing around the restaurant trying to remember where they'd sat last time. *OK!* 'Let's get a taxi. We could have a drink.'

⋅⇥⧟⊟⧟ ⧟⊟⧟⇤⋅

The taxi dropped them a short distance from the restaurant. Gabriel was a considerate man. He'd shortened his pace to match hers and minced along in Chaplinesque fashion. She disguised her amusement and responded to a rush of affection by slipping her arm through his. 'This is nice.' Thankfully, Gabriel relaxed into the first step in Lorri's plan. Ever the gentleman, he opened the door. Lorri chased away her reaction and stepped inside.

They ordered a drink at the table and after discussion decided on a set meal. The food, when it arrived, was plentiful and delicious.

'This was a great idea, and actually there is something I need to talk about.' Gabriel refilled their glasses.

'I'm all ears.'

'Remember Riikka?' continued Gabriel.

'The bookshop Riikka?'

He nodded. 'We bumped into each other, last week, at the bookshop. Thing is, we went for a drink and she fainted.'

'Goodness…'

'She'd had a previous episode.' Lorri was smiling now. 'I did resist the GP responses, honestly,' he said.

'I'm sure you did.' She was intrigued, where was this leading? 'And?'

'And then, I was trying to discuss her fainting fits and Celia,' he pointed to his head, 'she kept interrupting me. I lost it.'

'Lost it?'

'I told her to shut up. I actually spoke out loud – "Celia, shut up".'

Lorri held her breath.

'I thought Riikka was going to pass out again.' Gabriel ran his hand through his hair. 'And then she came out with this – I don't know how to describe it – revelation, confession?'

Lorri sat back and held out her hands as the circle expanded to enclose another player; the game changed.

Gabriel leaned forwards. 'Riikka said she'd met Cissy and Celia at Isabella's funeral...'

Lorri sat back stunned. A few dozen pieces of the puzzle fell into place, and now there were a thousand more in the box.

He was animated. 'There's more.'

Lorri closed her dropping jaw. 'Please...'

'She has an unwanted cerebral guest too, name's Sarah.' Gabriel sat back, a self-satisfied look on his face. 'How about that?'

How about that. Lorri was speechless. Evidently, Gabriel, Finn and Riikka were connected in some way by their imaginary friends, and this amazing Riikka was gifted to see them all. She collected her thoughts. How to respond...

'Well, that's a first.' Gabriel tapped the table.

Lorri refocused her gaze, catching the amused look in his eyes. 'I really don't know what to say, what you have shared is mind-blowing; literally, breath-taking.'

'I've been dying to tell you. Sorry if I've hijacked our night out. It felt like we would need time to reason it out.'

Lorri was thrown. Her agenda, that she'd wanted to discuss her promise to Bella, and was this the right time for her to leave, all of this seemed greyed out, no longer of consequence.

Meanwhile, Gabriel had a lot to say. 'Don't you see how incredible this is?' He didn't wait for a response. 'Celia, all of the weird stuff, it can't be a figment of my imagination.'

Lorri had no idea how he'd managed to sit on this for a week. 'Why didn't you say something earlier?'

He shrugged his shoulders. 'Waiting for the right time?

'I need time to think. Could we walk home?'

⇢⊷⊷⊛ ⊛⊷⊷⊶

Gabriel carried the mugs of coffee to the lounge. Lorri was stretched out on the sofa, eyes closed. She spoke. 'Talk to me Gabriel. What about this Riikka? Did you tell her more about Celia? How did she react?'

'It took me a minute or two to let in what she'd said. She was worried about telling me, in case I sent for the men in white coats… Some chance.'

'But you must have said that Celia was real enough?'

'I did, of course…'

'I have to meet this Riikka. This whole thing is incredible.'

'That can be arranged. I did tell her you'd stayed on and seemed to be very accepting and knowledgeable about these bizarre events.'

Lorri sipped her coffee. 'I'm beginning to see what Bella meant. She said she felt something was holding her here. Knowing her it would be a concern about family, and now there's you and Finn with imaginary friends and a casual acquaintance who's met them, and she has one too. But why, why did Riikka "see" Cissy and Sarah? Why are your ghosts revealing their connections? And why am I starting to feel like…' She hesitated. 'An interpreter?' Her eyes clouded over. She yawned. 'Regrettably, bed for me. I need to sleep on this.'

Gabriel stood. 'Me too, and thanks again for tonight.'

Chapter 19

FINN AND HIS best mate Liam sat on the towpath behind Finn's house. The canal was brown and still, littered with discarded plastic. Even the ducks seemed listless. Winter was expected. The air was dormant, as if paused while Mother Nature dozed, waiting. Liam was impressed by Finn's secret escape route. It had taken Finn weeks to prise three feather boards from the fence behind the garden shed. Finn knew that his parents wouldn't approve and had sworn Liam to secrecy.

The boys sat side-by-side holding fishing rods made from elder twigs and string from the potting shed, the scaffolds for two hapless worms. They sat like old men, chatting and dipping their rods in and out of the water. They discussed siblings, a hot topic with Liam whose elder brother was a constant source of grief.

'He's such a jerk.' Liam slapped his stick in the water to emphasise his feelings. 'He thinks he knows everything and he's always pinching my stuff.'

Finn nodded, although he rather liked his baby sister. In deference to his friend's point of view Finn was happy to agree and stirred the pot.

'You're lucky, at least you can talk to your brother. Billie gabbles all the time and when I tell her to shut up she gives me this dumb look and screams, or worse, giggles.'

The conversation drifted back and forth and moved on to kids at school. Liam edged closer to Finn, looking up and down the towpath to make sure they were alone. 'Last week, Susie Turner wanted to see my thing, you know.' He pointed at his crotch.

Finn was intrigued and definitely envious. Susie was amazing. 'Did you let her?'

'No way! And she threatened to get me after school with her mates if I didn't.'

'What did you do?'

Liam shrugged his shoulders. 'I told her I would if she did.'

'Wow, and...?' The grin on his friend's face said it all.

Finn caught his breath and coughed, feeling a familiar rattle in his chest. He'd have to borrow his granddad's listening tubes again.

'My grandma coughs like that,' said Liam, eyeing his friend accusingly. 'But she smokes, all the time. My mum says it's bad for her and Grandma tells her to mind her own business.'

Liam was interrupted by Finn's mother shouting from the house.

'Finn, five minutes, then in please, it's lunchtime. And tell Liam his mum wants him home.'

Silence from the boys.

'I better go.' Liam dumped his rod and line in the water. 'See ya...'

Finn was about to follow his friend's example when he noticed a dead fish floating on the canal. He still had most of his five minutes and it would only take a second to reach it with his stick. He leaned forwards, arm outstretched... The water slapped his face as he fell. It was really cold and smelly. For a split second Finn couldn't work out what had happened. The first lung-full of canal soup brought him back, retching, his feet pounding the water for a place to stand and finding none. He couldn't swim and started thrashing, yelling, panic-stricken. He could see a silhouette, a tree line with a church spire and then nothing as he sank below the water's surface. As he resurfaced he could see the trees again. When the horizon disappeared for the second time he felt less driven to struggle.

⋯⊶ ⊷⋯

Beth was irritated; why did she always have to repeat herself? She was half inclined to leave the boys to it but she'd promised to send Liam back. The call from his mother had taken up too much of her precious free time. She crept to the foot of the stairs and listened, no sign of wakefulness. She pursed her lips, at least Billie was a good baby. She strode through the kitchen and out the back door. Finn spent too much time behind the garden shed; she resolved to ask Patrick to fence it off.

She caught her ankle on used clay pots as she stepped between the fence and the outbuildings. 'Shit.' No Finn. 'What...' And then she saw the missing boards. 'The little...' She peered over the fence. No Finn. And then her heart flipped as her son's hand appeared from the canal's surface. She screamed his name and tried to squeeze through the gap. Seven-year-olds needed less space than a recently pregnant mother. She howled in frustration and clawed at the fence, losing a fingernail in the process. Two boards were quickly dispatched and Beth ran to the towpath. She didn't hesitate. Slipping off her shoes as she ran, she leapt into the water. Immediately, her searching hands found Finn's sinking form. The canal was deep, maybe eight feet. Holding Finn to her chest she allowed them both to sink until her legs flexed; she pushed her feet into the slimy mess below and made for the surface. Kicking hard she flipped on her back, spun in the water and heaved Finn onto the towpath. Choking and beside herself with fear and anguish, Beth levered herself out of the filthy waterway.

Her calls had roused fishermen a short distance away. They arrived as Beth, sobbing, turned Finn onto his back. The fates smiled on Beth that day, they were off-duty firemen. They managed to revive Finn and within an hour he was in the local A&E.

→══◎ ◎══←

Finn was feeling pretty bad. He'd broken just about every rule in the book and was lucky to be alive. From his first fit of choking when the men had got him breathing again, to realising what had happened, and worst of all, seeing his very upset (and very wet) mum. He felt miserable. He'd sat with his mum in the ambulance and choked and retched for the first half of the journey. She was shaking and crying and it was all his fault.

With the help of really kind nurses they had both removed their soiled clothes. His mum had been encouraged to take a shower and Finn was bathed. When he emerged from the hospital bathroom his dad had arrived.

His dad looked flushed, as if he'd run the whole way. 'Jesus, Finn... What...?'

'Patrick.' His mother appeared with wet hair and wearing a hospital gown. She reached for his hand. 'He's still with us and that's all I can cope with for now.'

Finn coughed, apologetically, tongue-tied, unable to frame a reply. His punishment was severe. For the first time in his short life he had no excuses and was experiencing guilt in large measure.

After loads of tests Finn was declared fit to return home. There was not a scratch on him. His mother, however, sported several injuries: painful reminders. Her hands were bruised and grazed by her attempts to remove fence panels, she'd cut the bottom of her foot, and there was the missing fingernail. The journey home in the car was purgatory. Finn feigned sleep. In truth he doubted he would sleep for some time.

⟶⟶◉ ◉⟵⟵

With Lorri's help Gabriel was coping with a rather irate Billie. Their attempts at bottle feeding had proved to be a dismal failure. Billie wanted her mother's milk. They'd received word that Beth was on her way back from the hospital. Gabriel was relieved – at least the boy, and Beth, had no serious injuries.

Raising his voice to counter Billie's protests, he spoke to Lorri. 'When they get back I suggest we let Beth settle this little one, and would you mind taking Finn to bed?' It was almost seven pm. Gabriel wanted to get the full story from Patrick.

'Of course.' Lorri took Billie and danced on the spot. 'The main thing is Finn and Beth are OK.'

Any further speculation was cut short as the very subdued Carey family stepped over the threshold. As planned, the children were whisked upstairs leaving Patrick and Gabriel to talk and prepare a meal. Gabriel poured them both a measure of whiskey, which was quickly dispatched. Patrick was past contributing to any culinary efforts and so he parked himself on a kitchen chair. With a nod to Gabriel he poured another glass. 'We were lucky not to lose him. It will haunt Beth for years. If she hadn't gone to find him...'

'Is Beth OK? She was limping, and her hands...'

'When she grabbed Finn in the canal she touched bottom and must have kicked against broken glass. She'd already lost a nail and badly grazed her fingers ripping boards from the fence. Unbelievable.' Patrick shook his head. 'I was at work for God's sake. Hadn't a clue.' He straightened his back. 'One thing's for certain, as soon as he's well enough, it's swimming lessons. I should have taken him before.'

Lorri appeared. 'Could you go and chat with him Patrick? The lad is riddled with remorse.' She noticed the whiskey bottle. 'Hate to be a fish-wife, but should you both be drinking? Patrick may need to drive.'

Patrick emptied his glass and shrugged his shoulders. 'You may be right, but we needed a drink.' He edged towards the kitchen door. 'I'll see to Finn.'

Gabriel fumbled and dropped the peeling knife. 'Damn!'

Lorri picked up the fallen implement and placed it on the worktop. She had an implacable Italian look on her face. She'd made a decision. 'Finn said something when I was helping him into bed. He seems to think that Cissy has left him. Don't you think that's strange?'

Gabriel was not sure what to think.

Lorri continued. 'Why would he think Cissy had left? It doesn't make sense.' She walked across the small kitchen and closed the door. 'I think we should keep a close eye on that young man.'

Chapter 20

NEXT DAY BETH came across a drawing as she helped tidy Finn's room. She was making an effort to forgive his canal episode. Finn had apologised, albeit in his own way, and they'd reached an unlikely truce. 'Finn, this is very good.'

She held the picture, admiring the work. It was the first time she could remember Finn creating recognisable figures.

'Who are they?' She pointed at the figures.

'It's me and Cissy, and Granddad.'

'And…' His mother pointed to Celia. 'Who's this?'

'Somebody Cissy knows.'

'Well, whatever, this is a fine drawing. Why don't you give it to Granddad?

Finn sat down on his bed. He felt sweaty and his head hurt. 'I need some of Granddad's water medicine.'

'What do mean? Are you poorly?'

His mother reached over and laid her hand on his forehead. 'You are hot.' She sat next to him on the bed. 'I tell you what, your dad will be home soon. He can look after Billie and you and I could take the picture to Granddad's, and I could pop out and get some more water medicine. But only if Granddad says you need some.' She ruffled his hair. 'We finished the last lot.'

Finn had no enthusiasm for journeys. The dunk in the canal combined with the massive "being found out" episode had been exhausting. He coughed, half-heartedly; his chest was hurting too. Billie shouted from the room opposite.

'Sorry Finn, better go and sort your sister out.' She turned at the door. 'Want to come and help?'

Finn shook his head and flopped back on his bed. He was knackered.

⊷▰ ▰⊶

Lorri was surprised to see Beth and Finn in the house when she returned from her walk.

'Hey guys, didn't expect to see you today.' Finn looked listless and wandered off to the sitting room.

Lorri frowned. She whispered, pointing at his rounded back. 'What's wrong?'

Beth was pulling on her coat. 'Another infection I think. Not surprising really. Dad said he would take a look when he gets back.' Lorri could see she was concerned. 'I'm going to the chemist, Finn will only take the dissolvable pain killers. Would you mind looking after him? He's refused to come with me.'

'Of course, no problem.' Lorri helped Beth with her coat. 'How's the hand?'

'Truthfully, it bloody hurts, and so inconvenient.' She flexed her foot. 'Like the shoes?' She laughed. She was wearing the only thing that fitted, a pair of green Crocs. 'Listen, I'll be fifteen minutes max.'

Lorri tossed her jacket over the newel post and joined Finn on the settee. 'Mum tells me you're sick again.' He nodded, clutching a piece of paper. 'What's this?'

'It's for Granddad.'

'Can I see?'

He held out the drawing.

Lorri looked at the four figures. She moved closer. 'Let me guess…' She pointed. 'Bet this is you.'

Finn grinned, an improvement. 'No, that's Cissy. This is me, and that's Celia.'

'What name did you say? The last one?'

'Granddad's friend, Celia.'

Lorri could feel the small hairs rising on her arms. 'Do you know her?'

The half-smile again. 'No, not exactly…' Finn traced his finger across his picture.

Lorri sat back and closed her eyes, she wasn't expecting Finn to endorse his grandfather's revelations.

'Did Granddad tell you about Celia?' Finn looked puzzled and shook his head. Lorri led Finn into the kitchen. 'Let's get a drink and you can tell me all about it.'

'But grownups don't believe in this stuff.'

'Maybe this grownup does.'

Lorri heard the front door close as Finn concluded his tale.

'Hello?' Finn's eyes lit up at the sound of Granddad's voice. He headed for the hall.

'Finn…' Lorri was holding his picture. 'Don't forget this.'

Chapter 21

THE COMPUTER SCREEN held her attention. Riikka was curious. She'd opened the appointment folder for Doctor Campbell. It was the entry for ten o'clock that held her attention: Finn Carey, and a note, "possible chest infection". She glanced at the display, it was already nine forty-five.

Irene was humming, one of her yesteryear favourites. Riikka decided to confirm her suspicion. 'I see Doctor Campbell is seeing Doctor Newman's grandson this morning. Will the man himself be coming do you think?'

Irene drummed her fingers on the desk. 'Indeed he is, called me yesterday to make the appointment. Poor lad has another chest infection.'

Riikka didn't miss the soft Edinburgh emphasis on "called me". She looked out the front window. The disclosures in the wine bar, their shared experiences. She still couldn't believe she'd had the nerve to talk about Sarah and her companions. She was sure that their entanglement had a purpose.

Further speculation was cut short as the surgery door opened and Finn bustled in, followed by Gabriel. Finn dragged his grandfather to the booking-in screen. Riikka was amused by the pantomime as Finn repeatedly tapped in the wrong information. Irene stood and adjusted her skirt. She wandered across reception.

'Can I help you young man?'

Finn studiously avoided Irene's attentive gaze.

Irene was positively glowing. 'Let's see now. "C" for Carey, that's right, and then your birthday month?' Finn looked at Gabriel again.

Irene prompted. 'Is it January?'

Finn nodded.

'So we need to press this one, Jan, that's short for January.' Finn stabbed at the screen. 'And last of all, are you a boy or girl?'

Riikka smiled as Finn giggled, pressing his finger the final time.

'And there you go, you will need to take your granddad upstairs to the waiting room.'

Gabriel steered Finn towards the stairs. He kissed Irene's cheek. 'Thanks Irene, we would have been here all day.' Finn was climbing. 'Better go…'

'No problem, lovely to see you both.'

Riikka was starting to feel like a fly on the wall, unseen and all-seeing, when Gabriel turned his head and waved. Riikka waved in response, surprised at the relief she'd felt, being noticed.

⋯⋯

The access stairway doglegged and opened out into a square-shaped seating area. Finn hated this part, everyone staring. There was an old lady who'd let herself go and couldn't close her legs properly, and a teenager with holes in his jeans and a scary grin. Finn was intrigued by an old man with watery eyes. His head jerked like a nodding dog. The room could have doubled as a freaky sideshow or creepy waxworks. Finn was relieved when Doctor Campbell appeared.

'This way Gabriel, Finn.'

Doctor Campbell's room was like a corridor, a shoebox. His desk sat at the far end next to the window. Finn sat in a chair next to his granddad and waited for someone to tell him what to do. He felt shy of doctors, apart from his granddad.

'So tell me, Finn, how are you?'

Finn shrugged his shoulders and glanced at his granddad, who sat forward. 'I thought I'd bring Finn in as his cough seems to be a permanent feature, and he fell in the canal…' The ex-partners exchanged a knowing look.

'Let me listen to your chest, Finn.'

Finn obliged, lifting his tops. The stethoscope was cold as it dabbed across his back.

'Deep breath for me.'

Finn endured the pointy thing in his ear and a wooden stick on his tongue as he said 'ahhh…', and then his tummy was prodded as he lay on the bed.

Doctor Campbell resumed his seat as Finn dressed. 'I'm reluctant to prescribe more antibiotics. Finn's ears are clear and his tonsils look fine. There's a bit of a rattle in his chest but nothing alarming. No temperature.'

Finn looked at his granddad again.

'What about the constant fatigue?'

'What are you suggesting, Gabriel?'

'Could we take some blood, see what's happening?'

'I can't see why Finn should be anaemic, but sure, we could do that and I'll write up another prescription for Amoxil. Tell Beth not to use it unless his temperature spikes again.'

Finn's ears pricked up. Tests and now medicine, maybe he should try his luck. He nudged his granddad's arm. 'Can I stay at home this week, until I'm tested?'

Both adults looked in his direction.

Doctor Campbell leaned over. 'Seems like a good idea Finn.' He turned to Gabriel. 'Ask Beth to keep him at home the rest of this week. Hopefully by Friday we'll have the results and it will give him a chance to rest up, avoid any further infection.' He turned and faced Finn. 'And no further dips in the canal.' Finn was not amused. 'Could you ask your mother to call me on Friday?'

Finn and Gabriel nodded.

Doctor Campbell picked up his phone. 'Jane, can you squeeze in a blood test for me? Yes? Great. It's Finn, Finn Carey. OK, thanks.' He turned to Finn. 'Right, you take your granddad back to reception and wait for the practice nurse, she'll take a small amount of blood from your arm. Just a tiny pin prick, promise.'

The wait outside the nurse's door reminded Finn of waiting to see his grandma. Eventually, the nurse appeared and led them inside. He closed his eyes as she reached for his arm. 'This will sting for a second.' She was quick, chatting as she worked, asking lots of questions about Billie and school. He was still struggling to remember his teacher's name when she announced that everything was done. She reached behind her chair. 'Is it OK to give this young man a treat?'

Chapter 22

BETH SLAMMED THE receiver into its cradle. 'Bloody phone's still engaged.' The heated declaration was wasted, there was no one else in the kitchen. She tapped her fingers on the worktop. She considered calling her father, but on reflection she was inclined to leave it. Finn had been so much better since his visit to see Robert Campbell earlier in the week. The infection must have cleared up. No need for test results. The key pad beckoned, a final tap? *Sod it, can't make the call if their phone's always busy, she thought.* She lifted the kettle and turned on the tap. The seemingly insignificant actions marked a turning point. The phone rang. It was the surgery.

'Is that Mrs Carey?'

Beth recognised the voice. 'Irene? Is that you?'

'Indeed it is. Doctor Campbell asked me to call.'

Beth waited. *Come on…*

'He would like to call by after surgery.'

'Sorry, what did you say?' A knot was forming in Beth's stomach. Her free hand slid behind her back as her fingers crossed.

This time Irene sounded flustered. 'Doctor Campbell wondered if he could call round after surgery. He wants to talk about Finn's test results.'

Beth had heard correctly. 'Why can't he tell me now? Why can't you tell me?' The latter request was unfair and desperate. Beth steadied herself.

Irene persisted. 'I'm sorry Mrs Carey, Dr Campbell has patients with him. He said to see if five-thirty would be OK?'

Beth gripped the back of a chair to avoid stumbling. She reset the kettle on its stand, tea long forgotten, and whispered into the handset. 'Yes, five-thirty is fine.'

⊷══◉ ◉══⊷

Patrick reached across the car and picked up his phone. It was Beth. He knew better than to ignore the call and pulled into a layby.

'Patrick, I need you to come home.'

'What's wrong?'

'The surgery rang. Robert Campbell wants to see us about Finn's test results at five-thirty, he's coming to the house.' Beth's emphasis – 'coming to the house' – made Patrick realise that his well-laid plans for the remainder of the day were crumbling. He was pretty certain there would be a good reason for the call, and the visit. He was unwilling to speculate further, shifting in his seat to steady the butterfly in his chest.

'I'll be there, no problem.'

'Patrick…' His heart sank as Beth's voice broke. 'What if…
you know…?'

'Steady, Beth, one step at a time. Listen, call your dad and
see if he can make it too.'

He could hear Beth thinking. Her voice steadied. 'I don't
think so, I'd rather you and I hear what Robert has to say. Then
see what's to do.'

Patrick, the bringer of good tidings and solver of problems,
assumed control. 'It may be nothing. Robert may be giving us
the "private" service treatment, because of the history with
your dad.' He could tell she was not convinced; he was not
convinced.

'Come home, soon as you can. Please…' The line went
dead.

Bollocks! The last bar had disappeared, no signal.

Patrick, the white knight, continued his slide into denial. He
closed his mobile and pulled out into the traffic. He rationalised,
surely there must be some mistake? It'll be nothing. Typical
of Beth to assume the worst. The doctor was on his rounds,
that's all. Unfortunately, the sick feeling in his stomach said
otherwise. His eye caught the crucifix dangling from the rear-
view mirror. Automatically, he crossed himself.

⟶▬◉ ◉▬⟵

Beth paced up and down the hallway. No sign of Robert
Campbell's car.

Patrick sighed. 'For pity's sake come and sit down. He'll be here soon enough.'

Beth was wound up so tight she couldn't reply. The waiting was intolerable and Patrick's repeated attempts at reassurance were not helping. She thought. *How will I cope if it is bad news?* Beth gazed at the children playing on the living room carpet. Billie was such a good-natured baby and Finn always seemed to have time for his sister: fetching and carrying, building and rebuilding brick towers. She could feel the burn of emotions she was not prepared to deal with, not yet. Maybe Robert was being thoughtful, popping in, saving them a trip to the surgery. After all, Finn was much better. A bit tired maybe. The doorbell rang.

--➤ ◉◄--

Riikka placed the last of the new books on the playroom shelf and stepped back to admire her handiwork. Familiarity had subdued her anxiety about the "Sarah" effect. After all, everyone seemed to be in the know. Riikka looked around the children's playroom and smiled, waiting, predicting the itch that preceded Sarah's return. The odd thing was she felt so much better. No headaches and her sex life was amazing. Physically, she felt fit and there'd been no repeat of the fainting fits. Every time she felt concerned about her mental state it was quickly followed by a contradictory certainty that all would be well. And then, of course, there was Jonathan.

'Could you read this to me Rikky?'

Riikka snapped out of her reverie and addressed the small, thin figure tugging at her hand. Maisy was eight years old and back for her final chemo session. Riikka took the book and led the waif to the large blue beanbag snuggled in the corner of the playroom.

'Of course I can. You read, I'll sit and listen and help if you get stuck.' As she relaxed Riikka was certain that Sarah was hovering. She had an overwhelming sense that Maisy needed to sleep. At that precise moment the young girl's head leaned into her arm and the reading stopped. *Well, well…* Riikka removed the half-open book from Maisy's hand and wriggled deeper into the beanbag. She stroked the remains of her hair and watched as her small eyes rolled behind closed lids. *Sweet dreams, honey.*

⊷⊷⊷⊶

Gabriel drummed his fingers on the steering wheel and checked his watch anxious to be home. Lorri was late. She had requested a pick-up from the supermarket at five. He was about to call when she appeared at the entrance with a loaded trolley.

'Sorry Gabe, it's hellish in there.' Gabriel hefted the produce into the boot with rather too much gusto. Bottles clinked.

Lorri gripped his arm. 'Steady. What's wrong?'

'Sorry?'

'What's on your mind?'

He reached up and closed the boot. 'To be honest I'm worried about Finn.'

'Why?'

'It may be nothing, but the run of chest infections concern me, and the lad doesn't look well.'

'I was expecting Beth to call me,' continued Gabriel as they drove away from the shopping centre. 'My ex-partner had organised some blood tests and the results were due in today.'

'Could you call Beth?'

'Maybe. I'm not sure I should, she'll only get anxious.'

Lorri settled into her seat. 'Then we'll wait.'

Chapter 23

BETH LURCHED TO her feet. *At last.* Her hand was shaking as she reached out and twisted the latch. Robert Campbell stood facing the open door.

'Hello Beth.'

If Beth was searching for reassurance she couldn't find any. Robert's face had the usual implacable GP look, and there was no attempt at pleasantry: a reluctant half-smile and no eye contact. She waited.

'Can I come in, Beth?' Another forced smile.

Beth shook her head. 'Sorry, please, come in.' She stepped back.

Patrick was standing as Doctor Campbell followed Beth into the kitchen. An uneasy silence followed as they sat at the table.

'Can I offer you a drink?' Making coffee was the last thing Beth wanted, nor did she want the conversation that was coming.

Robert Campbell touched her arm.

'I guess you know it's unusual, calling like this.' He shuffled forward in his seat. 'There's no easy way to break it to you I'm afraid.' He sighed. 'The results, the lab results have confirmed there are a number of suspicious cells in Finn's blood. His white blood count is very high. We've spoken to the children's hospital and made an appointment for Finn to see an oncologist, Dr North, Monday, first thing.'

Lifeless fingers squeezed what was left of hope. Beth glanced at Patrick, willing him to break the spell. He spoke…

'But Finn has been feeling so much better this week. Surely there must be a mistake?'

Beth had to know, hear the word confirmed, and know her adversary. 'Is it cancer?'

'Too early for a firm diagnosis but the first opinion is leukaemia I'm afraid, it's why Finn is so tired. Dr North will explain.' Robert dropped his head. 'I'm sorry to have to break the news. The thing is, prompt treatment is very effective these days.' He placed an envelope on the table. 'It's the test results. If the diagnosis is confirmed treatment will start quickly. Could you make sure Dr North has this when you see him?' He pointed at the envelope. 'Ask for oncology when you get to the hospital.'

Beth had questions. 'Have you told my father about this?'

'Apart from staff at the surgery, you're the first to know. Do you want me to tell Gabriel?'

Beth shook her head. 'How certain is the lab, of the diagnosis?'

Robert scratched his chin. 'The results fit the profile for leukaemia.' This time he didn't avoid eye contact. 'There could be a mistake, but I doubt it.'

Beth stood and gripped the back of her chair. 'Then I think we should tell Finn.'

Patrick shook his head. 'For pity's sake, let's keep this to ourselves at least until after the appointment next week.'

Beth looked at her husband, trying not to despair at his unwillingness to face facts. 'Patrick, if we're going to deal with this we can't hide our feelings from Finn. What we say and how we feel need to fit. I can't lie…' She turned to Robert. 'Would you help us tell Finn?'

'Of course, where is he?'

⋯▶▬ ▬◀⋯

Finn was playing with Billie. His sister frowned, the concentration required to place one brick on top of another all-consuming. Her podgy hands could barely grip and manoeuvre the wooden cubes. She was fond of yellow. Finn noticed that when her supply of yellow bricks ran out she would sit back, a look of amazement on her face. Then she would stare at Finn and beam. It was a game they played. He would reach behind and pick up a hidden yellow brick, Billie would scream, reaching forwards to take the sun-coloured cube. Carefully, she would set it at the top of the tower. Admiring her handiwork, she always reached the same conclusion: that the process was far more interesting than the result. Her face at this point split into a huge smile as she demolished the construction, and started building the tower once more.

Finn played the game with a different motivation as he needed to see his sister smile. It warmed him up, made him tingle, forget tiredness and coughing in case his chest hurt. It did have a downside. Watching his sister was a reminder that a carefree part of his life was passing. He'd no idea what that notion meant, only that when he woke most days he was more inclined to reach back for sleep than wake and see what the morning had to offer. And then, of course, he had to face the reaction of his parents and their obvious concerns when he felt unwell. He felt like they always needed him ever bright and cheerful, and in good health.

'Hello Finn.' Doctor Campbell came into the room, followed by Finn's parents.

Finn nodded. His mother looked upset and his dad had a strange grin on his face. Finn resumed his game with Billie, certain that he wouldn't be involved in talking with the doctor. Finn guessed that he would need to go back to school. He'd enjoyed his week off and was feeling much better, but he missed his friends. Be good to get back…

⤙▰ ▰⤚

Lorri stirred the rice, adding more stock. She tipped the bowl of frozen peas into the mix. This was Gabriel's favourite risotto. The kitchen clock showed seven. She assumed that the absence of a call from Beth was preying on Gabe's mind. The pan fizzed, the chicken stock almost boiled away. It was done. Lorri flicked off the gas and stirred in the cheese.

'Ready Gabe.'

As he stepped into the kitchen the doorbell rang. Gabriel tensed. Before he could move or speak Lorri handed him a serving spoon.

'I'll get it. Leave some for me.'

It was dark in the hallway and Lorri couldn't make out the figure beyond the patterned glass. As she opened the door the acrid smell of stale cigarettes fell into the house. Grace twisted her foot and feigned surprise.

'Lorri, I was looking for Dad.'

'Then you'd better come in.'

They exchanged a cursory hug. Lorri could make out the track of dried tears on Grace's powdered cheek.

'He's eating in the kitchen.'

Grace gripped her hand.

'I have bad news.'

Gabriel's head jerked up as they entered. 'Grace. What on earth are you doing here?' Her face painted a clear enough picture.

'There's no easy way to say this Dad so I'm going to come straight out with it.'

Lorri felt her departed sister's hand on her shoulder. Unconsciously, she covered the familiar gesture with her own and waited.

Gabriel dropped his spoon. 'It's the test results… What did Beth say?'

'She called me, asked me to come over… It's really bad, they're pretty sure it's leukaemia.'

Lorri watched Gabriel's barely recovered spirits fade. She sent a silent plea to Isabella and felt her steadfast response. She reached out to Grace. Gabriel shook his head. 'Dear God, not again.'

→▶◉ ◉◀←

Patrick watched, unable to deal with or participate in the scene playing out before him. Beth and Robert were explaining things to Finn.

'We think we know what's wrong with you Finn, why you've been feeling tired and sick.'

Their voices faded in and out as Patrick wrestled with his demons, bitterness pushing back fear: where the fuck is the justice in all this? To his credit Finn seemed to be absorbing the news with remarkable stoicism.

Beth sat behind Finn on the floor and stroked his hair.

'We have to go and see a special doctor next week. Make sure we know exactly what's wrong with you.'

Finn seemed preoccupied; Billie was trying to reach the last yellow brick. He broke away from his mother's bear hug and helped his sister complete her tower.

'Does that mean I have to miss more school?'

Patrick needed to get outside. 'Would you excuse me for a second, I need to…' He pointed upstairs. He wasn't sure if they'd heard or if it mattered. The whys kicked in: why Finn, why an innocent, why my son? He staggered into the hallway and got as far as the stairs before he had to sit. The familiar pattern on the wallpaper seemed to be sliding across the wall. He closed his eyes thinking he should get back. The weight of the crucifix around his neck lessened as he held it in his hand. With a single jerk he broke the chain and stared at the silver effigy. Carefully he laid it on the hall stand and marched into the kitchen. He grabbed a bottle of juice for Billie and Finn's favourite from the fridge, a carton of blackcurrant with a straw.

Beth looked up as he re-entered the room.

He lifted the drinks. 'Got something for the kids…'

Finn jumped up and grabbed both containers, placing Billie's bottle between her outstretched hands. 'Thanks, Dad.'

Robert Campbell stood. 'Listen, I should go.'

Leaving the children to their drinks, Patrick and Beth watched as he stepped out of their house and disappeared into the gloom. Closing the door, Beth spotted the spoiled cross. She picked it up.

'The chain's broken?'

Patrick lowered his head, unable to respond.

Beth, as usual, took charge. 'Let's have a minute together, work out what's to do.'

He followed her into the kitchen, his discomfort increasing as he wrestled with a desperate need for someone or something to blame.

'I hope the quacks have got it wrong, but I guess it's doubtful.' Patrick slumped into a chair. 'I think you should call your family. We're going to need all the help we can get.' He forced a smile. 'I feel out of my depth.'

'We're both out of our depth on this one.' She responded.

The supporting declaration didn't help. Patrick could feel a rising panic that threatened to undermine all his carefully laid coping mechanisms. He couldn't vocalise his greatest fear: that it was all his fault, his punishment. Logically, he knew such thoughts were ridiculous. The problem was his background. He wasn't exactly a devout Catholic but this challenge was going to test what remained of his faith, and some. The broken chain, the guilt, and the dreadful notion that he was going to lose his son battled for a front seat.

'Patrick.'

'Patrick!'

The thud of Beth's fist on the table bought him back. 'Sorry… a drink…' He needed to move. 'Right, what do we need to do first?'

Chapter 24

THE FOLLOWING WEEK Finn and his parents attended their first appointment at the children's hospital. Finn was beginning to feel like a celebrity. The missing fence panels, the dip in the canal, all seemed to be forgiven. He'd never had so much positive attention. The three of them sat in the oncology department reception area. Finn knew the word. His mum had explained. A nurse at the reception desk winked at Finn. He blushed. She picked up a phone and looked again in Finn's direction. Grabbing a file she marched over. He was mortified.

'Are you Finn?'

He tugged at his mother's sleeve; she did the talking with strangers.

'Lost your voice? Better add that to your file.' The nurse removed a blue pen from her pocket and clicked the top.

'It's not lost, he's a bit on the shy side.' Finn relaxed, grateful that his mum had spoken; gratitude that dissipated as the nurse stooped and held his hand.

'Well, Finn, Bruce North is ready to see you. Shall we show your mum and dad the way?'

The nurse's smile was infectious. Finn stood and followed, hand in hand. He glanced behind to make sure his parents were attached. The nurse smelt of soap or hand cream.

'You must be Finn?' Bruce North closed the file in front of him and the nurse guided Finn forwards. He continued. 'Come and sit next to me, and your mum and dad can sit there.' Finn climbed onto the grey plastic chair and watched as his parents shook hands with the bearded doctor. Finn noticed two things about him straight away: he had extremely white teeth and his eyes smiled.

'Finn, we are quite a friendly bunch here and we call each other by our first names. So I want you to call me Bruce. OK?' Finn nodded, he was starting to like this doctor. Bruce addressed his next comment to his parents. 'And we have a policy of being direct with our patients. I hope you won't object?'

Finn was puzzled by the word direct. *What does he mean?* Apparently, Bruce could read his mind. The experience was not a new one, remember Cissy?

'What I mean is that we know that our patients are children, but whenever we can we treat them like grownups.' Finn nodded.

The idea that a grownup was offering to talk to him like a grownup was intriguing, sort of scary but exciting. Bruce opened the grey file on his desk. 'The blood test your GP organised is not conclusive, but together with the other physical symptoms, tiredness, repeated infections and so on, there are strong indications that we are dealing with leukaemia. To confirm the diagnosis we'll need a full blood count and bone marrow samples.'

Bruce turned and spoke to Finn. 'Bone marrow is like a red jelly in the middle of your bones where your body makes new blood cells. Yours seems to be on a go-slow.' Finn guessed that "go-slow" was like a joke as his parents were smiling. 'We'll take the bone marrow under a general anaesthetic, put you to sleep.'

The doctor turned to his parents again. 'Finn would appear to be anaemic and his white blood count is way up. So we should make a start, and quickly. If the diagnosis is confirmed he'll be vulnerable to new infections until we get the white count down. You should keep him away from school for the time being.'

Finn lost the plot at this point and sat gazing out the window. The view was not that interesting – red brick walls, drainpipes and flaking paintwork. A pigeon bobbed on a windowsill, and as Finn watched, the bird released a grey and white mess from its rear end. Finn smirked. *Wonder where that landed?*

Eventually, his parents and Bruce North concluded their conversation. 'See you in two days. Theatre time is booked.' He turned again to Finn. 'Did you get all that?' Finn had no idea and shrugged his shoulders. 'We have to do the tests to make sure we understand why you are feeling so tired and keep getting infections. See you back here in two days so we can make a start. You'll be staying here for a few days and your mum and dad can stay with you. OK?'

⇢═◉ ◉═⇠

The drive home was uneventful and boring. Finn could sense his parents wanted to talk but for some reason were not. He chipped in.

'I liked Bruce. He's got a nice face.' His mum and dad looked at each other. Finn noticed his mum biting her lower lip. It was his dad who replied.

'Yes buster, he is, and no school until the hospital have had a chance to sort you out.'

Finn struggled to remember everything Bruce had said. Something was not quite right. 'But if you both stay with me, in the hospital, Billie will have to come too.' The words left his lips like a thought that bounced around the car. He hoped his parents had heard. He fingered the seat belt strap. There was more. 'And what about my school friends, when am I going to see them?' Finn half heard his mum's response. For the first time in a long while Finn needed Cissy. She'd been absent for ages. 'What if I don't like it…?' Finn shifted his gaze and stared out of the window. The question drew no response from his parents and Cissy remained elusive. 'When's Granddad coming? I'd like to talk to Granddad.'

⊶⊨⊚ ⊚⊨⊷

Gabriel was thankful for his medical training. He'd spent the afternoon at the library, using the computer. He'd read a number of research articles on the latest drug protocols. Things had changed since his stint as a trainee doctor. He'd made copious notes and was starting to feel a little more in control. The papers were spread over the dining table. One piece of the jigsaw was missing: he desperately needed to know Finn's detailed diagnosis. It would be the best part of a week before the first batch of tests were completed. A glass of red wine appeared and an unmistakeable fragrance. For a brief moment Isabella's absence was unmasked.

'Looks like your studying is paying off.' Lorri sat in the opposite chair. 'I've something I'd like to discuss.' Gabriel removed his reading glasses. Lorri continued. 'I wanted you to know that I'm happy to stay... For as long as you want me to.'

Gabriel sat back in his seat. He felt uncomfortable – reconnecting the dots was uncomfortable. Connecting Lorri's face to her sister's was uncomfortable.

Lorri frowned. 'What's up?'

Gabriel pushed the wine away. 'It's the perfume. Isabella...' He felt churlish. 'For a second there I thought...'

'That Isabella was placing the wine?' He nodded, unwilling to pursue the notion that Isabella was close by. Lorri paused and then spoke. 'I hear her all the time.' She reached over and lifted Gabriel's chin. 'Would you like to know what she has to say?' He nodded. Lorri moved closer and kissed him. With his eyes closed it could have been Isabella: the same tenderness and warmth.

He raised his head, his gaze raw with feeling. 'I miss her.'

Lorri stood and drew him close, whispering. 'She knows...'

Chapter 25

FINN JUMPED ONTO the bed and sat cross-legged. Today he was having tests, whatever that meant. In the bed across the ward a girl about his age was watching TV. She waved. A tube was sticking out of her chest and the other end came from a plastic bag hanging on a metal stand. There was another tube up her nose. Finn wrinkled his own in sympathy, thinking how bad it would be to have tubes. He definitely didn't want tubes.

A nurse stood at the end of his bed holding a clipboard. 'Hi Finn. My name's Mae and I'll be looking after you today.' Finn didn't know what to say.

The morning was a blur of activity. Bruce North came in for a chat. Finn had to wear what looked like a nightdress that did up at the back and then Mae reappeared.

'Right Finn, you come with me. Your mum and dad can wait here. We're going to fit a small tap to the back of your hand so we don't have to give you lots of injections.'

Beth stood as Finn slid off the bed. 'Shall I…?'

Mae smiled. 'Best if Finn and I do this together.' At this point Finn was warming to Mae. Earlier she'd let him hold this amazing gadget that went in his ear and showed his temperature.

Finn was directed to a chair and Mae sat next to him. She pulled over a trolley with lots of scary-looking things on it. She tore open what looked like a plaster and stuck it on Finn's hand.

'This will stop the needle stinging.' Then she opened another packet and Finn shot out of the chair. Mae was holding one of those things that his grandma had in the back of her hand when she was bleeding in hospital.

'I don't want one of those in me, they make you bleed.'

'Finn, sit down please. What do you mean they make you bleed?' Finn backed away towards the door. 'OK look. I'll put this away.' She dropped the half-opened box on the trolley and pushed it out of reach. 'Now come and tell me about this bleeding.'

Reluctantly, Finn sat and recounted the story of his visit to see his grandma and how her hand and the pillow were all red.

Mae held his hand and peeled off the anaesthetic patch. 'Can you feel this?' She tapped the back of his hand. Finn shook his head. 'If we're quick you won't feel me fit the cannula and I have some extra-sticky tape, like a plaster, that will make sure it doesn't come loose and make your hand bleed. OK?'

Finn nodded.

'What I'd like you to do is close your eyes and trust me. Can you do that? Think of it as playing a game.'

Finn suddenly thought of Billie trying to reach behind his back for the last yellow brick. The sound of her laughter was comforting…

'Finn.' He opened his eyes. Mae slipped off the plastic gloves she was wearing. 'Look.'

He held up his hand. It was all done. A slow smile spread across his face.

Mae took his other hand. 'Let's show your mum and dad.'

Soon they were wheeling him down to the operating theatre. Finn counted the ceiling lights and had nearly got to twenty when they arrived. Mae pushed his bed through some doors and into a small room. A lady with a cloth hat approached.

'So this is Finn.' She held his wrist above the thing in his hand. He jumped. 'Don't worry, I'm going to give you something to make you sleepy.'

Finn nodded. He felt hot and anxious.

The lady with the hat squeezed his hand while she attached a tube with white stuff in it. 'I want you to count for me Finn. Start at one could you?'

'One, two…'

→▭◉ ◉▭←

Riikka noticed Finn as she walked into the oncology unit. He was sitting on a bed halfway down the ward, his wild curls like a beacon. She approached the nursing station.

'Who's the new boy?' Riikka pointed.

'His name's Finn, possible leukaemia. We're waiting for test results.'

Leukaemia. Finn. The two words rattled in her head like the sound of cracking bones. She turned and left the ward, mumbling about something she'd left in the car. She found a quiet corridor and sat. The players joined hands: Gabriel, Finn, Cissy, Sarah and Celia. Riikka felt giddy and wondered what was going on. She could see that the disparate parts seemed to be forming into a coalition, but with what purpose? Her companion was silent, not a word spoken to add to the debate; she had to speak with someone. It would need to be Gabriel, and maybe Lorri.

She turned her attention to a more practical problem. She knew Gabriel's address, she'd taken it to send the book-signing invitation, but she could hardly turn up uninvited. She needed to get back to the ward. She picked up her bag and retraced her steps. Finn was still sitting on his bed watching an overhead TV screen.

'Riikka?' She turned. It was Gabriel. 'Good grief, what are you doing here?'

Riikka, flustered, responded. 'I think I told you? I volunteered to play with the kids.'

'Sorry, you did say. I didn't realise it was oncology.' He looked towards Finn's bed. 'We've had a bit of a shock this week.'

'So I see.' Riikka was lost for words and then, inspired, she moved closer, lowering her voice. 'Maybe there's more to these imaginary characters…'

Gabriel, half smiling now, agreed. 'We should talk and I'd like you to meet my sister-in-law, Lorri, she's quite a character. She has an interesting perspective on the whole issue. I'll pop into the bookshop next week to organise something.' Gabriel paused. 'By the way, I haven't mentioned anything about our discussions to Finn's parents. Could you not...?'

'Sure, of course, won't say a word, and I'd love to meet Lorri.' She glanced across the ward at the playroom. 'I should take up residence with the kids.' She hesitated as clumsy thoughts delayed the inevitable platitudes. 'I'm sorry about Finn.' The words sounded flat and meaningless, but she had to say something. 'You take care then, and see you soon.'

'I will, and thanks.'

⊶⫸ ⫷⊷

The playroom was empty and a mess. Riikka tidied away games and books, reflecting on Finn's surprising appearance in the unit. Death was ever-present in oncology. There were no guarantees that the rigorous treatments would work, and there was no good reason why any of the children she'd met had contracted cancer. Riikka struggled with the apparent injustice. As far as she could tell, their lives were a living and dying lottery: random events that settled grim choices on innocent shoulders.

She'd learned to stand back, to be a rock, but even so the suffering she witnessed replayed in her dreams. Now Finn and his family would have to take this same journey. Sarah seemed unwilling to contribute to her internal wrangling, although

Riikka could sense her attention, raking through her thoughts like some cerebral comb. The last book was returned to its place.

The door opened and Riikka's favourite patient, Maisy, and her dad, Rod, stepped in.

'Hey Rik.' Rod seemed to prefer single syllables. He eased his considerable frame onto a battered sofa. Maisy was asleep, wound around his twenty stone corporation, her head resting in the crook of his arm. Even though she was nearly eight years old Rod had no problem accommodating the youngster. He was heavily tattooed, no hair on his head and a ZZ Top beard. Maisy was asleep in the safest spot in the world.

'Hey Rod, how is she? Riikka marvelled at the size of his hands and the tender way he ran his finger through Maisy's new hair.

'All good, in remission.' A rare smile lit his face. 'We hope not to see you again. No offence...' More smiles.

'None taken. I'm so pleased, she's such a sweetheart.'

Maisy yawned and opened her eyes. 'Rikky!' She slid off her dad's lap and tottered to Riikka.

'Rod stretched. Listen, I could do with a leak and a brew. Could I...?

'Yes, and mine is no sugar, just milk.'

Riikka addressed Maisy. 'Let's find a book shall we?' They had barely buried themselves in their favourite spot, the beanbag, when the door opened and Rod reappeared. Maisy stood and headed for the basket of Lego bricks. Riikka took the mug of tea.

'I have another favour to ask.' Rod pulled a pack of rolling tobacco from his jeans and glanced in Maisy's direction.

Riikka winked. 'Sure. Listen, there's a new boy on the ward, looks like he may have the same diagnosis as Maisy. Would it be OK if I introduced them? It would be good for him to see that the treatment works.'

Rod looked at his daughter engrossed in building. 'As long as it's all right with Maisy I have no problem with that.'

Riikka walked across the ward with Maisy. Finn was watching TV and Riikka recognised the woman sitting with him. 'Hi, sorry to butt in.' Finn looked up. 'I'm Riikka, I help out in the playroom. She pulled her little companion forwards. 'And this is Maisy, she wanted to meet you Finn.' Maisy jumped onto Finn's bed; he looked apprehensive. 'And I think you must be Finn's mum?'

'Yes I am. Have we met before?'

Riikka pulled up a chair. 'Not exactly, I was at your mum's funeral. I came with Irene. I work with her at the surgery. Listen, I don't want to intrude but I thought it might be nice for Finn to meet Maisy. She's finished her treatment and she's in remission.'

Beth smiled. 'So Maisy's at the end of the process, so to speak?'

'She is. Is Finn OK to walk?' Beth nodded. Riikka turned to Maisy. 'Why don't you take Finn and show him the playroom.'

Maisy slid off the bed and grabbed Finn's hand as he followed.

'Nice of you to do that.' Beth stared at her son as he disappeared behind the playroom door. 'Nice for me too. To be honest, this is all new...'

Riikka hesitated. 'I'm here every other week, Wednesday afternoons. Feel free to talk if you need to. I can't offer any medical advice, not qualified for that, but I'm a good listener.' Riikka stood. 'I'd better keep an eye on those two. See you soon.'

'Thanks, and send Finn back when you've had enough.'

⊷⊷ ⊷⊷

'Do you mind if I take notes? Old habits…' Gabriel opened his notebook. Bruce North nodded. 'Help yourself.'

Beth and Patrick shuffled in their seats and Finn yawned.

'First of all, sorry that I had to drag you in before breakfast.' Bruce pulled a pen from his top pocket. 'The preliminary diagnosis is confirmed I'm afraid. Finn does have leukaemia.'

Gabriel's hand shook as he picked up his pen.

'Unfortunately, the white cell count is very high and the leukaemia cells have a chromosome abnormality. When we put the treatment protocol together Finn will be classified as high risk.' Bruce sat back in his chair and glanced in Gabriel's direction. 'However, and it's important you all know this, the expected prognosis is still good. Most children in the high-risk group respond well and achieve full remission.'

Gabriel was about to speak when Beth broke in.

'When will his treatment start?'

'What we'd like to do is have Finn back in theatre this afternoon. It's the reason for the early meeting. No breakfast or drinks please.' Bruce turned and tapped Finn on the shoulder. 'We want to fit a cannula like the one you had in your hand yesterday. Only this time we're going to put it here. He pointed to Finn's upper chest, near his left shoulder. This one will stay in until your main treatment has finished. It will save you having a needle fitted every time you come in.'

This time it was Patrick who spoke up. 'And after today, the treatment starts?'

Bruce closed Finn's file. 'As soon as we're happy that Finn has recovered from the anaesthetic I think you should all go home for the weekend. Let's start the chemotherapy Monday.'

Gabriel held back as Finn and his parents filed out of the office. 'Could I have a quick word?'

'Sure.' Bruce resumed his seat. He tapped Finn's file. 'If someone close, in my family, was in Finn's position I know how I'd feel. I'd want to know everything.' Bruce removed a sheaf of papers from the file and placed them before Gabriel. 'These are the lab results and the treatment protocol that's been agreed with the team. Bruce smiled and leaned across his desk. 'I can't let you have these, but if you want to take a quick look and make notes that's fine with me.'

Gabriel visibly relaxed. 'Listen, I won't make a nuisance…'

'Let's agree that if you have any issues with Finn's treatment you'll come and talk to me. Please don't challenge the nursing staff, unless there's an emergency. Do we have an understanding?'

'Thank you. Yes of course. That's generous of you…'

'Return the papers to the top of the file and no doubt I'll see you again?'

It was Gabriel's turn to smile now. 'Try to keep me away.'

Chapter 26

LORRI WAS ENJOYING a morning alone. So much had happened since Isabella had died: Billie's arrival, Gabriel's out-of-character moments, and Finn's dramas. Every time she'd considered her promise to Isabella fulfilled, along came another reason to stay. She'd given up a counselling job to respond to Isabella's call, and had been happy to do so, but her small pot of savings was fast disappearing. Fortunately, she'd qualified for a state pension that summer and although it was only a few hundred pounds a month it was enough to cover the basics. She was grateful that there had been no prior relationships to consider. For almost ten years she'd lived alone.

She'd received letters from friends in Scotland. The correspondence was easy reading but Lorri knew they were fishing, they wanted her back. Sooner or later she would have to make a decision: stay or return.

Lorri needed to meet Riikka. She had the makings of a cornerstone in Gabriel's unfolding mystery. Each new drama affecting the family appeared to relegate the previous to a lesser status. Gabriel's dreams and visions, his internal visitor, slipped into the background. All eyes were on Finn now. Lorri was convinced that Riikka held the key. There were too many loose ends, she needed to bring the threads together and make sense of the weave.

⊷≡◉ ◉≡⊷

When Lorri entered the living room Gabriel was examining a small card. 'Something interesting?' Lorri licked cake crumbs from her fingers.

Gabriel stared at the card. 'It's an invitation to a book signing.'

'From Riikka?'

Gabriel nodded.

'Could I come? I assume Riikka will be there?'

Gabriel re-read the invitation. 'Don't see why not. And yes, you will get to meet Riikka. Guess we could do with a break.' Lorri could see that he was preoccupied. He probably needed space.

'Listen, I'd like to run through my notes again, and I'm really tired. I'm going to call it a day. Beth and Patrick are going to spend a quiet weekend with the kids. I got the impression they don't want to talk.' Lorri crossed the room and kissed his cheek.

'Sweet dreams, Gabe.' She stood back. 'Are you sure it's OK if I come along tomorrow?'

'Sure.' Gabriel placed the card in Lorri's hand. 'I don't recognise the author but I could do with the distraction and it would be great if you could meet Riikka.'

Lorri read the invitation.

You are invited to attend a book-signing event...'

She skipped the details, her eyes drawn to a scrawled message.

'Should have sent this weeks ago. Hope you can make it. R.'

The date of the event was the next day. She dropped the card on the table and stretched. 'I'm going to turn in too. Goodnight.'

⋅⇥▭◉ ◉▭⇤⋅

Gabriel watched Lorri bend and retrieve her wrap. The gesture was so familiar. He missed Isabella with a vengeance. He'd no conception when she was alive how she'd held the family together. Living without her was like walking on glass with bare feet – painful. He was unable to retrieve a single memory of when he'd thanked Bella for her unconditional support. The realisation was beyond depressing.

As his thoughts edged towards despair a strange thing happened. There was only one light in the room, a standard lamp, and as his head dropped, bowed by the weight of his concerns, the bulb expired with a soft click. Gabriel closed his eyes; Celia was preparing to speak. *Right now I need to sleep. Can we talk another time?*

'Sleep is good, makes no difference. We can speak there too...'

⋅⇥▭◉ ◉▭⇤⋅

Gabriel stared around the bookshop and this time he knew he was dreaming. He grabbed a copy of the book from a stand, a review from a national paper stood out on the back cover.

'Alexander takes the often times overworked subject of the dream state and adds his own compelling twists. This is not another read for the self-righteous seeking an alternative lifestyle add-on; this is a well-researched, well-thought-out, and for a change, well-written piece that deserves to be read. I was pleasantly, and surprisingly, surprised! If you're curious about the significance of your dreams and would like to read an intelligent point of view on the whole active dreaming genre, this may be a book for you...'

Well, well.

He stood in line. It was past closing time and a reporter was finishing his interview. The manager stood to make a short announcement.

'Thank you for bearing with us. Alexander is free to sign now, and don't worry, we'll stay open until you get your book signed.'

The queue started to move. As he edged forwards he caught sight of Riikka, who waved. He was distracted by a discreet cough from behind and made up the missing steps. Soon enough it was his turn.

Alexander took his copy of the book. He hesitated before placing the volume on the desk. 'A name?'

Gabriel stared at his face. 'Gabriel...'

Alexander scribbled a few words across the page, closed the book and made to hand it back. As he reached out he touched Gabriel's arm.

'It's strange, don't you think, that no-sense has become nonsense?' He tapped the closed book. 'Nothing's as it seems...'

Without waiting for a response the author switched his attention to the next in line. Gabriel opened the book reading the barely legible scrawl. Alexander had repeated his remarks.

'You made it then.' He looked up as Riikka walked over. 'Did you get a signature?'

Gabriel, still puzzling over the author's comments, responded. 'Yes, I did. Thanks for inviting me.'

'Are you with anyone?' He shook his head. 'Then why don't we get a drink?'

Without waiting for a reply she turned and walked across the room. Gabriel was sure it was Riikka and yet there was something about her that was different. She was more confident and there was something else, she was playing a part. He joined her at the drinks table.

'Red OK?' Gabriel nodded and took the glass. He'd no idea what was going to happen next and yet he could direct his attention, drink or not drink, and apparently do all this whilst dreaming.

The wine seemed to have quite a lift. The shop was packed for the event and it was difficult to hear Riikka speak. She leaned over.

'Why don't we take a look around the upper floor? It's quieter up there. Give me a minute.' He watched as she walked over to the manager. They looked over. Gabriel dropped his head, feeling embarrassed. Riikka threaded her way across the crowded room.

'Follow me.' Voices receded as they climbed the stairs. 'I'm over here.' He followed the sound of her voice, picking his way between tables filled with books. Gabriel's pulse picked up. Downstairs it was difficult to hear. Upstairs it was difficult to see. Light filtered through from the street below.

'This is better, take a seat.' She was sitting in an area of the upper floor set out for shoppers to relax and read. There were two sofas facing each other.

Gabriel eased himself into the soft upholstery. Riikka had draped herself on the opposite couch. She leaned forwards, arm extended. 'Before we settle, would you mind? Another glass would be a treat.' Gabriel stood and she maintained her grip.

'Be sure to turn the key in the downstairs door when you come back, it's in the lock.' Her face was expressionless.

The shop was emptying as he refilled their glasses. The manager broke off his conversation with Alexander and turned in Gabriel's direction. 'I hear you're helping Riikka lock up tonight?' Gabriel picked up the recharged glasses. The precursor of a smile crossed the bookseller's face, animating his various chins. It was not too difficult to make out the barely concealed sneer that followed. 'Have a good night...'

Gabriel pushed his way through the fire door to the top floor; as it closed he remembered the key. Even though Gabriel continued to believe he was dreaming he was concerned that he was stepping into storylines that were outside his comfort zone. He mused, why was he locking himself in a room with a woman younger than his daughters? He watched as his fingers closed around the key and turned. What the hell, he was past caring. It occurred to him that his thoughts made no difference anyway, in fact, were they his thoughts? If he was losing his grip on reality, losing it in close proximity to Riikka would have its compensations.

He turned and climbed the stairs. Riikka was still on her sofa. He handed over the glass. Sitting, he stroked his chin, unperturbed by the smooth skin, no beard, and no myopia. The situation reminded him of some distant encounter. The memory had no face but it did evoke feelings. He sank back into the sofa, refusing to close his eyes.

Riikka stood and discarded her clothes. Gabriel no longer felt like a rather charming old gentleman. She looked hungry and Gabriel found himself responding.

⋯⊷⊚ ⊚⊶⋯

Gabriel shifted his weight, adjusting to the feel of stones beneath his skin. He heard the approaching surf, the sound mingled with something close, something intensely intimate, something mindful. The warm ocean scooped him up. His eyes opened as he was dragged under. Floundering, he struggled to stand. The water retreated, allowing him to touch the seabed with his feet, retching water and rubbing his eyes. The sun's heat drew him out. His eyes feasted on the ocean view, blue against blue.

'Congratulations.'

Why was he unsurprised? Celia was sitting under a parasol. She patted a vacant chair. 'Come, sit with me, we should talk.'

As soon as he stepped free of the tide he remembered the dream. 'Where's Riikka, and where am I?'

'She's close by, with Sarah, and you're still dreaming, but on a different level.'

Gabriel scanned the beach in both directions; no one to be seen.

Celia was apparently enjoying his confusion. 'I assume your little tryst was enjoyable? I should add that it must have been for you to be here.' Celia poured water from a frosted bottle. 'There are a few things I want to say, a sort of explanation...' She tapped the table. 'I could tell you much that would make no sense at all...' More table tapping. 'But my guess is you are wondering why the three of us and the three of you are conspiring in such inexplicable activity. Shall we place our cards on the table?' Gabriel shrugged his shoulders. Celia continued. 'This is going to sound like prevarication, but it's not. There are places where it's possible to access ideas that are yet undiscovered. People who can do that have eureka moments, they've no notion where their ideas come from. They are able to do this, are facilitated to do this, because they have the capacity to engage with other levels of consciousness. It's there that the knowledge they seek is freely available. Finn has this facility. In a limited way we are protecting him, or more truthfully, his abilities. Unusually, you and Riikka are required to assist in this protective process.' Celia stood. 'And you may be interested to know, but will find it hard to believe, that Sarah, Cissy and me, we have no separate identity, we are not physically present, we are ideas.'

Gabriel stared at his hands. 'Well, you're right, dead right. If this situation were real, I'd say that what you've just said was a load of rubbish, but as it's a dream I guess anything goes.'

When he looked up Celia had disappeared. On the table was the red box. As he reached across the glass surface the lid flipped open.

Chapter 27

LORRI FOLLOWED HER sister as she headed for the staircase. Grandmother's instructions rang out clear as a bell. Isabella was obviously asleep, but walking, just as Grandma Lucca had predicted. Lorri paused to pull on her slippers. Isabella stopped half way up the flight of stairs. When she turned to speak Lorri had to grab the banister to avoid falling. This was not her sister. An old woman stared back.

'You fool, you're following the wrong person, wake up!'

Lorri woke. She heard a noise. *Shit!* Someone was walking downstairs and then silence. She pulled on her shift and opened the bedroom door. It was cold. She grabbed a throw hanging over the newel post and wrapped it round her shoulders. The shuffling sound resumed. Lorri was a fairly robust character, but heroics were definitely off the agenda. She rationalised that it must be Gabriel. Even so... She switched on the landing light and descended the stairs.

There was enough light from the hallway to make out Gabriel lying on the living room carpet. At first Lorri thought he must have passed out, but then he moved. Reassured, she covered him with the throw. She smiled, how could she wake him, or leave him to wake, without traumatising the poor man: he was stark naked. And what about Grandma Lucca's timely call to action?

She sat the other side of Gabriel and laid her hand on his chest. What a strange place to sleep. Lorri resolved to leave him to complete whatever he'd started. He shivered. At least she could make sure he was warm. She retraced her steps and returned with her duvet and pillows. Carefully, she manoeuvred Gabriel so that he lay on the edge of the king-sized duvet, miraculously he slept on. She curled up behind his back. Spooning seemed the most appropriate way to warm him up. She rested their heads on cushions, covered herself and Gabriel with the remaining half of the quilt, and waited.

Gabriel did warm up, but despite her best efforts she could not sleep. Aside from Gabriel's nasal toots, the floor was not exactly comfortable. It was almost day break and she was thinking about breakfast when he woke.

'Damn!' With amazing agility he sat bolt upright and stared ahead. 'I've seen inside that retched box.'

Lorri rubbed her eyes and waited. Gabriel drew his hands from under the quilt and pinched his arm. He still seemed half-asleep. 'This can't be a dream.' Then he saw Lorri, gazing expectantly. 'Whoa… Why are we on the carpet, and together?' He lifted the duvet. 'Dear God…'

Lorri burst into laughter. 'You went walkabout again.' She yawned and stretched. 'I stayed with you to keep you warm…' She couldn't resist teasing. 'I don't suppose you remember?'

'Remember what?' He looked apprehensive. 'I remember the dreams well enough, never had such vivid dreams in my life.'

Lorri pulled the remaining cushions from the sofa so they could lean back. She was intrigued by the lift in his spirits. 'Well then, I'm not moving from here until you tell me all about them.'

Gabriel skipped over his adventures in the bookshop, but he gave enough away. Although he'd not mentioned the outcome of his time with Riikka, Lorri assumed that sex had raised its predictable head. She hoped there was more to Gabriel's transformation than copulation. Gabriel continued his monologue, recounting the dream conversation with Celia. This time he could remember what happened with much less circumspection. 'She more or less said Finn was a budding genius. Complete rubbish...'

'And the box?'

'The box?' Now it was Gabriel's turn to tease. Lorri jabbed him in the ribs. 'The box is nothing. It's what's in the box...'

'So...?'

'Well, after Celia had done her usual disappearing act, she must have left the box on the table and the lid opened, by itself. Inside,' continued Gabriel, his eyes closed, 'it was incredible. Inside the box is a small globe, like a glass marble, only it spins, and it has clouds.' Gabriel was obviously enjoying the retelling. 'I wish you'd been there. The clouds were grey-blue and underneath I could see a burnt orange. And then the best part, it lifted from the box and moved to my left. As I watched it stopped between me and the horizon and faded.'

'Good grief…' Lorri was finding it difficult to keep pace with the images his description conjured.

'There's more. My eyes were riveted to the spot where it stopped and as I watched a planet-sized version rose in the sky: burnt orange deserts with grey-blue clouds. It was unbelievable. Gabriel relaxed into the cushions. 'I feel twenty years younger. I've no idea how, why or what happened, but last night was incredible.'

Lorri couldn't believe the shift in his energy. 'And was it getting laid or finding out what was in the box that jump-started your change in mood?' Much to her surprise, Gabriel's expression changed, he looked embarrassed. Actually, he looked physically uncomfortable, or maybe both. Lorri pealed back the duvet. 'I need the loo I'm afraid.' She noticed that Gabriel was less than keen to part company with the bedding. His expression was priceless. 'You OK?'

Gabriel avoided Lorri's gaze. 'Sure, I'm going to rest up for a few minutes.'

Chapter 28

LORRI WAS APPREHENSIVE. Although Gabriel's recent escapades were fascinating, and entertaining, for the first time in many years she was starting to feel out of her depth. Maybe she was reading too much into Gabe's antics? As they approached the bookshop she almost made feeble excuses and left. What if her insight infected the outcome? She definitely wanted to spend time with Riikka. Perhaps she might hold the key to the mystery?

As they entered the bookshop she recognised the author. She said nothing to Gabriel, but she'd an inkling she'd known him years before. He was posing for a photographer. He was not the man she remembered; ageing had not been kind. His hair was thinning but he still sported what was left of his shoulder-length locks. The greying strands looked out of character with the man she'd known. He turned and caught her eye. There was no spark of recognition. When Gabriel gripped her arm she was relieved.

'Lorri?' She turned. Gabriel was standing next to a young woman. 'Lorri, can I introduce you to Riikka?'

'Sorry. Hi Riikka, I was miles away. Is that Alexander?'

'Would you like an introduction, later perhaps, when the formal part is over?' Riikka's offer was not appealing.

'Thank you, but I think not.' Lorri moved closer. 'Sometimes it's better to leave the past behind the present. If you see what I mean?'

Riikka smiled. 'No problem...'

Gabriel picked up Alexander's latest book from one of the strategically placed tables close by. 'Listen, I'm going to buy this and get it signed. Might as well make the most of being here, and it would give you two a chance to get to know each other.'

Lorri chuckled as Gabriel joined the queue. 'Well then, where shall we start?' Riikka's facial expression was conflicted: an uncompromising directness combined with older talents. Lorri was intrigued.

Riikka leaned over. 'Why don't we find a quiet place to talk upstairs?' She pointed to a door at the back of the shop. 'There's another department, a reading room, through the double doors.' She took Lorri's drink. 'Follow me.'

Riikka switched on lights, climbed stairs and guided Lorri to facing sofas. 'Please take a seat. It's a relief to be away from that melee downstairs.' She sat and immediately discarded her shoes. 'My feet are killing me.'

Lorri was incredulous. 'Sorry, this is so off the wall...'

Riikka looked confused.

Lorri needed to backtrack. 'I hope you don't mind, but Gabe has told me about Cissy and her friends, Celia and Sarah.'

Riikka didn't look phased. 'I guessed he would. He said you might be able to make sense of it all?'

'Not sure that I'm in that league. However, last night Gabe had a dream about you, and he described this room, these seats, and even you kicking off your shoes.' Riikka looked up as Lorri continued. 'To be honest, everything points to some sort of connection between you all, but I have no idea what it might be, what it means.'

'Maybe we're all going mad, group hysteria.' Riikka replied. 'Or perhaps we've forgotten that we've met and then meet again, but with no recall that we are already acquainted?' She shook her head and patted the seat. 'Please, would you mind…?' Lorri placed her drink on the table and sat next to Riikka. 'To be honest with you, this is all getting a bit beyond me.' Lorri was surprised to see tears formed in Riikka's eyes. 'It was difficult enough to cope with Sarah's visits, before Gabriel, Celia and Finn appeared. At least then the trickery was contained, inside my head. But now, the dreams, Gabriel's experiences… It feels like I'm trapped inside a wider experience and I'm not sure I want to be part of it. I feel like I'm boxed in and can't get out. Am I making any sense?'

Truthfully, Lorri did not know how to respond. A single tear ran down Riikka's cheek and descended, uninterrupted, to the carpet below. 'I don't know what to say. Making you feel better is what I want to do, but that seems incredibly patronising.'

Riikka met her gaze and seemed to take encouragement from Lorri's words. 'But I've seen things, been places, places no sane person would go.'

Lorri willed Riikka to carry on… And then, slowly at first, all of Riikka's pent-up misgivings, and strange experiences unravelled.

'At first, this is really going to sound off-the-wall. I started feeling horny, a lot of the time.' Riikka wiped her face and grinned. 'Sarah,' she hesitated, obviously embarrassed, 'she seemed to feed off the energy. God, this is difficult… I mean I did enjoy it.' More embarrassment. 'But most of the dreaming stuff seemed to happen after sex.' Riikka's expression changed. 'Actually, just an orgasm seemed to kick things off.' Riikka laughed. 'I can't believe I'm saying all this. Can't believe what a relief it is, to be able to…'

Riikka was sitting with her back to the door so she didn't see Gabriel poke his head through. Lorri did. She gave him her bugger-off-in-a-nice-way look and he seemed to take the hint. The door closed as he withdrew. Riikka took a sip of wine and held onto the glass.

'All sorts happened. When I first "met" Sarah, she rescued me when the car broke down. Then there was a weird shopping thing, and not knowing if I was going in or going out. I mean she still seems to encourage the sex thing, but now it's changed.' Riikka paused.

Lorri felt encouraged to chip in. 'I can't imagine how you must feel, but you wouldn't believe how much synergy there is between your experiences with Sarah and Gabriel's with Celia.' Lorri tapped her fingers on the sofa. 'There seems to be a pattern of sorts. Tell me more.'

'Well, it's funny you should say that, about patterns. I was trying to make sense of it all after meeting Gabriel, when I passed out in the bar.' Riikka became animated. 'Sarah's more of an advisor now. Which is strange as it sort of changed when I started at the hospital, helping out in the oncology ward. I couldn't believe it when Finn turned up.' Riikka sat back. 'What is happening to me?'

Lorri reached a decision. 'We should go and rescue Gabe. How would you feel about continuing this conversation at Gabe's house?'

Riikka nodded. 'No problem. I'm not officially working tonight so, yes that would be good.'

Chapter 29

WHILE LORRI AND Riikka were conversing in the bookshop, Finn was wide awake and not happy. His repeated efforts at reaching Cissy had failed. He felt abandoned. He needed to know what cancer was about and was savvy enough to realise that his parents were not up to that conversation. His thoughts drifted. What would his grandma say? She'd had cancer... The fact that she'd died from the condition was not food for present thoughts. He switched off the bedroom light and waited for sleep.

'How are you sunshine?' That's what his grandma said, or... 'How's my favourite grandson?' He liked that one, even though he was her only grandson. 'What would you like me to say?' Now that was an interesting question.

He whispered in his head, like talking with Cissy. 'Tell me about cancer.' He waited.

'It's when something unwanted grows inside you and it makes you sick if you don't stop it.'

'How do you stop it?'

'It depends. Doctors like your granddad use medicine and other stuff…'

Finn was tempted to open his eyes, but the prospect of seeing his grandma died was too scary. 'Then why did you die?'

'Because it was my time to go and the cancer came along at the right time to take me.'

'Will this be my right time?'

'That's something you'll have to wait to find out.'

'Grandma?'

'Yes, Finn.'

'If it is my right time will I be lonely, afterwards?'

'It's not the end, it's a new adventure. And I'll wait for you, don't worry.'

Finn opened his eyes. There was nothing to see except the vague shape of his chair in the corner and a litter of discarded clothes on the carpet. Light from the landing filtered through cracks in the closed door, reminding him of less pleasant, tomorrow things: taps in his chest, chemo something, and the possibility of his right time. Either way, right or wrong, it seemed he had options. His roving gaze settled on the room divider. It was too dark to see his submerged friend.

'Night Freddie…'

Chapter 30

GABRIEL WATCHED AS Lorri and Riikka emerged from their sojourn upstairs. The shop was almost empty. He was enjoying his second glass, and was relieved to see Lorri and Riikka arm in arm wandering across the shop floor. He was also intrigued, they'd been together for almost an hour. He stood as they approached.

'That must have been some conversation. I'm jealous.'

Lorri replied. 'Well it's not over yet. I've invited Riikka for supper, we can fill you in…'

'Excellent.'

Riikka seemed preoccupied. 'I'd better let the staff know that I'm leaving.' She glanced at Gabriel. 'Would it be OK if I came back with you? I don't have my car with me.'

Gabriel didn't hesitate. 'Of course, definitely, we'll wait.'

Riikka turned to Lorri. 'Are you sure you don't want to meet Alexander?'

Lorri shook her head. 'When I came here tonight I thought Alex might be drawn in, but it was the three of us getting acquainted that was the key.' Lorri smiled. 'Definitely not…'

During the journey back, chat was limited to small talk. When they returned to Gabriel's house any further dialogue was paused while supper was prepared. Having coped with his bizarre experiences pretty much alone, Gabriel was unsure how he would address his thoughts on the subject without feeling embarrassed, or stupid, or both.

Lorri picked up the baton. 'If I can make a suggestion?' She rolled a band from her wrist and tied back her hair. 'Riikka, why don't you tell Gabe what you told me? As far as I can see your "visitors" seem to have a common purpose, but it's you guys that seem to be drawn together. So…?'

Riikka gathered her thoughts. 'For me, it all started about the time I imagine you were dealing with Isabella's illness. I had weird… not dreams exactly, more like being somewhere else, unreal. There was this voice in my head, always the same character, Sarah. She seemed a bit obsessed at first…'

Gabriel noticed the unspoken exchange between the women. Obsessed about what? Riikka continued. 'But what I'd like to discuss is the overlap: things that have happened to me, that Lorri tells me have also happened to you Gabriel?'

Gabriel frowned. Where was this leading? 'Such as?'

'The orange planet with beautiful clouds; waking up inside a dream on a beach; passing out; shall I go on?'

Gabriel was astounded. 'Grey-blue clouds?'

'Yes.'

'And what about the red box, did Sarah give you a red box?'

Riikka shook her head. 'Sorry, no red box…'

'Wait, I'll show you.' Gabriel walked across the room and opened a drawer in the sideboard. He rummaged. 'Lorri, did you move it? I always keep it in here.'

'No, haven't seen it for weeks.'

'Unless I'm completely losing my marbles that's where it should be. I must have put it somewhere else.' Gabriel resumed his seat. 'Anyway, the red box was given to me by Celia – my imaginary friend – and somehow, even though she's a figment of my imagination, it was a real thing, Lorri could see it.'

Riikka frowned. 'What was in the box?'

'That's the interesting part – we couldn't open it. It was quite small, a cube.' Gabriel held up his thumb and forefinger. 'About this big.'

'So the only evidence you have about the contents of the box is a dream?' Riikka mused.

'I guess so...'

Lorri sat forward. 'And what about Finn? And Cissy?'

'And,' Riikka cut in, 'by sheer fluke I had started helping out at the children's hospital, when Finn was admitted for treatment, and I had taken up a job at your old surgery.'

Lorri was smiling now. 'More coincidence?'

Gabriel lifted his hand. 'OK. So we all have cerebral companions, and we are all experiencing strange dreams, for want of a better description. Three of us and three of them.' He removed his glasses to rub his eyes. 'Obviously, we have become connected, and more importantly, now we know that we are connected. I'd like to know why we are, and what's next.

He directed his next remark at Riikka. 'But what about the imaginary threesome? Are they connected in some way?'

Riikka was animated now. 'Yes, yes they are… I saw them all together at Isabella's funeral.'

Gabriel was almost lost for words. 'You saw them where?'

'Isabella's funeral, just before we left. They suddenly appeared in front of me, Celia, Sarah and Cissy. It was extraordinary.'

'Dear God, this is getting worse…' Gabriel slumped back in his seat.

Lorri seemed to reach a conclusion. 'Don't overthink this. In fact I only have one piece of advice.'

Riikka and Gabriel voiced their needs together. 'Which is?'

'Well,' said Lorri, tapping her head with a forefinger. 'Grey matter can only deal with mystery in one way, by rationalising, figuring stuff out, looking for an explanation. In short, by attaching meaning.' She paused for effect. 'What if there is none? Or what if the journey you are on would be compromised in some way if you knew what was going on?'

Gabriel recognised the response. He rounded on his sister-in-law. 'You sound just like Celia.'

Chapter 31

FINN CONTEMPLATED HIS second hospital visit with trepidation. Even the approach of Christmas packed no punch. Billie faced him in her car seat. She had an engaging habit of staring, and today her company offered some relief from the nervous rumbling in his stomach – no breakfast, again. She flicked at the straps of her seat and grinned, a wrinkled thumb slipping from her mouth. Finn reached across and played with her toes. She kicked his hand away. The game continued, repetitive and comforting. Finn had almost mastered his nerves when the car slowed and stopped.

His mother's head appeared between the seats. 'We're here.'

So the hours he'd estimated for the journey were only minutes. Finn sighed and released his seat belt. Curiosity about what would happen next was insufficient to prompt him to move. He waited for instructions…

Finn didn't like the squeaky sound his feet made as he followed his parents along the hospital corridor, it had an unsettling, familiar quality. They were going to fit a tap to his chest. Finn was no plumber, but walking around with even a small version of their kitchen tap poking from his body was more than disconcerting. He was drawn to Billie's company for solace, for distraction.

'Can Billie stay, please?'

His parents exchanged glances.

'For a while. Your dad is taking her home later and Granddad will be here with me when you wake up from your operation.'

'Will it hurt, the tap thing?'

'Maybe, for a day or so. I'm sure you'll get used to it.'

Finn knew what was going to happen this time and somehow this knowledge made matters worse. He couldn't stop it, he couldn't run circles round this dentist's chair. Billie sat with him on the bed and screamed when the nurse led him away to have the needle in his hand. When he returned she'd gone. His dad had gone too. And this time the needle thing had hurt. He curled up on the bed and waited for the next part to begin. There was a dull, albeit scary, monotony about the process. It was almost a relief when the counting part came.

⇥▤◗ ◖▤⇤

When he regained consciousness Finn was really thirsty. His mum helped him sit. No sign of Granddad.

'You can only have water Finn.'

He took a sip. It was horrible, warm.

'Can't I have juice?'

'Soon, we have to wait a few minutes.'

Finn's interest in drinking quickly dissipated when he noticed there was a strange pulling feeling at the top of his chest. He lifted his shoulder to ease the sensation and if he dipped his nose he could see a big white plaster stuck to his front.

Bruce North appeared. 'Hi Finn.' He pulled curtains round the bed. 'Let's take a look.' He removed a corner of the dressing from Finn's shoulder. 'It looks fine. Good. As long as you're feeling OK you can go home at tea time.' He turned to Beth. 'We'll need Finn back as soon as we have a bed free. My guess is a couple of days.'

Finn prodded his chest. He could feel a lump.

'Be careful, Finn. The cannula is there so we can give you medicine without having to give you injections. So,' he lifted Finn's hand, 'we can take this out now.' Bruce stood. 'So far so good. The team will give you spare dressings Beth, and show you how to keep the wound clean.' He scribbled on the clipboard hanging from the bottom of Finn's bed. 'See you in a couple of days for your first chemo session.'

⋯⋙ ⋘⋯

Patrick stared at the cross and broken chain that lay unattended on the hall dresser. Finn's diagnosis had challenged his faith and it was a while since his last confession. Without comfort from his forgiving God he felt unbearably lonely. He was struggling to stay positive and felt certain Finn would deteriorate. He couldn't shake off the disturbing notion that it was all his fault. What had he done? Perhaps, and more to the point, what had he not done? Forgiveness, he'd been advised, flowed from confession and penance. Self-doubt forced him to face within. The world without had become remote. He'd found it easy to step back and let Beth and her family organise the complicated coming and goings.

Beth appeared. 'Patrick, are you OK?'

He stared at his wife, unable to find the words that adequately described his anxieties. He'd been dispossessed, lost hope, lost the knack of asking for help. He decided to say nothing.

Beth reached out and dropped a prescription in his hand. 'The chemist closes in twenty minutes. Could you please go and get Finn some more of his pain killers?'

Preoccupied, he picked up his car keys and made for the front door. He wanted to reclaim his faith, but guilt had stirred the pot. The broken icon was left untouched.

'Patrick.'

This time he turned.

'This is hard for all of us, you know.'

Patrick was lost in an unwelcome fog. Somehow, the need to empathise with someone else's feelings was too much. 'I won't be long.'

As he drew away an approaching car flashed its headlights. He wiped the windscreen to remove condensation. As the shops came into view he almost drove past. He was half convinced no one would miss him if he did.

⋅⊷⊶⋅

Grace and her sister embraced. Grace was puzzled. 'Did I see Patrick drive off?'

'Yes, he's gone to the chemist.'

Grace could see her big sister was upset. 'And?'

'I'm not sure he's coping too well.' Beth lowered her voice. 'He's been a bit odd since we got the news about Finn.' She lifted the cross and chain from the hall table. 'Also, he hasn't been to confession for weeks.'

'I see.' Grace pointed upstairs. 'Where are the kids?'

'Finn's reading to Billie in his room. They seem to be inseparable. Sweet really.'

Grace led the way into the kitchen. 'I don't suppose you could get Patrick to talk to the priest? Why don't you give Father Conway a ring, I'm sure he'd be happy to pop round.' Before they could discuss the matter any further Finn appeared in the doorway.

'Did you close the stair gate Finn?' He nodded, smiling at his aunt.

'Can me and Billie have a drink?' He wandered over to the fridge and pulled out two cartons of juice.

'Give this to Billie. She's had enough juice today.' Beth handed her son Billie's sucky-cup filled with water.

'Hi Finn. I'll come up and see you both in a minute.' Grace was intrigued by his posture. As he disappeared upstairs she couldn't help but comment. 'Did you notice?'

Beth returned the spare carton to the fridge. 'What, his passion for juice?'

'No, not that. Is the cannula causing discomfort? His left shoulder is lifted.'

'It is, but the wound seems to be OK. He doesn't like it when I try to clean it mind. And that's another thing, Patrick can't hack it. I asked him to help me and he almost passed out.'

Grace bit her lip. *You're stuck with wet-nursing them all.* 'We should talk about the practicalities. That's why I've come over. Dad and I can help. We'll need to get organised.'

The front door closed and Patrick wandered in. He placed the pack of analgesics on the table.

'Hi Grace.' His eyes never left Beth. 'Will you excuse me, I'm going down to the study, have a kip. I'm knackered.'

Beth held Grace's hand. 'What am I going to do?'

⋅→▭ ▭←⋅

Finn was sitting on the floor with his back against the bed. Billie had fallen asleep between his legs, leaning into his chest. It was painful. The pressure added to the discomfort from the implanted cannula but he didn't attempt to move his sister. Her blond curls slipped between his fingers, exposing the last patch of cradle cap. His mouth watered. He loved picking at the dead skin, but it was prohibited. Even so, he couldn't resist peeling back a loose bit. He flicked it onto the carpet as Billie whinged and scratched her head. He left the rest alone.

Apart from the barely audible snuffles from Billie, it was quiet. His thoughts turned to Cissy – was she really an idea in his head? He'd not seen her for ages. He stared at the chair and his mind wandered. What would he do, what would happen if he didn't get better? Like his grandma he didn't want to end up in a box buried in the ground. The thought touched a raw nerve. A desperate panic closed his throat just as a small hand pushed at his chin.

Billie was awake. She grinned, and her smile gave him a lift. Maybe he could get better? Finn preferred this optimistic viewpoint. He rallied. 'Shall we go and see Mummy?' Billie's shrieks of approval nailed any lingering despair. 'Come on then.'

Chapter 32

LORRI COULD SEE that Gabriel was immersed in his notes and was preoccupied with Finn's treatment. Since their conversations with Riikka, Gabriel appeared to be more settled; or perhaps he was elsewhere, preoccupied, being granddad GP. In any event, Lorri felt quite the opposite. She felt that she was left holding the mystery. She had a real need to know what was going on. For the first time since Isabella's death she was starting to regret her promise to stay on and support Gabriel. Added to which, now that she had a wider appreciation of Riikka's entanglements in the Newman family dramas, she felt more, not less, confused.

'Gabe?'

He dropped his pen and turned. 'Sorry, a bit engrossed...'

'Don't apologise, I could do with a minute or two to talk.'

'Of course.'

Lorri wandered over and rested her hand on his shoulder. 'I'm going upstairs to meditate, could you stick your head around the door in, say, an hour? When you've finished.'

'No problem. Do you want to talk now?'

'No, an hour's fine.'

⟶⟩⟩⟫ ⟪⟨⟨⟵

Gabriel was pleased. He felt settled that all was being done that could be done to treat Finn's condition. He closed the file with the copies of Finn's notes and considered Lorri's request. He'd had precious little time to consider his sister-in-law in the past few weeks. He'd flipped from erstwhile husband to grieving widower and on to God knows what, all within the space of one year. He knew that Lorri did not share his more conservative viewpoint on many topics, but even so he felt they'd managed well together.

The light in Lorri's room was still on as he rounded the top of the stairs. Aware that his knock was unnecessary he tapped the door and waited.

'Yes? If that's Gabriel come on in, otherwise, bugger off.'

Gabriel grinned as he entered the room, he loved the irreverent humour. Lorri was reading. She removed her glasses and waited as Gabriel sat on the end of the bed.

'All done? Are they doing a good job for Finn?'

'Yes, as far as I can tell Bruce and his team seem to know what they're doing.' He shrugged and repeated the remark. 'As far as I can tell…' He knew that there were no definitive treatments for leukaemia.

Lorri, ever the one for cutting to the chase, didn't waste time on chit-chat. 'I've spoken to Beth and she's asked me to stay at their house for a few weeks, while Finn's in and out of hospital. I can take care of Billie so you guys are free to take shifts with Finn.'

'I see.' Gabriel knew she wanted a response, not a platitude. He lifted his hands to hold his words. 'I agree. Sounds like a good idea, but I will miss having you around.' There was more he wanted to say. 'Will you promise me something?'

Lorri removed her glasses. 'Depends…'

'I have a feeling, and I may be wrong, that there will come a time when you'll need to return to the glens.' Lorri shrugged her shoulders. 'You've already made a huge difference,' he added.

Lorri smiled. 'Don't worry. I'm here for love not duty. And can you really see me being a victim of any situation?'

Gabriel stifled a laugh. 'I'm still going to need your support with all the off-beat stuff, and I imagine you'll have Riikka to consider as well. You've no idea what a relief it is to have your insights. There's no way I could talk to my daughters the way I talk with you.'

'Interesting.'

'Sorry?'

'That was my follow-on request that you start to open up with the girls. They might surprise you.'

⇢▬◉ ◉▬⇠

Sarah was experimenting with feelings, Riikka's feelings. The process was fascinating. She particularly liked the sensation called relief. Since Riikka's conversation with Lorri and then with Gabriel, she had experienced relief. The thought that led Riikka to this conclusion was the realisation that she was not isolated and that Gabriel in particular had similar, shared experiences. She was not alone, she was not "ill", and as a consequence she was relieved.

When Sarah had made the first, tentative links with Riikka she had been surprised. Riikka, Gabriel, and to a lesser extent, Finn, lived their lives within a framework of logic that determined the survival of the individual was prime. And yet, Riikka's evident pleasure when she realised her unexplained encounters were shared flew in the face of her primary obsession: separation, self-protection, the paranoid position.

Why unusual?

Sarah was impressed and surprised at Riikka's interjection, she seemed able to discriminate, separate out her lodger's thoughts even though rudimentary shields were in place to protect them. 'I shall have to take care. My thoughts are not my own…' She allowed a minor flood of unrelated ideas to show themselves.

Hey, take it easy, too much. Now I'm confused again.

'You seem more at ease. Am I right?'

Yes, I am, and no doubt you know why…

'Lorri is quite a character, she's like you… Must have been a telling conversation as your anxiety levels have dropped. Tell me, why do you think you are being drawn together?'

Always the easy questions. I have no answer, and before you pick up your script my guess is I can only speculate, or read the autopsy.

'Nicely put, but it's good that you know you are not alone.'

You've finally said something I can understand. Yes, it is good and I am relieved.

Chapter 33

FINN WATCHED AS a nurse hung a plastic pouch on the drip stand next to his bed. His first chemotherapy session was about to start. She'd connected a long plastic tube to the cannula on his chest.

'Right Finn, I think we're ready. Let me know if you start to feel sick and we'll give you something for it.'

Finn flinched, nobody mentioned being sick. The connecting tube ran through a machine. She switched it on. The red stuff in the bag slowly worked its way down the line. Finn watched, fascinated, a cold feeling spreading into his shoulder. The hum from the pump was hypnotic. He waited, watching the steady drip until he could no longer map the progress of the red line – it had disappeared into his chest. After an hour, he started to feel sick, really sick, and the worst thing was he couldn't be sick. His mum reached over and wiped his face. He was sweating.

'How're you doing Finn?'

'Not good.'

'Let me get the nurse. She said to let her know.'

The nurse returned and injected medicine into the tube. Finn felt miserable, he couldn't figure out why the cure felt worse than the illness. How could this be making him better? He turned to his mother. He considered asking the question but couldn't quite turn the bad feelings into words. He shrugged his shoulders and turned over. When the red stuff was gone they replaced the bag with water. He heard something about kidneys and rehydration and had no idea what they were talking about. The sick feeling was still bad but the other medicines did seem to be taking the edge off. Eventually, he slipped into a fitful sleep.

When he woke it was much darker. He panicked, where was his mother? A new nurse was checking the tubes. When she looked at him he noticed her eyes were black. He shivered. He didn't like the look of her. She bent down to adjust his pillow and ran her finger down his cheek – it felt cold where she touched. He twisted away from the sound of her voice. 'Go away.'

'Finn, what are you saying?'

Someone was holding his hand. This time it felt OK. His mum's face came into focus.

'Where is she?'

'Where's who Finn? There's no one here, just you and me.'

⊷▦◉ ◉▦⊶

The next day Finn had a welcome visitor, his friend Liam, and he was in good form. The grownups had left them to it.

'This is so spooky, all of these sick kids.'

Finn noticed that Liam was staring at the girl in the next bed, who had no hair. 'It's the medicine, the chemo, it makes your hair fall out.'

'But yours is still there.' Liam observed.

'They said it might be a few weeks before mine goes. Chemo is pants.' Gradually, the boys re-established their banter. Finn was eager to find out about school, find out what was happening, what he was missing. Liam handed him a card; all the kids in his class had signed it.

'Look, all the girls put kisses next to their names, all of them!' As they talked Finn gradually caught up with the class gossip, who was in love with who.

'When are you coming back?' Liam asked, dropping his head. 'We were wondering, you know, when you'll be better?'

Finn looked at his friend with a blank expression. 'They've only started really. So far I've felt worse not better.'

In time they exhausted conversation and sat watching TV. They were rescued from a state of mutual silence by a frequent visitor to Finn's bed.

'Hi Finn, hi.' Maisy sat next to Finn and stared at Liam.

Finn decided to put him out of his misery. 'This is Maisy. She's had her treatment and will be going home next week.'

Finn smiled. His friend was furiously avoiding eye contact. Their parents arrived.

'Sorry boys, I'm afraid that Liam will have to go now.' said Finn's mother. She turned to Maisy. 'Could you keep Finn company until his granddad arrives? He should be here soon.'

Maisy grinned and nodded. Finn exchanged a knowing look with Liam. He could see that Maisy impressed him. She looked really neat in her tee-shirt and jeans. Finn tried to avoid a parting kiss from his mother, and watched his friend and family disappear through the doors at the end of the ward. Maisy tapped his hand.

'I think Bruce is coming over.'

The doctor was talking to the nurses and kept looking in their direction. He walked across.

'Hi Finn. No family today?'

'They left. I'm waiting for Granddad.'

'Well I have good news for you. Your first treatment is finished and if your temperature stays normal you can go home tomorrow.'

Finn was relieved, good news at last. 'Have I finished then? Am I better now?' Bruce rested his hand on Finn's leg.

'Sorry Finn, not yet, but we are making progress.' Bruce stood. 'Could you ask your granddad to arrange things with the nurses when he comes? I'm sure it'll be fine for you to go home tomorrow.'

⇥━⊙ ⊙━⇤

Finn's temperature didn't spike and he was happy to find himself back in his bedroom. It took him a day or two to get used to being at home. In an odd sort of way he missed the nurses, the other kids on the ward, and Maisy. A few of his friends visited, including Liam. Finn had taken on a hero status at school. He couldn't go back yet – something about infections – but slowly, he started to feel happier.

The chemo had altered his taste, eating was a chore. Some foods tasted like metal, horrible. His mum worked hard to find things he could eat as it was important he didn't lose too much weight. His favourite food was tinned tomato soup. Meat and most vegetables were a definite no, no.

Billie followed him everywhere. She could crawl now, and Finn didn't mind her attention. Somehow she seemed to know that he was unwell and was content to sit and be with him, even if they watched television. In the quiet of his own room Finn recalled the times he'd spent with Cissy. It seemed ages since he'd last seen her. He posted entries in his diary every day. His hospital experiences poured out. Eventually the diary became a Cissy-substitute; he imagined her standing behind him, reading the words as he wrote. Every time he opened the diary he half expected to see a reply.

It was almost a week after his return home that Finn had a feeling all was not well. He felt hot. He kept the discomfort to himself as he didn't want more hospital, not yet. Fortunately, his mother was looking out for changes in his behaviour. As he lay on the sofa she placed her cool hand on his forehead.

'Finn, you're burning up!' She rushed out of the room, returning with a thermometer. She tucked it under his tongue. 'Don't take it out!' She waited. 'Oh my God, it's a hundred and two.' She held Finn's hand. 'Bruce warned us this might happen. I'll call the hospital.'

Lorri was on hand to take care of Billie, and Finn watched in despair as his mum packed a bag.

When they arrived at the hospital the doctors confirmed he had an infection. Worst of all there was no free bed in oncology, so he had to go to a different ward.

'But how long will it be 'til I can go home?'

'It will take a day or two until they find the right antibiotic, Finn. We'll have to make the most of it.'

'But Bruce said it was OK for me to go home. I'm hot, that's all.'

'It's a bit more complicated than being hot. The chemo kills off the good cells in your body as well as the cancer cells. Without the good cells your body can't fight the nasty germs and bugs we all come into contact with every day. The different medicine you're taking now will do that for you until your own antibodies grow back.'

Finn was unconvinced, fed up and not ready to be sensible.

'Well I think that's stupid. Why would Bruce make me better by making me sick? I was much better before all this hospital stuff started. It sucks…'

Chapter 34

RIIKKA GAZED ACROSS the surgery reception, watching Irene charm another anxious pensioner. Riikka was sure that she could never apply herself with such dedication. She was also preoccupied with Jonathan's next visit. He'd agreed to take a week off, and as neither of them was in funds they were going to spend their time at her flat and find their entertainment locally.

She was apprehensive. What if Sarah or her cronies orchestrated some sort of stunt while he was with her? How would she explain things? She'd grown fond of him and didn't want that particular boat rocking. Of course, she could try to explain what had been going on... She tried out a few approaches in her head, but couldn't see how Jonathan would make any sense of it all.

Riikka decided she needed another Lorri fix. Pleading a pee break she made her way to the kitchen at the rear of the property and placed a call. Lorri answered second ring.

'Riikka?'

'Hi, I'm calling from work so I don't have much time. Could I ask a favour?'

'Shoot.'

'I need to talk… I don't suppose you could make coffee later?'

'Sure. Beth is handling the kids today… You know I'm staying at Beth's for a few weeks? To help out.'

'No, I didn't. Then why don't you come over to my flat, I'll cook something.'

'Sounds good. Text me your address. I'll come over about seven if that's OK?'

'Brilliant, see you then.'

Riikka folded the phone, text on its way. She realised with Lorri she'd no fear of Sarah causing mayhem, quite the opposite.

⟶⟨⟩⟨⟩⟵

Riikka was nervous. Her hands were sweating. She took a deep breath, working slowly, afraid the knife would take her fingers not the pinioned carrots. The talk with Lorri was approaching, and she felt like a star turn in the school play, about to go on. She imagined this must be the itch that drove smokers to light up. Without thinking she uncorked the wine on the worktop.

A thought popped into her head that Jonathan was going to call and delay his visit. She stared at the mobile and jumped as the doorbell rang. She placed the wine glass on the worktop and headed for the door.

Lorri was in good form. They chatted over dinner, inconsequential things. Soon the meal was finished, the dish holding the remains of the lasagne a vacant plot.

'Well, this is nice,' said Lorri. 'Billie is a sweetheart, but I do crave adult company.' She lifted her glass. 'You wanted to talk?'

'I did. Shall I dive in?'

Lorri sat back. 'When you're ready, no rush.'

Riikka fiddled with a napkin. 'I'm starting to feel nervous about… you know.' She tapped her head. 'Sounds stupid… but Sarah, the rest of the weird stuff, will there be an end to it?' Lorri remained silent. 'My boyfriend, Jonathan, has no idea. What if something happens when he's with me? How would I explain?' Riikka fingered her glass, an unfamiliar burning behind her eyes.

'What are you really afraid of?' Lorri reached across the table and smudged the tears from Riikka's cheek.

'I thought, you know, that being alone was preferable, but Jonathan… I don't want to lose him.' Riikka squared her shoulders, underlining her realisation. 'I really don't want to lose him.'

Lorri smiled. 'Being in love is not such a terrible thing. Have you thought that your concerns have contributed?'

'What do you mean?'

'Would you have allowed yourself to have feelings for Jonathan without your recent adventures to nudge you along?'

The thought was engaging. 'Before you came tonight, I was sure that he was going to ring, delay coming.'

'But no call, right?'

'No call.'

Lorri continued. 'As far as I can see, your guest,' she pointed at Riikka's head, 'and Gabe and Finn's imaginary friends, all seem incredibly friendly. I don't see any lasting damage being done. If anything they're like facilitators.'

Riikka considered her friend's remarks and had a further realisation. 'Is this about trust?'

'What do you think?'

Riikka shrugged her shoulders. 'Maybe it is. Maybe I should take a risk or two.'

'Only two?' They laughed.

Riikka stared at her friend's face. 'How do you smile like that?'

'Like what?'

'You don't smile, your face lights up.' Riikka said.

'And if your face lights up what generally happens?'

Riikka grinned. 'Depends. That sort of openness is risky.'

'That's the advantage of a wrinkled visage, permission to smile freely. It's why the menopause was such a gift for me.' Lorri fixed Riikka with her green eyes. 'Men, and some women, stopped reaching for my underwear...' Lorri chuckled. 'That's not to say I can't enjoy myself when roused, but it sure as hell is a freeing experience, having more choice.'

'Life begins at fifty...'

'No, no, not begins, it changes. My change, as far as I can see, was for the better, and life as a consequence has been less complicated, more fulfilling. So,' she reached for her glass, 'I can smile, and weep, with a measure of safety. Me, I'm happy to be overlooked in that way.'

Riikka refilled their glasses. 'Change of subject? I know we've touched on this before, but have you any idea what Gabriel and I are mixed up in?'

Lorri's expression changed. 'To be honest with you I've no idea. If you remember, I was keen we didn't overthink the issues or try to make sense of them. However, these last couple of weeks staying at Beth's have been instructive. I do like things nice and tidy. Enigma is not my cup of tea and yet I am truly baffled. But, I have started to realise that the answer to the question "why" is not going to provide the solution we all seem to crave. We want beginnings and endings. What if neither actually exists?'

Riikka frowned. 'Not sure I get what you're saying. There definitely was a beginning for me and I'm not sure I would miss Sarah if she vacated her room.'

'Well, it's a thought.' Lorri glanced at her watch. 'Sorry, old habits… I have to be up at six in the morning to breakfast Billie. Has any of this helped?'

Riikka pursed her lips. 'According to the oracle I should take more risks and figure out what's to do, or not do, if there's to be no endings.' She laughed. 'I may call on you again...'

Lorri grabbed her car keys from the bookshelf and dislodged Riikka's mobile. Thankfully, it fell into a waste basket. 'Sorry…'

Riikka retrieved the phone. 'That's odd, no power.' They looked at each other.

'Where's your charger?'

Riikka rummaged behind a pile of books and pulled out the required lead. She flicked the switch, plugged it in and waited. The flashing image confirmed that all was well, the phone was charging. It made a familiar ping. Riikka couldn't believe her eyes, she'd missed a call, from Jonathan.

Lorri had brushed aside the apparent coincidence: that the message had been from Jonathan, that he had called and he was going to be delayed. After all, they would still have most of their week together. The hospital couldn't rejig his hours so they would lose half a day.

Riikka had dismissed the possible twist of fate when Lorri was with her, but on reflection it had felt like a setback. Nights were bad enough without this complication, the apparent ability to prophesy. Thoughts danced about in her head and she no longer trusted their provenance – was this Sarah's notion or her own? Was she about to have another peek into the future?

She took a deep breath. In a few days Jonathan's train would arrive and he was the perfect distraction. Perhaps Lorri was right, overthinking didn't solve anything.

⋯⟹ ⟸⋯

Jonathan could sense that Riikka was asleep. There was no light in the room and he lay, wide awake, concerns about patients and paying his rent forgotten.

'Please don't wake her.'

What the fuck!

'There's something you should know, so please listen and for God's sake don't make a noise.'

It was Riikka talking. He flicked on his mobile, the light from the small screen illuminated Riikka's face; she was lying on her back, apparently sound asleep.

'Hope you've a good memory, I can't keep this up for long.'

Jonathan scratched his head. 'Come on, Riikka, stop taking the piss.'

Her eyes were definitely closed, but she was speaking. 'I said be quiet, I'm not Riikka.' The light from his phone clicked off.

Fuck…

'I'm not sure Riikka will be able to discuss things with you, so, I've decided to organise this little intervention.' Riikka's hand moved across the bed and a single finger traced a line on his thigh. He flinched. 'Now listen.'

He considered a cold shower at this point convinced he was dreaming.

Riikka stirred. 'You must tell Riikka that Sarah spoke to you and I don't care how you rationalise this conversation. Your mind will think of something.' The finger moved again. 'She's involved in matters that are causing her some anxiety and if she does manage to explain you should listen. There's no need for white coats or pill popping. Got that?'

Jonathan didn't know how to respond. Although he'd been told that you shouldn't wake someone who was sleep walking, he had no idea what he should do if someone was sleep talking. He nodded into the darkness. 'Yes…'

'Good.' More stirring and an arm draped over his chest. Now her voice whispered into his ear. 'What's my name?'

Mindful, he whispered back. 'Sarah?'

'And what do you need to do?'

'Listen.'

The arm withdrew and Riikka's breathing resumed its familiar sleeping rhythm. Jonathan stared into the darkened room, unable to make sense of their conversation.

When he woke the next morning his head ached. He could feel Riikka's warm body folded into the contours of his back. The memory of their nocturnal chat was clear enough in his mind. Riikka moved. He was not convinced he should say anything.

Any further prospect of talking was quickly abandoned by the slow progress of Riikka's hand towards his groin. He groaned, content to ignore the sleep talk.

Chapter 35

HIS NOTES HAD proved useful after all. Gabriel patted the cover. Finn's diagnosis and treatment were examined, researched and he couldn't fault the hospital's conclusions. Everything depended on how well Finn responded to chemotherapy. As far as he was concerned – so far so good. The phone rang as he descended the stairs, it was Beth.

'Hi Dad. I'm leaving the hospital with Finn.'

'How is he?'

'The infection responded to second-line antibiotics. He's anxious to get home, and so am I. Why don't you come over? Lorri's texted, she's preparing a meal for us all. Grace is coming…'

Gabriel didn't hesitate. 'Of course, I'll be there for six.'

The prospect of seeing his family was enlivening. This, combined with his satisfied feelings about Finn's treatment, contributed to a general sense of wellbeing, one that he'd not had for months. Perhaps, he thought, we are turning a corner.

When Gabriel arrived the house was in turmoil. Billie was screaming with delight, her brother was back. Grace was in conversation with Beth and he found Lorri and Patrick in the kitchen. Patrick looked stressed.

'Gabriel, thank God you've arrived. Could you take over as commis chef while I find some pain killers?' Patrick threw him a tea towel and kissed Lorri's cheek. 'She's a hard task master, but I must fix this headache. I swear to God, Billie's screams are going to split my head open.'

Gabriel caught the towel and tapped Patrick's shoulder as he passed. Lorri stood back from the cooker.

'Finn's looking much better.' She winced as Billie released another squeak. 'And how is the good doctor?'

Gabriel took the spoon from her hand and tasted the remnants of gravy. 'Well, thank you.' He waved the spoon. 'This is good.'

Lorri smiled, recapturing the wooden implement. 'I'd rather hoped you would be. But I need you to be useful, not good.'

'Hi Granddad.' Finn waddled in, shoulder raised.

Gabriel ran his fingers through the boy's red curls. To his dismay the returning hand was not empty. 'How you doing? Infection cleared up?'

Finn sighed. 'Hospitals suck. We were in a different ward. I didn't get to see my friends or the nurses I know.' Billie rounded the kitchen door on her knees and grabbed Finn's leg.

'Looks like Billie's missed you.' Gabriel bent and picked up the lively infant. She immediately started pulling at his beard. 'Hey, steady on.' Gabriel winced as she tugged again. He appealed to Lorri. 'Give me a second will you? This tyke needs her mother's attention. Come on, Finn.'

·→▸══◉ ◉══◂←·

It was a familiar ache, hidden from most, but there all the same. Gabriel's close family sitting down to dinner: seven at the table and there should be eight. The cross-talk allowed Gabriel to sit back and stay with his feelings. He drifted, hearing Isabella's responses as her ghost added to the confused chatter.

'Gabe?'

The call was clear enough, but he was not ready to come back. Clear as a bell he could see Isabella standing behind Lorri's chair. She lifted her hand and stroked her sister's hair. It lifted, enlivened by unearthly static. He wanted to speak, to bring Bella back, but this was not a time for speaking.

She walked around the table and Gabriel's resistance crumbled as she bent and whispered in his ear. 'If you don't speak soon you'll be wheeled out on a stretcher...' Bella's remark acted like a switch. He blinked and when his eyes opened the room was filled with sound.

Grace was shaking his arm. 'Dad. Dad, I can't...'

Gabriel was physically shaken. He grabbed Grace's hand. 'Sorry... Completely blanked out.'

'Jesus, Gabe, we thought you were off again, you know...' Patrick tipped his head towards the children, scrapping over the last slice of pizza. He mouthed the rest. 'Sleep walking?'

Gabriel caught Lorri's eye. She was certainly not alarmed, in fact she was smiling behind her napkin. Beth however... 'For God's sake Dad...' She hesitated, more consideration for the kids' feelings.

Lorri stepped in. 'Blissing out I think. Tell us what you saw Gabe.'

Lorri's challenge was too specific, there was no way he would share that nugget. He was also peeved, did she know? 'I was enjoying my family. This is the first time we've all been together socially since, well, you know...' Even the children chose that moment to be quiet.

Lorri filled an empty glass and lifted her own. 'Then let's bring her into the ring.' She gazed around the table her head moving with the salutations: 'Your mother, your wife, my sister,' She smiled at Finn, 'your grandma...'

Finn had the last word on the matter. Grinning from ear to ear he held up his carton of juice. 'Cheers.'

Grace was still holding her father's hand. She squeezed, hard, knowingly; I understand. Gabriel was relieved when the banter resumed. Lorri pushed back her plate and tapped the unclaimed glass with her own. Gabriel could almost hear her exchange with Bella. The thought triggered a memory. He was prompted to speak. 'I imagine that's the sort of thing Celia would see.' The words tripped out before he could hold them back. The adults at the table assumed a co-ordinated silence. Beth and Grace smiled in that 'so who's this Celia then?' way. Gabriel was flustered, embarrassed, found out, and then rescued.

'Granddad was jealous.'

'I beg your pardon?' Beth was half smiling now. Gabriel was sure she had tuned into his discomfort, but what was Finn going to say?

'My Cissy said Granddad had a 'maginary friend too, and she knew her name, Celia.'

Gabriel was unable to contribute to his rescue bid. Lorri, however, could speak and did. 'As I recall, Celia is a Granddad imaginary friend. As you say Finn, your Granddad wanted one too…' She tossed a refugee chip in Finn's direction, she had his attention. 'Am I right Finn?'

He nodded and added. 'Are there any more chips?'

Beth was apparently unsatisfied by the exchanges. 'What would this Celia see? I don't get it, and I don't approve.'

Gabriel finally found his voice. 'Of what?'

Beth lifted her eyebrows.

Grace reached across the table and transferred her uneaten potato fries to Finn's plate. 'Well, I think it's really sweet of Dad. And anyway, if Dad says he has an imaginary friend then I guess he does.' She challenged the room to disagree, before continuing. 'So, Dad, what would Celia have seen, or said?'

With a further prompt Celia provided closure. Gabriel addressed the room. 'She would have picked up the unspoken thoughts.' He waited for a frustrated Billie to vent her feelings as Finn downed the last fry. 'That we missed Isabella…'

Irreverent perhaps, but timely nevertheless, Finn had his mind on more basic concerns. 'Any pudding?'

Chapter 36

RIIKKA WAS CONFUSED. Her walk to work was taking an unexpected turn. She was sure the road she'd taken connected with High Street. She was going to be late. Stopping to take her bearings she leaned against a wall and removed a shoe. The inverted footwear released its cargo, a small stone. An unseasonable breeze picked up litter and twisted the paper flecks, lifting them into the air. Something was wrong. She replaced the shoe, looking for someone to ask for directions. An elderly woman approached dragging a small child. The young boy seemed agitated.

Riikka approached the odd couple. 'I'm sorry to bother you.' The woman walked past and then stopped. Riikka called after them. 'Could you give me directions to High Street?'

'High Street, did you say High Street?' Riikka nodded, disturbed by the old woman's tone. It had an edge, accusative. 'Lost are you?' She took a step closer, the tendons on her arm standing proud, peppered with liver spots. Again Riikka nodded. 'Well now, I seem to remember a High Street, end of this road and left. That way.' She stabbed a bent finger. 'But you'll have to hurry.'

Riikka stared as they continued on their way. What was she talking about, you'll have to hurry. She glanced at her watch, ten am. There was no way it could be that late. She'd left in plenty of time. A walk had seemed like a good idea and yet she was already an hour late. At this rate she'd be turning up at lunchtime. She tried to unwind the journey in her head, unable to make sense of her predicament. How could she be lost? She took the same route each week. And yet she was lost. Agitated, she headed to the end of the street and turned left. A lone taxi was parked at the curb. At last, normality beckoned, surely the driver would know?

Riikka tapped the window. No response. She peered through the murky glass and could barely make out the driver, who appeared to be sleeping.

'You'll not get much from him.'

'Shit!' Riikka slipped and twisted her ankle as she turned to see who was speaking. A young man lounged against the cab.

'Haven't heard a word from Freddie for years.'

Riikka lifted her foot. 'Bugger…'

'I hear you're looking for High Street?'

She didn't know how to respond. What the hell was going on?

'You seem to have wandered off-track.' He pulled a dog-eared *A to Z* out of his pocket and thumbed through the pages. 'According to this you've missed High Street.'

She backed away. *Sarah, if this is some sort of sick joke… How can I miss a fucking street?*

'So you missed it then?' The old woman had lost her companion and was now eyeing Riikka's coat. She shuffled forwards and lifted a searching finger. Her nails and finger ends were black. Once again Riikka retreated.

The youth returned the book to its pocket and took a pace in her direction. 'Hetty likes that. You should let her have the coat.'

'It still has the light.' Hetty reached out again. 'I do like that. Don't see much light round here.'

Riikka was panicking. 'Listen, I haven't got a clue what either of you are saying, I'm going to retrace my steps.' She started walking, casting backward glances every few steps. They were still standing by the taxi when she reached the junction. She turned right and came to a dead stop. The buildings either side of the road moved towards each other and formed a cul-de-sac. She felt sick. It was like watching a film, except this film had started as a walk to work. She was trapped. An insistent prodding in her back caused her to scream; she knew it was the old woman.

'Why don't you come with us, we'll look after things…'

'Get the fuck off me!'

Ahead, at the point where the two sides of the street had met, a crack appeared. Riikka was transfixed. Now what? A large pair of hands emerged, lamppost-high hands, the fingers pushed outwards, moving apart, like someone drawing curtains. The buildings crumpled as if made of paper. Riikka reeled as her sense of scale was challenged. A figure emerged from the rendered gloom and continued the destruction of the street. It was Sarah. Riikka was looking at a space that was a remarkable likeness to the inside of her flat, her bedroom. The change in perspective was unnerving. Riikka had lost her coat; she'd lost all her clothes. Jonathan lay at her side, blissfully unaware. There was no way Riikka was going to wake him.

Sarah filled in the spaces, answered her question: why the sideshow? 'It was necessary to provide you with a demonstration. It seems that your natural defences are breaking down.'

What's that supposed to mean?

Sarah approached the bed. 'Certainty.'

Pardon me?

'From now on you will have to assume that nothing is certain.'

Shit… could you please be straight with me?

'That's tricky. As far as I can see you don't have the words to describe this straightness you desire. I could say that you are opening up to lost skills, or dipping in and out of other realities, but it's more than that.'

Riikka sighed, Jonathan was stirring. Sarah's parting words were all she was going to get. She disappeared from view without further comment.

Jonathan stretched and ran his hand down her back. 'Hey… Morning.'

Riikka closed her eyes and banished Sarah's remarks. It was a bad dream and nothing was going to spoil morning sex. 'Give me a minute, need to brush my teeth.'

⊷⊶⊷ ⊶⊷⊶

It was their last day. The week had flown by. Riikka picked at the scrambled egg, she was going to miss him. 'I had such a weird dream last night. This horrible old woman wanted my coat and I couldn't find my way to work.'

'I slept like a top, but at least you didn't wake me again.'

'What do you mean, again?'

'You woke me up, talking in your sleep.'

'You're joking?' Riikka knew he wasn't. She had to know. 'What did I say?

'Weird stuff. You said you were someone else, get this, someone called Sarah.'

Riikka's heart flipped.

'Something about you going through a difficult time and protecting you from the white coats.'

Riikka dropped her fork. 'Would you do that? What if I really was heading for the happy home?'

Jonathan laughed and then stopped as he noticed the drawn expression on her face. 'Hey, what's this all about?'

Time to take a risk. She took a deep breath. 'I've been hearing this voice, in my head. It's a she, Sarah.' She ploughed on. 'It's like having someone else talking to me, and I've had really bizarre dreams.'

Jonathan paused, a fork full of egg half-way to his mouth. 'And?'

'Well, what do you think?'

'Truthfully?' Riikka nodded. 'This is not my speciality, you understand, but it doesn't sound like Sarah is a personality split.

You have conversations with her, for God's sake.' He pushed his plate away. 'Are you going to eat that?'

'Jonathan, this is important, am I going mad?'

'No, you're not. We are having a perfectly rational talk about it, about her, and I don't see you harming yourself, or anyone else for that matter. You haven't woken up with a knife in your hand.' He was grinning now. 'Actually, maybe I better check this out in future, see which one of you it is, you know...'

The ridiculous, boyish expression on his face was beyond irritating – he was not going to take her seriously. At least he was not concerned and that was a huge relief. For counsel she would have to rely on Lorri. She composed her face, trying to assume a Sarah look. 'What makes you think we haven't switched already?'

Chapter 37

THE WARD WAS quiet when Finn woke, it was night time. The steady hum of the pump and the pull of the line attached to his cannula was enough to bring him back. This was not home. He felt sick. Finn looked at his granddad fast asleep on the camp bed next to his bed and threw up. The pitiful remains of his supper sprayed across the bed. Exhausted, he lay back on the pillow shivering, a cold sweat breaking out on his face.

'Finn? Sorry Finn, we need to change your bed.' The duty nurse stood over Finn and gently shook his arm as he squirmed, reluctant to move his aching head. The bile had burned his throat and nose and still coated his tongue.

'Leave me alone, I want sleep…'

His granddad, awake now, joined in, lifting Finn clear of the soiled bed. Soon his pyjamas were changed. 'Steady buddy. We need to tidy up then you can sleep.' Finn felt the welcome touch of a scented wipe as it cleaned his face. It smelt really nice. He was relieved when his granddad lifted him back on his bed.

The nurse spoke quietly in his ear. 'Finn, I'm going to add something to your drip, it will help stop the sickness.'

He heard his granddad answer the nurse and as he started to drift back to sleep his body was racked with cramps and more nausea. He reached out, his face delivering the message. His granddad grabbed a bowl and helped him sit, supporting his back as he heaved and retched. Finn gasped for breath, arching his back, desperate to feel better, to lie down, to sleep.

'Lean against me Finn, keep sitting or you'll choke.'

Eventually, the sickness drug took effect. Finn tugged at his granddad's sleeve. 'Can I lie down Granddad? I think I feel a bit better.'

'Sure, let me know if you feel poorly again.'

Finn stared at the ceiling as his granddad straightened the sheets. 'I want to sleep. I think I've forgotten how to do it. And my belly hurts.' He turned away from the nearest light.

⊷▬◉ ◉▬⊷

Gabriel stayed awake with Finn until it was almost dawn. The boy looked completely drained. Even though the sickness had stopped the drugs seemed to have changed his demeanour. He looked depressed. Gabriel desperately wanted to help, but had no idea what to do. The doctor had nothing left in his bag of tricks. As far as he could see it was a waiting game. Wait for the drugs to do their job, wait for sickness to pass, and deal with infections as they come along. Easy enough to document, quite another matter for his grandson to live through. Assuming he survived the malady, how would he survive the experience unmarked?

'Hold his hand.'

Gabriel rolled his eyes. *Celia, please, give me a break…*

'Don't be smart, hold his hand.'

Gabriel took Finn's hand. It was damp and lifeless.

'Now close your eyes and imagine you are a hollow bone. What Finn needs will pass through you. Not from you, through you.'

Too tired to question Celia's instructions he concentrated. It all seemed a bit strange.

'Not good enough. Open the other hand, palm up. Good. Now imagine there is help, a source of healing. Last part. Get out of the way. Intend that this healing finds Finn through you…'

At first Gabriel felt ridiculous, but then he felt a strange warmth in his hand. It moved up his arm and across his shoulders. Finn's hand started to feel different. After a few minutes he risked a peek – Finn was sound asleep.

⇥ ⇤

Gabriel had no idea what had happened, he couldn't explain it. Celia, as usual, had offered no further explanation. Ironically, Gabriel found he no longer needed to sleep. Finn was still fast off. The pump continued to hum and Gabriel could see that staff must have added a bag of water in the night. Time seemed to have slipped, he must have slept. At least they'd stopped pumping vincristine. Gabriel had researched the side effects, some of which were far more threatening than nausea. He yawned. The saline solution would flush out Finn's kidneys.

He was about to make a drink when he noticed the plastic line running across Finn's body. A series of air bubbles worked their way towards the port on his chest. Gabriel moved quickly, switching off the pump. *Shit!* The whole family had received instruction on aspects of Finn's treatment, matters that needed vigilance. Bubbles in the line were a real no, no. Gabriel knew that if the air reached Finn's blood stream the resulting air embolism could have serious, very serious, consequences.

A nurse passed the end of Finn's bed and smiled at Gabriel. He called her over. This time the drama was contained. Finn slept on as the various components were replaced and reassembled.

When Finn did wake he was tired, but appeared to be in much better humour. Gabriel drew curtains round the bed and handed him a disposable bottle. 'Finn, you have to wee in the bottle, we have to measure how much fluid comes away.'

Finn pointed at the curtains. 'All right, I won't look.' Gabriel left Finn to it. Time passed.

'I can't do anything.'

'Give it a minute, Finn.' Gabriel turned on the nearest tap and was gratified to hear a productive response.

Between them they worked through the rest of the morning routine, including brushing of teeth – Finn always complained – cursing toothpaste that tasted like petrol. 'OK, I'll do it!' Finn snatched the toothbrush and started to brush. With his mouth full he spluttered. 'Look…' Finn pointed to his eyes in the wash room mirror; even his eyelashes had started to fall out.

'Your hair will grow back.' Even before he made the remark Gabriel regretted the wider deception. Finn's hair would grow back, but would he ever forget the experience? Would he still believe that there will always be a tomorrow? Or would he be marked by the illness, an older man too soon? It was something that was starting to play on Gabriel's mind. Surprisingly, given his occupation, he'd been well into middle age before he realised that there really were no unlimited tomorrows. His grandson would have to grapple with this sobering fact at an early age. They both needed a diversion.

'Come on, Finn. Let's get back to the ward. What about breakfast?'

⋅→══⊙ ⊙══←⋅

Riikka was standing by Finn's bed when they returned to the ward. 'Caught you both, at last.' Finn grinned. 'You're looking very smart Finn.' She tugged at his tee-shirt. Didn't know you were a football fan.' She turned his shoulders to face the playroom. 'Guess who's popped in to see you? She's waiting in the playroom.' Finn coloured up. 'Go on, off you go, I'm going to have a chat with your granddad.'

She sat on the edge of the bed. 'It's good to see you Gabriel.' Riikka waved at Maisy as she emerged from the playroom with Finn. They headed for the kitchen. 'I managed to discuss "things" with my boyfriend last week.'

'And how did that go?'

'To be honest he was a complete arse, but he didn't rush out for Prozac. It was no big deal really.'

'I had a similar experience. I rather stupidly mentioned Celia during a family meal.'

'I bet they were impressed.'

'Well yes, it could have been a catastrophe if it hadn't been for Finn. He saved my bacon.'

'Listen, the children look happy enough, could you take five minutes off and pop down to the canteen with me? The coffee is pretty awful...'

'Love to. Let's make sure they're not wrecking the kitchen first.'

Finn and Maisy seemed more than happy to escape adult supervision and Gabriel was grateful for the break. As the doors to the oncology ward closed behind him he reflected that he'd spent a good part of the past few years in and out of hospital. Riikka slipped her arm through his and this time there was no embarrassment or discomfort. They negotiated the serving counter and settled at a small table near the only window in the room.

⤙⫤ ⫣⤚

Finn watched Maisy measure blackcurrant juice into two beakers and top them up with water.

'Thanks.' It was perfect, she was perfect. It was a relief when his granddad had disappeared with Rikky. He wanted time alone with his friend. A distant wave of nausea greeted the juice as it reached his stomach. He grinned, sheepishly, and willed the sick feeling to go away. Maisy smiled.

'Try sipping. When I felt sick I found it helped.'

Finn took a deep breath. 'Thanks, this chemo stuff is pants.'

'Let's sit on your bed and talk.' Obediently, Finn followed. Maisy stacked pillows so they could sit together. She turned her head to speak, her breath a sweet mix of fruit and peppermint. Finn drank them in. 'What shall we talk about?' asked Maisy.

Finn was considering options when the nausea returned and this time it was difficult to ignore the inclination to heave. Maisy jumped from the bed alive to Finn's discomfort and a remedy. 'Where's your toilet bag?' He pointed. She took out his face cloth and soaked it in a nearby sink. 'My dad used to do this for me.' Tenderly, she wiped his face. Finn closed his eyes, the close proximity of Maisy and the sensation of the cool towel on his skin was wonderful. The sick feeling receded.

'You guys OK?' A nurse stood at the bottom of the bed.

Maisy took the lead. 'He was feeling sick so I…' She waved the cloth.

'You should be a nurse when you grow up, you're doing a great job.' She scanned his notes. 'Do you want me to get you something for the sickness?'

Finn shook his head.

'Well come and get me if you need help.'

They both nodded, in that moment a testament to the best they could be.

Finn had chosen his topic to talk about. 'D'you believe in imaginary friends?'

Maisy returned the face cloth to its bag. 'I guess so, but I've never had one. Why, have you? How exciting. Tell me.'

Finn was embarrassed but stumbled on. 'Mine was called Cissy. You remind me of her. I liked her a lot. Sounds stupid, but I did.'

'What was she like?'

Once he started all his old feelings returned. Maisy seemed fascinated and didn't interrupt as he talked.

She sat up, facing him on the bed. He'd talked for ages. 'That's some friendship, how sad she had to go away.'

'Sometimes I feel like she's close by, but I don't see her anymore. You're like her, not to look at, in other ways.'

'What do you mean?'

'The way you listen.' Finn dropped his eyes. 'I mean, we seem to get on...'

'Guess there's a big difference though?' Maisy moved closer to Finn, who made no effort to move away.

'What's that?'

'I'm real...'

Chapter 38

SINCE HER ENCOUNTER with Hetty and the gang Riikka had been reluctant to walk to work, and yet, regular as clockwork, High Street dutifully appeared. She doubted she would ever forget Sarah peeling back that fateful street scene. Today she was early to work, not late. She sat on the bench opposite the bookshop and waited for the key holder.

The sun had crested the skyline to the east. Riikka closed her eyes and enjoyed the warmth as shadows crawled down the street. When she opened her eyes she was surprised to see Lorri pushing past a customer leaving the store.

'Lorri?'

Lorri didn't turn and instead disappeared into the shop. Riikka stood, stretched and walked towards the open doors. She was confused, how had she missed opening time? She was about to follow Lorri when her extended hand hit an obstruction. *Shit!* She tried again, this time she was more circumspect. There was something blocking the doorway, but she couldn't see anything. It felt familiar: ironwork, it was the security grill. Touch claimed the day until a figure emerged, a well-dressed man who paused to check his watch and strode forwards. Instinctively, Riikka raised her arm and shouted, they were going to collide. Instead, he literally passed through Riikka and continued down the street. Riikka froze. 'What the fuck was that?'

'Riikka?' She was still grappling with the absurdity of the phantom shopper when Tommy, manager Tommy, grabbed her arm. 'What on earth are you doing? Who are you swearing at?'

As if by magic, Tommy's corpulent frame appeared. *Good God, Sarah, so this is what you meant, no certainty…* She managed a weak smile. 'Thought I could see a light inside.'

Tommy shook the security grill, it was still locked. 'Can't see anything.' The remark held a note or two of scorn. On this occasion Riikka had no counter, no riposte. She would only sound defensive, she certainly felt defensive.

Riikka stepped back, he could go first. 'Shall we take a look?'

⊷⊶ ⊷⊶

Lorri entered the bookstore at midday. Riikka stared in amazement as her friend approached. Fortunately, the manager was on his break so they had time for a brief exchange.

'Hi Riikka, any chance we could have coffee?' Riikka checked her watch.

'You bet. I have a lot to talk about. I can take my break now.' She was distracted as right on cue the well-dressed man appeared. Riikka watched as he stopped at the door to check his watch and then hurry away.

'Someone you know?' Lorri's interest was obviously piqued.

'Someone I've seen before. I'll explain later. Give me a minute, I'll get my bag.'

They decided to find a seat at Eleven, the café where Gabriel had first talked with Riikka. Lorri was intrigued. 'Who was the well-dressed lad in the shop?'

Riikka recounted the time shift she'd experienced earlier that day.

'Good grief.' Lorri was impressed. 'You're a seer. How fantastic.'

'You're kidding. I nearly peed my pants.' Riikka moved closer and lowered her voice. 'It wasn't the first time.'

Lorri sat back. 'What first time?'

'The phone call, from Jonathan, when you came over for dinner.' Lorri nodded. 'And then there was this really strange dream. It wasn't seeing the future, it was something else.'

'What happened?'

'I was walking to work and basically got lost. This old woman and another weirdo started following me. It was pretty scary. I turned into this street and the houses at the end of the road moved towards each other. It felt like they were closing off my escape. The old crone caught up with me and poked me in the back. I screamed.' Riikka paused to sip her coffee.

'Surely that's not all?'

Riikka grinned. 'Where the houses met this sort of crack appeared and two hands poked through, but completely out of scale. They were huge.'

Lorri nearly choked. 'You should write a book…'

'There's more. The hands pushed back the houses, the sky, everything, and Sarah stepped through, just like she was across the room.'

'What room?'

'Behind the street was my bedroom. I was sitting up in bed and Jonathan was asleep next to me. Sarah was standing at the foot of the bed.'

'Please tell me she said something.'

'She said that I needed to be careful. That I couldn't rely on certainty. She emphasised that word, certainty. And then this morning, when I was sitting across the street, I thought the shop was open and watched you walk in. When I tried to follow I couldn't. The security gate was still down, but I couldn't see it. I was watching the door three hours into the future.' Riikka opened her hands. 'Welcome to wacky street…'

Lorri seemed impressed. 'This is incredible. Whatever is happening to you and Gabe it's likely that you will need this new skill.' Lorri tapped the table. 'Be careful. If I were you I'd take Sarah at her word.'

'What, about certainty?'

'Exactly. My guess is we are headed towards some sort of crisis. If you are part of the solution, you don't want to end up in a psychiatric ward. I'm sure that's not part of the plan.' Lorri took Riikka's hand. 'Check out stuff with me if you need to. I'd be cautious about interfering, trying to change the future is a risky business.'

'Which leaves me where?'

'It leaves you, my sweet, exactly where you are…'

Chapter 39

LORRI WAS CONCERNED. The mood in the Carey household was bleak. Finn was back at the hospital with another infection, and this one was proving difficult to tame. Even Billie seemed subdued. She appealed to her sister. *If you're listening we could do with some help.* Lorri had long since abandoned the notion of divine intervention, but she'd eyed Patrick's crucifix, still a discarded relic on the hall stand. She sent a plea to the unknown source of all. It was the best she could do.

She braced against despair and entered the kitchen. Beth and Grace were hand in hand across the kitchen table. 'Am I disturbing you guys?' Of course she was.

Beth wiped her eyes. 'Of course you're not...' She managed a half-smile.

Lorri had stood by and watched as the past few days exhausted what remained of Beth's stamina, her last defence against hopelessness. Lorri wanted to love her up. Her hair looked as if it hadn't been washed in days.

Beth released Grace's hand. 'Is Billie OK?'

'Yep, a three-story bedtime tonight. She's still awake. Why don't you…?'

'I should… I don't want her to see me like this.'

'You don't need to hide your feelings Beth. Billie is a tough little cookie. Make sure she knows its Finn you're worried about, not her…' Lorri bit her lip, fearful she was over-egging her remarks.

Beth tossed the used Kleenex into the sink. 'OK. I'll go now before she falls asleep.' Beth ran a hand across Lorri's back as she passed. 'Thanks. You're a brick…'

Lorri dumped the soiled clothing she was carrying.

'This is such a bitch.' Grace opened her bag as she spoke. On the face of it she was in better shape than her sister. Lorri noticed her hands shake as she struggled to pull a pack of cigarettes from the Burberry. 'I'm sorry, I need this.'

'Come on, let's sit outside, the rains held off.' Lorri led the way.

Three drags and Grace seemed more composed. Lorri was content to sit. She wondered how Patrick and Gabe were faring at the hospital. 'Any news from the boys?'

Grace removed a tobacco flake from her tongue. 'That's why Beth is so cut up. Patrick called while you were upstairs with Billie. He was upset. Finn is past the worst, the last batch of antibiotics have done the trick, but Patrick is convinced their son is on a downward, slippery slope…'

'What do you think?'

Grace waved at smoke drifting between them. 'I think Patrick should grow up and take his fair share of the burden. Beth can't mother them all.' She looked at her aunt. 'Am I being too harsh?'

Lorri shrugged her shoulders. 'We can only stand by and support them. Strikes me that we are all carrying some of Patrick's fear. If Finn doesn't beat the cancer, it'll be difficult for all of us.'

Grace looked at her feet. 'I wish Mum was here. Days like today I really miss her.'

⊷⩥ ⩤⊶

For the first time that week Finn felt hungry. His granddad was in the ward kitchen making toast with chocolate spread. He was worried about his father sitting at the side of his bed, head in hands. He guessed he was fretting about the cancer and stuff. Finn missed Billie. She was too young to make much sense of his illness. Having said that, Finn knew she was affected by their parents' mood swings. Now he was feeling better, perhaps he could be more cheerful and then everyone would be better too. The notion was compelling. He tried out a smile and then a giggle.

'Here you go.' Granddad arrived with the toast and Finn attacked it with gusto.

'Patrick, why don't we get some fresh air while Finn polishes off his toast? You look as if you need a break.'

Finn answered for his dad. 'Could you switch on the telly for me, it's cartoons. And don't rush back, I'm fine now.' He watched as they disappeared out the door. He wanted to say phew, but there was no one to listen. It was hard work looking after grownups…

Chapter 40

BRUCE STOOD AS the Carey family trooped in. Why was it he never seemed to have good news for these people? He made a half-hearted attempt at reshuffling papers on his desk. Finn took his usual seat and Bruce laid a hand on his shoulder.

'I'm afraid we're reaching the end of the road with chemotherapy. Finn's white blood count is still way too high. We are also running close to the limits of antibiotics to treat his infections.' Bruce paused. The gallery of adult faces turned an unpleasant grey. He could see them sliding into disbelief and if not that then despair. They desperately wanted a miracle, and so did he. There was still one move to play. 'We're listing Finn for a bone marrow transplant. There are no other options I'm afraid.'

Beth was the first to react. 'Are you saying that without a transplant there's no possibility of a cure?'

Bruce nodded. 'That's about it…'

'Well take mine then. I'm his mother, for God's sake.'

'Steady, Beth.' Bruce was grateful for Gabriel's interjection. 'It's not that simple, none of us may be a close enough match.'

Bruce continued. 'That's right. We'll take a blood sample from all of you and we've already listed Finn with the major donor organisations.'

'So it's a waiting game.' Bruce was startled by Patrick's deadpan delivery. 'How long do we have?'

Beth glared at her husband as her father spoke again. 'We have as long as we have. It's not a question you should be asking at this stage. A donor may turn up tomorrow.'

Beth turned to her father. 'Dad, would you take Finn outside, the kitchen maybe, get him a drink.'

'Wait a second, please.' Bruce turned and faced Finn. 'Do you understand what we're saying Finn?'

Finn shook his head.

'The medicine we have been giving you is not working fast enough. Your bone marrow, where new blood is made, needs to be replaced. We'll see if someone in your family can let you have some of theirs, or someone else whose cells match yours.'

'So no more chemo?'

'That's right.'

Finn beamed. 'That's good isn't it?'

Bruce smiled. 'Let's hope so Finn. You are still very poorly, we have to try to find another way to make you better.'

Finn stood and followed his grandfather from the room.

Beth rounded on her husband. 'Please don't do that – take away hope – even if you have none. You have no right…'

Patrick raised his eyes and it was Bruce who spoke.

'We've not run out of options and we usually track down a donor in good time. My immediate concern is controlling

Finn's infections. His last nearly exhausted our options. There are only a limited number of antibiotics we can use. We're going to move Finn into a side ward to minimise the risks of cross infection. It's not necessary to isolate him at this point, but we need to cut down his contacts.'

'When do we have our tests?' Beth's voice was shaking.

'Soon, later today if possible. Best if you could all be here. We'll need to take a blood sample from Billie, and your sister as well.'

Patrick took a deep breath. 'OK, we'll be here. Please excuse me, I need to find the loo.'

Bruce sighed as Patrick left the room. Finn's parents were encountering a common enough problem; their son's predicament stretching their otherwise sound relationship to breaking point.

'Beth?'

'I'm sorry about that. I'm sure you have plenty to worry about without accommodating our problems.'

'We still have options Beth. All we can do is manage them as best we can.'

Beth seemed to find inner reserves. 'I'd better call my sister.'

'Sure. Would you like me to organise an appointment with a counsellor?'

'That's another reason I need to speak with my sister. We can talk.'

As Beth left the room Bruce scanned the path lab reports in his file. He prayed that he was wrong, that the science was wrong, but the odds were shifting, narrowing the chances of a much desired cure. He also nursed unspoken risks: that Finn's resident fauna, the bacteria in his gut, would overcome his fragile defences. In the end, it would likely be Finn that would infect himself, and for that there were only prayers and hope – and the wheel's spin - standing in the way of terminal infection. His old friend, the familiar black dog was watching. It was an uncomfortable realisation.

⊸⊚ ⊚⊶

Beth hardly noticed her father as she crossed the ward, waving his attention away. No sign of Patrick. She needed fresh air and time to think. She needed to call Grace. In her agitated state she missed a turn for the main entrance and was confused by a warren of unfamiliar corridors.

'Beth?'

She heard her name but had no enthusiasm for conversation. Hurried footsteps closed the gap. The touch on her arm was not unexpected, neither was Riikka's next remark. 'Beth, it is you.'

'Yes, sorry, I seem to have lost the main entrance.' Beth was finding it difficult to be civil.

'It's OK, I get lost myself on occasion. You need to turn around and take the next corridor on your right, then straight on.' Riikka moved her hand away. 'You OK?'

Beth turned her head. What should she say? Finn's face popped into her mind and she could no longer deny the feelings. She didn't realise her face was wet, that her chin was alive with the realisation that she might lose her beloved son.

'Hey… What on earth's happened?'

A comforting arm drew her close and, eyes closed, Beth sobbed. She was guided to a chair.

'Take these.' Riikka placed clean tissues in her hand. 'I didn't mean to pry…'

Beth drew in a deep breath, time to talk. 'It's Finn. We've been told chemo's not working.' She gathered the words spilling round her head. 'He's going to need a bone marrow transplant, if, you know…'

Riikka sat back in her chair, unable to respond. It was a long minute before she spoke. 'I guess the family will have to be tested, for a match?'

Beth nodded.

'I'm so sorry. I actually thought Finn was on the mend.' Riikka drew back the hair falling over her face. 'Can I help? God knows how but if I can I will. I've grown quite fond of Finn, of all of you.'

Beth managed a smile. 'Right now you could help me find the main entrance. I need to call my sister.'

They negotiated the grey-walled corridors in silence. Beth was grateful for the support of Riikka's arm. When they pushed through the glass doors Riikka spoke.

'How has Gabriel taken the news, and your husband?'

'Let's not dwell on Patrick's thoughts shall we, I need to stay positive.' Beth found a space on a bench and sat. 'But there is something you could do for me.'

'Anything.'

Beth flipped open her mobile, holding it motionless on her lap. 'Could you go back to the ward? It's Dad, he'll be worried about me.' Beth reached out and squeezed Riikka's hand. 'And he probably needs someone to talk to…'

'If you're sure you'll be OK?'

'I'm sure, and thanks. And tell Dad I'm calling Grace.'

Beth watched Riikka disappear into the hospital. She grabbed her mobile. Grace, she needed to speak with Grace.

Beth's conversation with her sister was short and to the point. Their father had spoken to Grace already and she was on her way. Beth resolved to wait near the main entrance. She couldn't bear to go back inside, not without Grace. She found an empty bench and waited.

The world outside flitted past: patients, visitors and staff spilled across her vision like a half-seen moving picture. Even though it was barely past mid-morning the light began to fail followed by a persistent drizzle. Beth ignored the rain.

'So now you know.'

Beth embraced the voice. *Mamma?*

Her mother responded as Beth imagined she would. 'Now you know what you must do. You must be a rock and believe that Finn can find peace and healing. Patrick, regrettably, is not up to the task. Not yet.' Silence. Beth needed more.

'Beth?' The world was shaking. 'Beth, wake up. It's me, Grace. You're soaking wet.'

Beth opened her eyes and shivered. She was wet.

'Christ, Beth, I'll have to get you out of those clothes. Come with me.'

Chapter 41

FINN HAD UNDERESTIMATED the impact of his move to a side ward. It was weird, there was no one else in there. He helped his mother move his stuff. There wasn't much to explore, although he did have his own bathroom. They were sorting out dirty clothes to wash when Finn's favourite nurse came in, closing the door. Mae sat on the end of the bed.

'Settled in?'

Finn shrugged his shoulders. 'Guess so…'

'Do you know why you've been moved?'

'Mum said to escape germs.'

'That's right. You can still see your family, but we'll keep this door closed.' Mae pointed. 'It will probably be best if other children don't visit for a while, or grownups that have a cold or other infection.'

Finn was worried about children being excluded. 'But not Billie or Maisy?' He blushed, his feelings for Maisy were a secret.

Mae looked at his mother. 'As long as Billie is well it's fine for her to come.' Finn was only part satisfied. 'And if Maisy wants to visit that's fine too, as long as she's not sick.' He was happy now.

'Beth, can you brief the family visitors to be vigilant? We really don't want Finn with another infection before a donor is found.'

Beth nodded. 'Sure, they know. We won't take any risks.' She dumped the rest of the laundry into a carrier bag. 'Can I ask you something? I'll follow you out...'

Finn watched them disappear through the door: the door that closed, the door that needed to stay shut.

⊷⊷⊶⊶

It was almost a week since Riikka had found Beth in a state, and she was dreading her next encounter with the family. As she entered the ward there was no sign of Finn. She headed straight for the nurses' station.

'Where's Finn?'

The duty nurse pointed to the far end of the ward. 'He's semi-isolated now, to minimise infection.'

'I see. Is it OK for me to visit?'

'Yes, but stay away if you are felling unwell, or if you've been in contact with someone sick.' Riikka nodded. 'And could you use the hand-gel dispenser outside the door. Oh, and one more thing, don't let any of the kids in.' The nurse smiled. 'We need to keep Finn away from infection if we can.'

Riikka stopped to chat with a couple of her little friends as she headed for Finn's new quarters. She opened the door and was surprised to see that Finn was on his own. 'Hi Finn, can I come in?'

His face lit up. ''Course.'

'So, how are you? Like your new place?'

Finn fidgeted. 'Bit bored. I miss the ward.'

'Who's with you today?'

'Aunt Lorri, 'til Dad comes later.'

The prospect of seeing Lorri was a bonus. 'I have something for you. Can you play DVDs in here?' Finn pointed to the screen and box on the opposite wall. She handed over the latest *Shrek* movie.

'Thanks…' He jumped off the bed as Lorri appeared with drinks.

'Riikka, what a surprise.' Lorri handed Finn his habitual carton of juice. 'A new video, I see.'

They helped Finn unwrap his present. Soon he was settled, giggling furiously.

Lorri pointed to the door. 'Finn, I'm sure Riikka has to get back to the playroom. OK if I go with her for ten minutes?'

Finn took a long drink from the straw. ''Course, don't forget the door…'

Riikka followed Lorri into the playroom. It was lunch time so no children. 'I've been dreading today,' she said. 'How are the family? Beth was in a terrible state last week.'

'It's been… stressful? Not sure how to describe the atmosphere. Everyone is trying to stay positive, but it's not easy.'

'Finn seems in good form.'

'God knows how, but he's managed to retain his sense of the now, if you see what I mean.'

Riikka knew exactly what she meant. 'Tomorrow, who cares, I'm fine right now...'

Lorri slumped into the playroom sofa. 'Wish I could embrace that belief. There's this unspoken agenda going on. No one is prepared to deal with it. Except maybe Patrick. Which is interesting as Beth is giving him a really hard time, and if anything he's the only person who's facing up to losing Finn.'

Riikka was anxious to speak with Lorri. There was no-one else. Her needs burnt through her reservations. 'I know this is really bad timing. Could we talk? I could do with another Lorri fix.'

'Sure. Anything to distract me. Please, go ahead.'

'Since I found out that Finn's treatment is not working I've been terrified that I'm going to have one of my episodes and see how things turn out. I'm not sure I can cope with that sort of knowing.'

'I don't think it works like that.'

'Like what?'

'It's a gift. You take what comes.' Lorri laughed. 'Sorry, I had this stupid idea, how do you refuse a sneeze?'

⊷▬◉ ◉▬⊶

Patrick was late. To compound matters the car park seemed full. Ahead a car pulled out and gratefully he entered the parking spot. It was only a small thing but the vacant space registered as a positive, maybe the first since Finn's diagnosis. He grabbed his overnight bag and headed for oncology.

He waved at the nurses on his way to Finn's room. As he approached the playroom Lorri and Riikka emerged.

Lorri's hug was welcome. 'Hope you like *Shrek*.'

'*Shrek*?'

Riikka responded. 'My fault I'm afraid. New video. You may be watching it a few times tonight.'

Patrick was unaffected by Riikka's levity; banter was not going to meet his needs. 'No problem. How is he?'

'See for yourself. A few minutes ago he was a very happy boy.'

They made their way to Finn's room. He looked up briefly as they entered. 'Hi Dad. This is a great video.' Patrick kissed his son, who wriggled away, trying to maintain eye contact with the screen. 'This is the best bit.'

Patrick handed Lorri cash and a slip of paper. 'Beth wondered if you could call at Tesco on the way back. This should be enough.'

'No problem.'

Riikka held open the door as Lorri grabbed her coat and carrier. 'Nice seeing you again Patrick. I need to get back to the playroom, books to sort.'

Lorri's parting communication was to the point. Patrick liked Lorri. She edged closer. 'If you've lost hope don't abandon possibility, none of us know where this is headed…' He could have fallen into her eyes.

'Thanks.' There was more, but the torrent of feelings held firmly in place would fill more than a parting minute. 'Thanks...'

Patrick never unpacked. He lived out of his bag. He preferred to sleep on the bedside chair. The mist of unreality that had grown in recent weeks was now a thick fog. It removed his ability to cope without digging deeper into denial. He watched his son, laughing, apparently in rude health, and yet he couldn't share the moment. Hope seemed a distant blur, like a mirage, no succour if you were thirsty.

Eventually, the film ended and Patrick attended to routine matters: beans on toast, brushing teeth, lights out.

'Dad?'

'Yes sunshine.'

'What if I don't get better?'

Finn's question was like a candle in a dark room. Patrick's own concerns, the shadows, were chased back. 'What do you think?'

'I asked Grandma.'

'And what did she say?'

'She said she'd wait for me, if I didn't get better.'

'You know we all want you to get better though?'

A strange stillness settled in the room. For a while Finn didn't reply, as if his father's question deserved proper consideration. Then he spoke. 'Well, if I get better I'll have you, and if I don't I'll have Grandma.' Finn reached for his drink. 'Could I watch *Shrek* again?'

Chapter 42

THE NEWMAN FAMILY'S blood tests provided no comfort – none of them was a close enough match to donate bone marrow. Two weeks after registration with the donor agencies and still no word. Gabriel couldn't bear more than an hour or two in Finn's room. It was not knowing, the constant, unrelenting anxiety. Would a donor be found? He was becoming paranoid about any change in Finn's demeanour, and the approach of each twice-daily temperature check was a torment. There was an unwritten agreement between Finn's watchers to text the all-clears. The rapid march of time had slowed to a crawl. If anything, Finn was the most resilient. Apart from gripes about his food the boy was amazing.

A rather portly man walked into the small hospital kitchen as Gabriel stirred his tea.

'Are you Finn's granddad?'

'Yes.'

His outstretched hand wrapped around Gabriel's. 'I'm Maisy's dad, Rod.' He moved closer. 'She's outside. Is it OK for her to visit Finn?'

'Have you cleared it with the staff?'

'Yes, no problem there, she's in good shape.'

Gabriel relaxed. 'Well, Finn will be pleased. Let's take her down.'

Finn was more than pleased. Maisy rushed over and jumped on his bed. They both turned and faced their minders. No words, the message came across loud and clear – go away.

Rod chuckled. 'D'you think we can trust these two alone?'

Maisy was not amused. 'Dad!'

Gabriel picked up the banter. 'Perhaps one of us should stay?' Now Finn was glaring. Gabriel and Rod left the youngsters and settled in the parents' rest room.

Rod's hands rested on his ample belly. 'Maisy seems quite taken with young Finn. She's told me about his condition, the transplant… I'd like to make a suggestion, an offer really.'

Gabriel was intrigued. 'I'm all ears.'

'I have a business. I sell mobile phones.' He reached into his jacket pocket and handed Gabriel a handset. 'Would you ask Finn's parents if he could have the use of this phone? It's been set up under my business accounts so there'd be no costs involved.' Rod raised his hand. 'I'll give Maisy a similar phone so they can text each other.' He ran his hand through his beard. 'She doesn't have a phone of her own, but she knows everything about them. I wouldn't recommend mobiles for nine-year-olds, but the circumstances are exceptional. Maisy's had more than her fair share of set-backs before remission was confirmed. She knows how Finn must be feeling.' He smiled. 'They've become good friends. This would give them a chance to talk to each other.' He hesitated. 'Especially, when Finn has his transplant and is isolated...'

Gabriel was touched by the offer. 'Beth and Patrick are bringing Finn's sister for a visit soon. We can ask them then, if you're not in a hurry. But we must make a financial contribution.'

'I've no plans until later tonight so I can wait, no problem. And I won't accept any money. As I said, the phone will run through my business account and there's no way they will run up large bills. I have thousands of free texts and calls on my account, which always go to waste.' He stood. 'If you'll forgive me for a minute, I need a smoke. Would you mind keeping an eye on Maisy 'til I get back? Ten minutes?'

⊷⊷◉ ◉⊷⊷

Finn was thrilled with his phone. His mother had taken a bit of persuading, but Maisy's dad had talked her round. There were ground rules. Maisy's dad would keep her phone at night, and she couldn't take it to school. Likewise, Finn had to surrender his phone at night. And outgoing calls to premium rate numbers were blocked. Maisy had spent the last part of her visit explaining how to text and call. Rod had discussed the use of the phone with the nursing staff, who had agreed Finn could use it as long as the ring tone was switched off, vibrate only, and Finn would have to turn it off if certain equipment was being used in his room.

At the nine o'clock watershed Finn switched off his new toy and laid it carefully in his drawer. His granddad nodded in approval. 'Maisy seems a nice person.'

Finn didn't disagree, but there was no way he would agree. For the last hour or so he had been feeling depressed. The phone was great, but he desperately wanted to go home. The visit from Billie and Maisy had reminded him there was still a world outside the hospital.

'Who's looking after Freddie?' Finn sighed. 'I hope they're feeding him.'

'He was fine last time I checked. Your dad is taking care of feeds.'

'When can I go home? I need to get out of this room.'

His granddad looked away. 'We need to wait until they find a donor. Hopefully it won't take too long.'

'I want to go back to school. I want to see my other friends. I don't want this cancer thing anymore.'

Before the conversation could continue a nurse appeared with an ear thermometer. 'Time to check you out Finn.' She handed him the primed instrument. Finn was an expert. When he handed it back she looked puzzled. 'Let me try.' When she checked the reading again she left the room and his granddad followed.

Finn yawned. He slipped off the bed and shuffled into the bathroom.

--»≡⊚ ⊚≡«--

Riikka dropped the book she was reading. This time it was her room that suffered a time shift. She could see through transparent walls into the oncology ward. Gabriel was talking with a nurse outside Finn's room. The nurse was speaking. 'His temperature is spiking. I'm so sorry. I'll have to contact Bruce...' She touched Gabriel's hand and left. The look on his face was heart-breaking.

⋯▶▬◉ ◉▬◀⋯

When Bruce North got the call he was resting. He listened to the message. 'I'll be there in ten minutes,' he said. 'Make sure Finn's file is available. Thanks.' It was the worst possible news. Finn's temperature was up. It could only be another infection. *Bugger!*

⋯▶▬◉ ◉▬◀⋯

'Beth? Bad news I'm afraid. Finn's temperature is too high. They're going to start intravenous antibiotics tonight. There's nothing you can do Beth... Finn is happy enough. Get some rest, I'll see you in the morning... OK, see you then, bye.'

Patrick was passing Beth as she placed her mobile phone, too carefully, on the hall table. She looked white as a sheet. 'Beth,' he said. 'What's wrong?'

⋯▶▬◉ ◉▬◀⋯

Maisy stretched, time for breakfast. Then she remembered her phone. Her dad was in the kitchen when she caught up with him. She held out her hand and squealed with delight as she switched it on. 'There's a message from Finn.' It was clear enough.

'!Got nothr fection txt later'

She handed the phone back. Rod read the message. 'Damn…'

Chapter 43

THIS TIME THE infection did not respond to antibiotics. The rattle returned. Finn drifted in and out of consciousness. He was aware that his condition was worsening and couldn't bear the look on the faces of the adults who stayed by his bed. Eventually, he closed his eyes and entered the space before everything changes. The dreams he had were more real and welcome than the real world held at bay: he joined Freddie for a swim, met Cissy again, and was reacquainted with Billie, newly born.

Soon enough, these familiar features faded and he entered a place where the visions were unfamiliar. They seemed to be preparation for a transition, and as time progressed this process appeared to be inevitable. It was like an unknown pathway where the only direction was onward, no turning back, which was why the voice was such a surprise.

'Finn, hang in there buddy...'

It was granddad. Finn stopped. Curiosity re-emerged as a viable thought process. What did he mean? Hang in where? In the far distance he could hear a weird sort of hum, and he could feel as well – he was hot. The sensations reopened the possibility that he could find a way back. Finn knew he needed to make a choice. This was it, back or forward? His granddad was close by, should he go back…?

'It's up to you sweetie.'

'Grandma, you kept your promise.'

'I said I'd be here, but you still have a choice. What do you want to do?'

⋆⟶⊙ ⊙⟵⋆

Gabriel regained consciousness to the howl from a monitor next to Finn's bed. He was still holding Finn's hand. The door to the room burst open and three nurses appeared with a crash cart.

'Sorry Doctor Newman, you'll have to leave.'

Gabriel released his grandson's hand and backed out of the room. *Surely this can't be happening?*

At the other end of the ward Patrick and Beth appeared. Gabriel had no time to compose his face. Beth dropped her shopping bag and raced down the ward. 'What's happening? Dad, what's happening?'

Despite his best efforts, Beth opened the door to Finn's room and disappeared. Her drawn-out, anguished 'No…' confirmed Gabriel's worst fears. Patrick, ashen-faced, followed his wife's call. Reluctantly, Gabriel joined them.

Beth had collapsed across Finn's body and was sobbing. Patrick looked lost, like Marley's ghost in mardi gras. Two of the nurses, obviously upset, were switching off their failed gadgets. Gabriel stood by the door. This was different to Isabella's passing. This was shocking, unexpected, and unfair. A nurse approached, Finn's favourite, Mae. 'I'm sorry, we couldn't bring him back…'

Incredibly, Gabriel smiled, and almost said it's OK. There was no remedy for the grief unravelling in the tiny room. Disregarding protocol, Mae stepped forward and embraced Gabriel who slipped, drowning in too much. He ended his tussle with reality and fell, at ease, embracing the impossibility before his eyes. It really was too much. The parting words from Bella's poem laid bare his feelings: I am enough. His legs give way, and he sensed Mae's failed attempt to hold his weight. He heard rather than felt the sickening thud as his head hit the floor.

Chapter 44

WHEN PATRICK HAD pushed open the door to follow Beth his recurring fears were confirmed. Weeks of fretting, of not knowing, of faith challenged, suddenly dropped away and he'd felt strangely relieved. Finn had gone. He'd taken two steps towards the bed and for the last time he'd hesitated as the vestiges of doubt had cleared away. The realisation was quickly replaced by guilt, how could he feel relieved, and then he'd heard Gabriel enter and, in a rush of clarity, he'd closed the door on his own misgivings and reached out to Beth.

When Gabriel had taken a tumble the drama took on the character of farce. It had all happened only yesterday, and yet Patrick was already finding the recall of the events difficult. The only person who seemed to be immune to the grief and stress was Billie. The toddler was intent on drowning her rubber duck, and howled with laughter when it resurfaced. Patrick finished rinsing her hair and lifted her from the bath. She stood as he gently towelled her down. Sitting with his back to the tub he rolled Billie in a warm towel and sat her on his knees. She snuggled up and Patrick found himself quietly weeping.

The house was still. Grace had taken Beth for a walk and Lorri was tending to Gabriel. Beth was angry. Patrick could see that she was trying to cope with the loss of their son, but she'd taken a step towards bitterness and he could sense that it was his turn to take responsibility for the day-to-day stuff. Lorri had recognised his new status in the family and, without saying, had offered her support. Patrick kissed the top of Billie's head, the wet curls tasting of bubbles. He was dimly aware that the front door had opened.

Lorri appeared. 'Hey you two. That looks cosy.'

Billie shifted, the spell was broken. She freed a hand and held it out to her great aunt.

'Shall I finish up?' Lorri offered. Patrick was unwilling to part with his daughter so he was non-committal. 'Or shall I make a start downstairs? Dinner?'

Patrick nodded. 'Dinner would be great. Could you warm up Billie's milk? We'll be down soon. 'The girls are out walking. How's Gabriel?'

'No change.' Lorri did her best to smile and repeated the reply. 'No change…' She swept up the discarded clothing, the wet towels and disappeared.

Patrick had felt no need to seek comfort from the Church. He'd surprised himself. There was no sense to Finn's early demise. However he rolled the dice, Patrick couldn't see how a loving God could countenance such loss. The only lingering guilt he felt was for his recurring relief at the ending of uncertainty. He half hoped that Finn would have a life beyond death, but even that promise held no lasting charge.

Billie started fidgeting as familiar voices filtered through from downstairs. The girls were back. Patrick struggled to his feet. It would be difficult for Beth. She'd been a rock when Finn was ill. Patrick could see it now, how he'd avoided responsibility, made a meal of his feelings. No matter, he was ready to make amends. He hoped they could heal the hurt, all of it...

Chapter 45

RIIKKA WAS GIVEN no foreknowledge of Finn's death, only his decline. She was blissfully unaware as she parked her car outside the surgery and entered reception. It was strangely quiet. No Irene and no patients. She checked her watch. It was early, eight-fifteen, but there was usually some activity at this time. Robert Campbell descended the stairs.

'Ah, Riikka. I'm afraid we've had bad news today.'

Riikka eyed Irene's empty throne in reception. 'Is Irene…?'

'No, it's not Irene. I'm afraid my ex-partner's grandson died yesterday, Finn.'

Riikka dropped her bag and gripped the back of a chair. 'Dear God. I had no idea he was so sick…'

'I'm afraid it gets worse.' Somewhere, a phone was ringing. 'It seems the shock was too much for Gabriel, he passed out and fractured his skull when he fell. The poor chap is in intensive care at the General. An induced coma.'

Riikka eyed Irene's seat. She would have taken the news none too well. 'Does Irene know?'

'She does. She took the call from the hospital. I've sent her home, not fifteen minutes ago. The poor woman was too distraught.' He straightened his back. 'So, can you manage reception for me? I've sent for reinforcements – they should be here soon.'

Riikka felt sick. Finn dead, Gabriel in a coma… The last thing she wanted to do was manage reception. 'Sure, I'll be fine.'

⤙⟞⟝⟞⟞⟵

It was twelve-thirty before Riikka could get away. She'd spent the morning coaxing the regulars – Irene called them "hypos", hypochondriacs – when all she'd wanted to do was find out how Gabriel was, and the rest of the family. She sat behind the wheel of her car trying to decide what she should do. She didn't want to intrude so Lorri seemed the safest bet. Riikka guessed she would be at Gabriel's house.

The journey was quick enough. Riikka parked and sat undecided: should she knock the door or leave it for a day or so? Really, there was no choice. Not knowing was the option she couldn't face. She locked the car and gazed at the Victorian semi. How could so much bad luck be visited on this house?

Lorri answered after the first ring, looking dreadful. 'So, you've heard, I hope?' She stepped back to let Riikka in.

'This morning. I still can't believe it.'

'It's a bitch. A total bitch. Beth and Patrick are destroyed and my brother-in-law is…' She couldn't find the words. 'Unavailable.' Riikka followed Lorri into the lounge; thankfully she was keen to talk. 'I was going to call over and see you later today. I cannot believe Finn has gone. A week ago he was fine.'

'Was it the infection?' Riikka immediately regretted the question. Of course it was.

'As far as I can tell Finn developed pneumonia and with no effective antibiotic the bugs ran riot.'

'And Gabriel, where's he?'

'Gabe's in the General. When he keeled over he fractured his skull. It's awful, he's away with the wee folk.'

'My God. What a fuck-up. Sorry...'

'That about sums it up fine. Don't apologise.' The phone rang. 'I better get that.' Lorri was gone for some time. Riikka could hear her talking in the kitchen. When she returned she looked strained. 'That was Beth. She sounded a bit more in control. Patrick has been coping really well. Reading between the lines I think he's taken over as mother and father. I did offer to have Billie. Ironically, the little one is probably the best therapy they could get.'

'So what can I do? Would you like to spend a few days with me? Would it be OK to leave this place locked up?'

Lorri smiled. 'You bet it would. I've been wondering what to do. No offence to my family, but it would be such a treat to have a break, a bolt hole.'

'Well, I've cancelled my next stint at the children's hospital so I'm free for the rest of the week. Shall I help you pack a bag?'

'I can manage...' Lorri gazed at the empty house. 'There's an air of unreality about all this. Shock I guess. I keep feeling that I'm going to wake up. How can any of this be true?'

⊷⫘⊷ ⊷⫘⊷

Gabriel looked terrible. Riikka stayed outside the ward, but she could see him through the glass panel that screened off the unit. He was surrounded by, and attached to, numerous monitors. Beth, Grace and Lorri were allowed to sit with him. Riikka could hear Billie's giggles as she toddled around the visitors' reception, refusing to let go of her father's hand. Riikka was struggling to control her feelings, and in particular the notion that Billie would not remember Finn. Lorri was right about Patrick, he seemed to be coping better than the rest of his family. Riikka watched father and daughter playing together and felt envious; what must it be like to be part of the drama and yet oblivious to the meanings, the attendant adult thoughts? She was certain Billie just accepted things as they were.

Beth and Grace waved to Riikka as Lorri stood, presumably to leave. Lorri looked more than a tad irritated as she emerged. 'That man needs to wake up.'

'Why "needs to"? I don't understand.'

Lorri sighed. 'He needs to wake like he did when he was sleep standing, before Bella passed on.'

Now Riikka was really confused. 'Sleep standing?'

'It's like sleep walking only standing still. Gabe has a history…'

'But surely this is different?' Riikka was still trying to figure out her friend's comments when Billie arrived. The toddler transferred her hands to Lorri's leg.

'Hey Billie.' Lorri directed her next remark to Patrick. 'Thanks for letting me sit in for a while. The girls said they'd be out in five minutes.'

Patrick looked preoccupied. 'How is he, any change?'

'Nope. He looks sound asleep. Beth said the medics don't expect him to resurface for a couple of days.'

'Right, no change then.'

Billie got bored trying to attract Lorri's attention, she wanted to see inside the room where everyone was going. She transferred her attention to Riikka's leg. Riikka was not going to miss the opportunity for a cuddle. Billie, perhaps realising that Riikka was not heading in the required direction, squirmed to be let down. Patrick offered to take his daughter. 'She wants to go in, to see her granddad, must be a bit confusing...'

'Then we should go.' Lorri handed Patrick a scrap of paper. 'I'll be at Riikka's place for a few days if you need me. Here's Riikka's number just in case my mobile goes AWOL. Let me know if there's any change.'

Patrick nodded. 'You take care.'

Lorri said little as they walked back to the car. Riikka held back until they were driving home. 'You were right.'

'About what?'

'None of this seeming to be real. I mean I know it is, but...'

Lorri cut in. 'Pull in to that supermarket.' She rummaged in her bag. 'I need a drink.' She gripped Riikka's arm. 'No more thinking tonight.'

Chapter 46

GABRIEL WAS CERTAIN he was close to the beach. There was a tantalising whisper of surf breaking on sand and he could swear there was ozone in the air. He knew who he was, but not where he was, and perhaps more importantly, where he'd come from.

'Time to wake up, young man.'

The instruction made no sense. 'Am I asleep?'

'As you have no unique viewpoint in this discussion, what difference does it make?'

Gabriel felt like a runner under starter's orders. 'Celia.' The voice had a name, a significant name, like a nugget in a silted pan. 'I was with Finn.' Another find. 'And I tried to help, held his hand again…' *Why can't I see?*

'Because you need to wake up. Open your eyes, it's easy.'

A startling insight punched through the confusion, switching on sight. 'What happened to Finn?' Gabriel asked, blinking. He was on the beach.

'He's beyond that crossroad.' Celia added.

Gabriel's memory returned in a rush. Fully briefed, there was only one question on his mind. 'Did the boy live? For God's sake Celia, is Finn alive?'

'Remember Riikka?'

'Of course.' *Why can't you answer my question!*

'Because, my dear friend, there is more than one answer. Wait for Riikka. Wait here if you like. You're safe enough, and trust me, enjoy this time, it's a rare treat to step outside choice. Relax.'

'No more riddles please. I have to know...'

'And so you will, so you will...' Celia left, her exit lifting Gabriel's anxieties and leaving him alive in his own questions.

Chapter 47

GRACE LISTENED AS Beth and Patrick discussed Finn's arrangements with the funeral director. Hardly a year had passed since they were having a similar conversation about their mother's internment. She missed her father. Surely he would recover? How would they cope if he slipped away? A cheap cliché butted in: everything comes in threes. Grace needed a smoke. Far from kicking the habit she had almost doubled her daily draws. She crept from the room, determined that the curse of three would have no power over her family's fortunes.

Lorri was sitting on the patio and Grace pulled up a chair. 'Do you mind if I smoke?'

Lorri shook her head. 'Carry on. I couldn't bear to listen to the funeral arrangements, it's too real. I can't believe Finn has gone.'

'Me neither. The funeral director person is a sympathetic chap, but I can tell that Beth is very close to losing it.' Grace took a long drag at her cigarette. 'How are we going to manage?'

'Do you have any belief in an afterlife?' Lorri asked.

'Not the religious sort, but yes, I sort of hope this is not it.'

'I've been thinking about Bella. I need to feel that Finn is not alone. I hope Bella was waiting for him.'

Grace reached out and held Lorri's hand. 'Amen to that.' The idea had a strange and compelling logic. The notion that Isabella was taking care of Finn was comforting. Faith planted a seed. Perhaps Finn would be guided to his happy hunting ground.

Their contemplation was broken by Patrick. 'Here you are.'

Lorri peered into the kitchen window. 'Where's Beth? Have they gone?'

'She's seeing to Billie and then wants to be alone for a while.'

Lorri and Grace frowned. Grace voiced her concern. 'Are you sure that's a good idea? I've been trying to get her to open up about how she feels for days now...'

Patrick opened his hands, juggling with his thoughts. 'Well, that's what she said, and to be honest you may need to be patient with the catharsis approach.' He smiled. 'This is about as bad as it gets. I have to trust that Beth knows her limits.' He reached for an empty chair and sat. 'Can't we just be around in case it all gets too much?'

'And what about you? How are you coping?' Lorri was engaged now. 'You seem to be doing remarkably well.'

Patrick stared at the patio, backlit now by light from the house. 'Truthfully, I have no idea.' He shrugged his shoulders. 'I'm finding it helpful to be supportive, helpful to me I guess. I'm not sure I'm ready to confront my feelings, at least not head-on.'

Grace was impressed that he'd deflected Lorri's "remarkably well" judgement. She wondered if Lorri had added the adjective to compliment or goad. Grace was sitting on a different judgement. She was tempted to ask Patrick if he was relieved. She herself felt relieved. It was the first thought that came to mind when she heard that Finn had died. No more suffering. And it was more than that, it was also that she no longer had to endure the unrelenting suspense: would a donor be found, would Finn catch another infection, would he survive? These were not feelings that Grace wanted to share. Even so, the daisy chain logic gave her an unexpected lift.

'I guess we'll all have to find our own path through,' said Lorri. 'No doubt it will be tough going.'

Patrick tapped his fingers on the table top. 'I better get upstairs. My turn for bedtime stories.' He pushed back his chair and hesitated. 'There's nothing remarkable about caring…' He seemed to think better of any further comment and disappeared into the house.

Lorri chuckled. 'Touché. I guess I deserved that. He's a good man.'

Grace stubbed out her cindered filter and consigned it to the borders. 'Keeps the slugs at bay.'

⋯▷▤◁ ▷▤◁⋯

Beth craved sleep. She had responsibilities, but while Patrick was coping she needed to escape. She dreamed most nights, and since Finn had passed all of her dreams were about him. They were bitter sweet. A recurring dream was of Finn recovering from his cancer, of a life that she would no longer witness in the waking world. For a few precious seconds each morning she would wake, bathed in the night's fantasies, until the physicality of her surroundings dragged her back and the living nightmare resumed.

She lay on their bed and listened to Patrick reading. Billie was such a sweetheart. Beth tried not to be negative, but she couldn't help being suspicious about Patrick's sudden resilience. When Finn was ill he'd been incredibly negative, depressed almost. Now that Finn was no longer with them she felt sure that he was relieved. Her husband, it seemed, needed certainty: death and taxes.

Through the back bedroom window she could hear Lorri and Grace talking. Suddenly, the notion that she needed time alone seemed redundant. She faced her reflection in the dressing table mirror and decided that makeup would do no justice to the damage. She wanted to talk. Passing Billie's room she blew the giggling toddler a kiss. Leaning against the door jamb she whispered to Patrick. 'I'll be downstairs…'

At one point in the journey down the stairs she reached a mid-point, a place where she could hear them all, the girls outside and father and daughter inside. She stopped. There were two steps left. Beth gazed at the worn carpet on the treads and had the strangest notion that if she took those steps, somewhere close by Finn would be waking from his own dream. She took the steps half expecting the redhead to emerge from his room or burst out of the kitchen with yet more juice, but there was no Finn in the house. It was like tossing a coin – it landed on tails and tails was absence of Finn. Beth sat on the bottom step and caught up with reality. Finn had died. She would never see him alive again. All she had left was memories and the endless choices to come. Beth weighed her future with Billie, Patrick, her sister, Lorri and her father. She decided it was enough. Somehow, she would keep Finn's memory alive for Billie's sake.

Grace walked past, heading for the kitchen. 'You OK?'

Beth nodded. 'I'm fine.'

'I'm making supper. Want some?

Beth smiled, nodded again. Her face tingled. *I must do more of this...*

Chapter 48

RIIKKA WAS SURPRISED to discover that familiarity had value after all. Jonathan was sound asleep. He was always bushed at the beginning of their weekends together. However, he was getting used to her needs. A process, she observed, that worked both ways. Taking care not to wake him she cupped his testicles in her hand. Putting aside the erotic consequences of her action, she contemplated the future generations that lay within her grasp.

As the night moved on, and the need to sleep was replaced by other needs, Riikka encouraged Jonathan to wake. He was a willing victim. This time Jonathan was rested and Riikka was not disappointed. Afterwards, sleep came quickly.

⊷⊷⊷

Sarah was waiting. 'We need your help.'

'We? I thought you guys were beyond help?'

'Gabriel needs to be reunited, to wake up.'

'United with what?'

Sarah hesitated. 'Shall we walk?'

The view ahead cleared and Riikka's toes curled into warm sand. It was dusk. The sun, some distant star, paid its respects and dipped below the horizon. The sky was alive with a cascade of local moons. Riikka counted four. 'Where is this place? Not your regular solar system?' Sarah stalled, no response. 'You're not going to tell me, are you?'

'Let's say that knowing where we are is of no consequence. The view is here to offer perspective, that's all. A bit of wonder is a stimulant, don't you think?' Sarah's question seemed rhetorical. She was still the same, well-manicured woman that rescued Riikka when her car had stalled light years ago. Walking on some off-world beach with a phantom was perfectly fine.

'How do we get to Gabriel? Isn't he in a coma?' Riikka was confused.

'He's having a vacation here, recuperating, but it's time to go back and we need you to take him.' Sarah paused. 'There's a complication.'

'What sort of complication?'

Sarah continued. 'Why don't you ask them?'

Ahead, Riikka could make out two people sitting at a white table. *Is that Gabriel?*

He waved. *How bizarre is this…*

When they arrived Gabriel stood. 'At last, a friendly face. I feel like I've been here for years.'

Riikka felt uncomfortable. After all, this was a dream, surely this was a dream? There were two vacant chairs so Riikka and Sarah sat.

Celia spoke first. 'Something incredible has happened.'

'And we can't elaborate.' Sarah continued. 'We've bought you here as we need you to fix something for us.'

Gabriel and Riikka exchanged glances. 'Any idea what these guys are talking about?' said Riikka.

Gabriel grinned. 'Can you remember anything other than we know each other, and these charming ladies?'

Riikka was dumbstruck. 'Shit. That's ridiculous... No, I can't.'

'That's the first thing I noticed when I arrived, whenever that was.'

'The thing we want you to consider requires that you act without your usual need to have a motive.' Celia looked deadly serious.

'Now wait a minute.' Riikka was having none of this. 'You mean we can't refuse?'

Sarah shook her head. 'Choice is a universal constant. There is always choice. What we are trying to explain is not that you have no choice, but that you will have no reason for doing as we ask and no expectation or knowledge of a particular outcome.'

Gabriel coughed, politely. 'I assume if we choose not to do "it" then matters will revert to the status quo, and if we do as you ask then the status quo will change in some way?'

Now it was the turn of Sarah and Celia to exchange glances. They replied together. 'Correct.'

Gabriel continued. 'So we will never know why. Is that assumption correct as well?'

'It is.'

Without the benefit of hindsight Riikka felt unsteady, and there was no way to reason or figure out what was being suggested. The rabbit hole beckoned.

Sarah responded. She was, after all, a resident in Riikka's mind, a fact that was shielded from her host's present deliberations. 'If madness is acting without reason then consider yourself crazy.' She waved at the view. 'This is all crazy.'

Celia leaned forwards. 'We are offering you a rare opportunity to act instinctively, without due consideration. And so,' she continued, turning to her companion, 'we would like you to choose.'

Riikka was still confused. 'Earlier I said this must be a dream. Now, I'm not sure I understand what that word means, even though I'm still using it. So, if the choice is between some sort of future resolution of whatever, or going back,' she looked at Gabriel, imploring him to make sense of her thoughts, 'what difference does it make?'

Gabriel clapped his hands. The sound startled Riikka. 'Let's do it. Living in the moment, in this fashion, is not what it's cracked up to be.' He grabbed Celia's arm. 'What exactly do you want us to do?'

Celia directed his attention to the ocean, almost black in the fading light. 'Walk into the ocean, together.'

'If we told you why,' added Sarah, 'it would interfere... with the process.'

Riikka stood. 'A swim is good. I can handle that.'

'There's a minor detail.' Sarah smiled at them both. 'You have to leave everything that is not you here.'

Gabriel laughed. 'I think that means we need to be naked.'

'Skinny dipping, even better.' Riikka felt like a player under direction, but she was not intimidated.

They removed their clothes and walked to the edge of the water. Looking back, they could see no table, no belongings, and no invisible friends. Riikka took Gabriel's hand and pulled. 'Shall we?'

The water was warm, masking their progress as they waded out deeper. Eventually, the seabed disappeared and they were drawn downwards, passing shadows.

Chapter 49

WAKING AFTER MORE than ten days of sleep was challenging. When Gabriel first opened his eyes he was convinced he was elsewhere. There was no one in the room. He was obviously on a hospital bed. There were a number of tubes and leads attached to various parts of his body. The catheter inserted in his penis was painful and he had a vicious headache. He'd no idea how long he'd been in the hospital, or why. Memories lay about his mind like scattered pages, none of them making any sense. Page one appeared, Finn was in trouble. Page two... Page two was a problem. It was blank.

The door opened and Grace wandered in, sipping tea. He watched her progress towards the only chair in the room. Gabriel had a vague notion that he should say something, but was content to watch his daughter place her drink on his bedside table and open a novel. She sat and read. There was something niggling away at the back of his mind and Gabriel had no energy to bring page two into focus. Grace, he thought, looked well enough. Maybe he could afford to have another nap?

⊷⊶ ⊷⊶

When Riikka woke, Jonathan was preparing breakfast. She could smell bacon cooking. 'It's out of date,' she said. There was no response. She pulled on Jonathan's tee-shirt and padded into the kitchenette. 'Jonathan, you can't eat that bacon, it must be over a week past its use-by date.' Jonathan was not interested. He attempted to lift the hem of her tee-shirt with a wooden spatula. Riikka grabbed the opened packaging and slapped his hand. 'Look!'

Jonathan lifted his eyebrows. 'I like my bacteria well cooked, don't worry. And anyway, it's an undervalued source of protein.' He tried a repeat of the tee-shirt manoeuvre. 'Want some?'

Riikka shook her head. 'I've a sudden yen to be veggie.' She moved his hand away again. 'And chaste, so no thank you.'

'More for me.'

When they eventually sat down to eat Riikka was feeling agitated. 'I had another of my dreams last night...'

'Your dreams – thank God they aren't my dreams.'

Riikka needed her man to be attentive. 'As your dreams oscillate between shagging and grabbing some bloke's balls in a scrum, I think I'll pass on sharing your fantasies.'

Jonathan grinned. 'Touché. So what was it this time?'

'I think I need to help Gabriel recover from his coma, or whatever...'

'And the dream? What has that got to do with waking Gabriel?'

'We were talking on a beach.' Riikka was starting to feel ridiculous. 'And before you ask, Sarah was there.' Jonathan zipped his mouth and continued munching. 'Before I woke we were swimming in the sea, and then we were dragged under the water. I had the strangest feeling, that I had to wake up, and then help Gabriel wake up.'

'Where is Gabriel?'

'He was in the General.' Riikka shrugged her shoulders.

'Would you like me to find out where? We could go visit.'

Riikka didn't want to intrude. 'Not sure, it's probably just a stupid dream...'

'Well, he's a friend, and we've got nothing on today.'

Riikka pushed the bowl of porridge away. 'OK, make the call. Thanks.'

⋅⟶▥ ▤◀⋅

Jonathan had threaded his way through hospital red tape and asked permission to visit Gabriel. They had agreed, thanks to a small white lie – Riikka was an out-of-town relative. Riikka approached the side room with some apprehension. The door opened and Grace emerged.

'Hi Riikka. What are you doing here?' Grace yawned. 'Sorry, Dad is still unconscious.'

'I was passing.' Another white lie. 'Thought I'd see if there was any change.'

'Why don't you sit with him for a few minutes? I need a break.' Another yawn. 'Dad's wired to all sorts of gadgets, any change and the locals will come running. I'll be back in ten minutes.'

Riikka had her chance, and with no idea what she should do, she agreed. 'Sure.' Grace wasn't joking about the gadgets and tubes. Tentatively, she sat and considered what to do next. Gabe looked peaceful. Surely he was asleep.

'You don't have much time.'

Sarah's interruption startled Riikka. 'Couldn't you cough or something before you speak?'

'Now you have even less time.'

'So what do I do?'

'What was the last thing you did with Gabriel?'

'In the dream?'

'Yes, yes…'

'We walked into the sea and, actually, we sank.'

'Were you together?'

'Yes, of course…'

'Because you led him to the sea you must lead him out.'

Riikka slid a hand under Gabriel's and waited. 'How do I do this?'

'Don't overcomplicate things. Make a connection and call him back.'

Riikka remembered the first time she'd seen Gabriel at Isabella's funeral. She started to realise why Gabriel needed to sleep, why the sea was so beguiling. He needed the rest, he needed to be at peace. *Why would you come back?* She leaned forwards and whispered in his ear. 'Time to come back Gabe, there's someone you need to see.' She tugged his hand. 'Open your eyes Gabe…'

The lifeless hand she was holding twitched. 'Riikka?' Gabriel's eyes squinted. 'Could I have a drink, my head's killing me.'

'Welcome back old friend. I'll have to check out the drink request with Grace.'

'Where is Grace?'

Much to Riikka's dismay tears were forming in the corner of his eyes. 'Finn's dead. That's how this happened.'

Gabriel was examining the wires attached to his chest and arms. 'I must have passed out.'

'That you did. You've had us all worried.'

'How long…?'

'About ten days.' Riikka smiled.

Gabriel seemed to have another realisation. 'Good God, I must have missed the funeral.'

The door opened and Grace came in. 'Dad, you're awake.' She stared at Riikka. 'How…?'

'He just opened his eyes.' The third and last white lie. Riikka slid her hand away and stood. 'Grace, I think you should…'

'But this is wonderful, you're back,' said Grace, looking at her father.

Gabriel managed a smile, but still looked confused. 'How is everyone? I should have been there to help.'

Grace frowned. 'Help? I don't understand, help with what?'

Any opportunity that Gabriel may have had to expand on his reasons was lost, like sand falling through fingers. Isabella's voice whispered in his ear. 'Enjoy…'

Finn burst into the room. 'Hi Granddad, why have you been asleep so long?'

Chapter 50

It was almost ten years since Finn's miraculous recovery from leukaemia. He was a young man now and still in remission. As far as Gabriel was concerned he was cured. Gabriel, however, was far from cured, the ageing process remorseless. He watched as Billie disposed of the remaining breadcrumbs.

Lorri interrupted his reverie. 'Do you remember when Finn turned the corner?'

Gabriel chuckled. 'Will I ever forget? When I woke up in the hospital I was certain Finn had died. I had lived and breathed Finn not being with us for ten days. It was extraordinary.'

'And now look at him.' Finn was tall, his curls tempered by chemotherapy. He was on his way back with Billie. The pilgrimage around the pond was an essential element of visits to the park with his granddad. Lorri gripped Gabriel's arm. 'You never did say what happened that day, when you were alone with Finn. Before you collapsed.'

'It's gone. I was never able to recall what happened. But I'll never forget the ten days that followed.' Gabriel shook his head;

he needed to change the subject. 'How's Scotland? I should make an effort, come and visit.' Gabriel eased his back.

'It's wonderful. Yes you should.' Lorri stood and stretched. 'Neither of us is getting any younger.'

The platitude, Gabriel knew, was well meant. 'You were a real friend in those difficult times. But you know that. At least I hope you do?'

Lorri checked her watch. 'If we're going to meet Beth we should go.'

Gabriel shaded his eyes from the sun. 'Tell Beth I'll be there in half an hour. I want to sit a bit longer.' He smoothed his hand across the wooden frame. It was difficult to believe that their bench was still in one piece.

Finn approached and laid his hand on Gabriel's shoulder. Gabriel never ceased to be grateful for these minor miracles. Absently, he reached back and patted Finn's hand. 'You should go. Take your sister, I'll be along soon.'

Finn grabbed his sister's coat. 'OK Granddad, no sweat. Let's go sweet-pea, we'll be late.'

As the threesome walked away Billie turned and waved. Gabriel's spirits lifted, she had such a smile, engaging, like she knew something, a secret. Her attention shifted, she seemed to be looking behind Gabriel. She waved again.

'Indeed she has.' Celia had assumed her position on the bench.

'Good grief Celia. To what do I owe this visit?'

'I feel that you deserve answers.'

Gabriel's long history with his resident guru had prepared him for the standard response, so the offer of an explanation was somehow shocking.

'You have been very patient.' Celia's voice faded.

Gabriel was interrupted by a touch on his knee. He'd nodded off, but Celia was still sitting on the bench. 'Best if you stay awake old man. Time is pressing.'

Gabriel yawned. He was tired, the sort of heavy tiredness that left footprints. 'Should I ask questions? How many rubs of the lamp do I get?' He smiled. 'I probably have a hundred or so...'

'Three is a good number. Let's go for three.'

'OK.' Gabriel rubbed his whiskered chin. 'My lost ten days. Where did I go?'

Celia's turn to smile. 'That's a dilly. We should probably back-track, to when you held Finn's hand again and asked for healing. You were heard. You drew back enough energy to do the job, and more.'

'More?'

'It's hard to frame an answer, but your actions caused a fracture in what you might call reality. From that moment a parallel version of here and now opened up and Finn died. You lived in that version and this version for ten days. You were split until Riikka called you back, put you together.' Gabriel's head filled with questions as Celia continued. 'Easy on the questions, you only have three. That other dimension continues and your family lost both Finn and you in that ten day period.' Celia sat forward. 'Without Riikka's intervention you wouldn't be here.'

'I guess you know this all sounds a bit fanciful, even if your explanation does fit the facts?'

'Nevertheless, it's what happened. Number two?'

Gabriel tapped the bench with his finger. 'Where's the beach?'

'There are places where the forces that hold the multiple versions of "real places" apart merge together. I guess you could call them a crossroad. The beach, more particularly the ocean, is such a place. So, to answer your question, it is real, but you couldn't point your finger to the sky and say "it's there". I took you there to facilitate the things we had to do. Last question?'

'Why was it so important that Finn had to survive?' Gabriel rubbed his eyes. He really was tired. 'More to the point, why were you sent to intervene, if that's what happened, and by whom?'

Celia raised her eyebrows. 'Can't you count? That's three questions. However, they all have the same answer. Consciousness evolves. There are very few places where physical conditions come into being that support the evolution of consciousness. Your planet is one such place. Sometimes, the genetic mutations that move things on have to be protected. Finn needed to be protected.'

Gabriel was not impressed. 'I see. So, you're galactic shepherds? Not sure I like the idea of being a galactic sheep.'

Celia laughed. 'Nice analogy. Look.' Celia pointed out across the river. A swan skipped across the water and landed. It started to swim in their direction.

Gabriel needed to ask one more question. 'Why are you telling me this now? Why not before?'

'That knowledge would have changed things. There are rules.'

'And now? Don't the same rules apply now?'

Celia moved closer. 'That, my friend, is a question you are about to answer.'

Made in the USA
Charleston, SC
12 March 2016